30 DATES
IN 30 DAYS

Praise for Elle Spencer

The Road to Madison

"The story had me hooked from its powerful opening scene, and it only got better and better. I feel like Spencer tailored this book just for me. For anyone who has read my reviews, it's no secret that I love romances that include lots of angst, and *The Road to Madison* hit the bull's-eye."—*The Lesbian Review*

"Elle Spencer weaves a tale full of sadness, remorse but one filled with those little moments that make you have the flutters. Her characters are well developed, the dialogue is seamless and natural, you really get thrown right into Madison and Anna's world. You feel what they feel. This book grabbed my attention and had me turning the pages through the night. A delightful story that I thoroughly enjoyed. I cannot wait for the next adventure Elle Spencer takes me on."—*Romantic Reader Blog*

Unforgettable

"Across both novellas, Elle Spencer delivers four distinct, compelling leads, as well as interesting supporting casts that round out their stories. If you like angsty romances, this is the book for you! Both stories pack a punch, with so much 'will they or won't they' that I kind of wondered how they'd turn out (yes, even though it's marketed as romance!)"—*The Lesbian Review*

"I was stunned at how Elle Spencer manages to make the reader feel so much and we end up really caring for the women in her novels…This book is perfect for those times you want to wallow in romance, intense feelings, and love. Elle Spencer does it so well."
—*Kitty Kat's Book Review Blog*

Casting Lacey

"The characters have a chance to really get to know each other, becoming friends and caring for each other before their feelings turn romantic. It also allows for a whole lot of angst that keeps things interesting. *Casting Lacey* is a compelling, sexy, angsty romance that I highly recommend to anyone who's into fake relationship books or celebrity romances. It kept me sucked in, and I'm looking forward to seeing more from Elle Spencer in the future."
—*The Lesbian Review*

"This is a very good debut novel that combines the fake girlfriend trope with celebrity lifestyle…The characters are well portrayed and have off-the-charts chemistry. The story is full of humour, wit, and saucy dialogues but also has angst and drama. I think that the book is at its best in the humorous parts which are really well written…an entertaining and enjoyable read."—*Lez Review Books*

"This is the romance I've been recommending to everyone and her mother since I read it, because it's basically everything I've been dying to find in an f/f romance—funny voices I click with, off-the-charts chemistry, a later-in-life coming out, and a host of fun tropes from fake dating to costars."—*Frolic*

By the Author

Casting Lacey

Unforgettable

The Road to Madison

30 Dates in 30 Days

30 DATES
IN 30 DAYS

by

Elle Spencer

2019

30 DATES IN 30 DAYS

ISBN 13: 978-1-63555-498-4

THIS TRADE PAPERBACK ORIGINAL IS PUBLISHED BY
BOLD STROKES BOOKS, INC.
P.O. BOX 249
VALLEY FALLS, NY 12185

FIRST EDITION: OCTOBER 2019

CREDITS
EDITORS: BARBARA ANN WRIGHT AND STACIA SEAMAN
PRODUCTION DESIGN: STACIA SEAMAN
COVER DESIGN BY TAMMY SEIDICK

Acknowledgments

First, a huge thank you to Rad, Sandy, and every member of the Bold Strokes Books team for all of your hard work and for making the publishing process so seamless for me. I couldn't ask for a more supportive, professional group, and I'm truly grateful to be part of the Bold Strokes family.

Thanks to my editor, Barbara Ann Wright, for your always on-point insight, guidance, and laughs along the way.

To Nikki, you fill my life with so much joy and laughter. So much love and affection. So much fun and excitement. I'm so lucky to call you my wife. Love you, baby.

To Paula, my BFF extraordinaire, I'm so blessed to have you in my life, on my side, and only a text or phone call away. Please stay my BFF forevs. Ride or die, baby.

To my family, your support is everything. Love you all.

And to my readers, thank you from the bottom of my heart for taking this ride with me. I appreciate each and every one of you more than you could know. Thank you, thank you, thank you.

For my wife, Nikki, who makes every date special.

Chapter One

Veronica Welch's hands were full. Literally. She heard that godforsaken ding again, but the elevator was so packed, if she tried to juggle her coffee and briefcase to look at her phone, she'd surely elbow someone in the ribs. It didn't matter. She knew what the little ding was. Damn Bea and her snarky notifications.

The offices of Belden & Snow were buzzing with activity already. Veronica hated walking in late. It gave the wrong impression. It hardly mattered that she hadn't left the office until eleven the night before. The partners didn't know that. They also didn't care. They'd probably been at home, having a cocktail with their spouses while they watched the evening news. That would be Veronica soon too—minus the spouse part. But making partner would happen within the year. Everything was running right on schedule. Just one more sleepless year (tops!), and it would be Belden, Snow, Miller, Baker, Anderson, Sheffield *and* Welch. Okay. She knew she wouldn't be a named partner just yet, but it really didn't matter anyway. Just ask Miller, Baker, Anderson, and Sheffield.

"Good morning, V!"

Well, at least someone felt perky this morning. Veronica traded her lukewarm to-go cup of coffee for the steaming mug her assistant had waiting for her. "You're a godsend, Bea, you really are, but you need to get that crap off my phone."

"Crap?"

"Don't play cute. You know exactly what I'm talking about." Veronica set the mug on her desk and pulled her phone out of her jacket pocket. "The crap that reminds me every day of the impending doom that is my thirty-fifth birthday." For the past week, Bea's daily alerts had delivered the same message in some new and clever way. *Reminder—in five months and eight days, you'll turn thirty-five. A gal on your arm shows the world you're alive.* She handed the phone to Bea. "Please. Take care of it."

Bea didn't take the phone. Instead, she asked, "Did you even look at what it said today?"

Bea reminded Veronica of a young Audrey Hepburn. She had the short bangs and the red lipstick and big brown eyes. Flamboyant skirts and dresses were the norm, along with a colorful cardigan because the offices were a bit on the chilly side. As meddling assistants went, Bea was straight out of central casting. They stared each other down for a few seconds before Veronica gave in with a huff and looked at her phone. Curiosity quickly morphed into horror.

Your whole life is planned
That much we know.
But you won't find a wife
At Belden & Snow.
I'm here to help you
Like it or not.
Your date is at eight
And PS, she's hot!

"Oh, God. No. No, no, no!"

"Hold on," Bea said. "Just hear me out."

"You scheduled a blind date? For tonight?" Veronica threw her hands in the air. "For me?"

"You said you wanted to be married by thirty-five."

"I was drunk when I said that!"

"Or at least on your way to being married by thirty-five." Bea sat in a chair by Veronica's desk. "Please hear me out, V. I have this so worked out you wouldn't even believe it."

Going out for drinks with her assistant wasn't something Veronica normally did, but they'd settled a big case the week before, and Bea wanted to try a new place that offered craft cocktails. That's what Bea called them. Craft cocktails. Apparently, Veronica was old-fashioned because she preferred her drinks with less craft and more olives, rosemary sprigs and lavender essence be damned.

Getting drunk that night was definitely not part of the plan. Spilling her guts about her private life wasn't either. For whatever reason—possibly the absinthe-soaked orchid leaves—it had happened. And now Bea knew that Veronica had put everything off for her career. Wife, kids, a home with a gourmet kitchen. Veronica told Bea about every single goal, want, and desire that had been set aside so she could focus on becoming a partner in one of the most prestigious law firms in New York City.

Veronica knew the clock was ticking. Biological and otherwise. She sat and looked Bea in the eye. "She'd better be amazing, this woman you've set me up with."

"She is. I mean, as far as I can tell from her profile."

Veronica lifted an eyebrow. "Profile?"

Bea put up a hand. "Hear me out, V."

"I already heard you out," Veronica interrupted. "When you said blind date, I assumed that meant blind to me, not you!"

"Well, I mean, technically, I never said it was a blind date at all."

At that point, Veronica was just this side of apoplectic. "Oh, don't you even try to lawyer me. Stay in your lane, Beatrice."

They stared each other down for a moment before Bea burst out laughing. "You realize that is literally not my name, right?"

"Of course I know that, Beadore."

"Also not my name. It's Bea. Just Bea. Always has been—"

"Always will Bea. Yeah, I know the joke." Veronica tried to look stern but knew she failed miserably. She smiled at her assistant. "Bea, I adore you, but you are seriously stressing me out right now."

"This will work. I know it will. Thirty dates, and you'll have found the one."

Veronica's eyes widened. "How exactly did it go from one date to thirty?"

Bea bit the tip of her finger. "I may have put you on a dating app called Ryder. It's strictly for lesbians."

Veronica's mouth gaped open. "Ride Her? You put me on an app called Ride Her?"

"Ha! No! It's called Ryder. R-Y-D-E-R. I hadn't noticed the pun until now, but I swear it's legit. They even vet you to make sure you're not some weird dude or homophobic creep." She pointed at Veronica's hair. "But you'll have to lose the bun."

"What do they have against buns?" Veronica absentmindedly smoothed down her hair. Yeah, so she wasn't like Bea. She only wore black, navy blue, and gray in the form of a suit or a shift dress. And the tightly pulled-back hair meant she didn't have to spend unnecessary time trying to style it. It looked professional, and that was all that mattered.

"The photo," Bea said. "Your hair's down in the photo I found for your profile pic. It looks pretty."

Veronica shook her head in disgust. Bea had overstepped her bounds. In fact, from the look of things, Bea didn't actually have any bounds. "Cancel the date tonight."

"But—"

"I said cancel it, Bea. I don't have time for one date, let alone thirty."

"You're a big hit on Ryder. Everyone wants a date with you. And I've set it up so that they all happen at the same time and place. Just thirty minutes. Coffee, a drink, whatever. And you'll be done with it in a month. Thirty dates in thirty days. Done. Married. Well, at least engaged by your birthday. Your mom will be so happy."

Bea had lost her mind. Was she trying to get fired? And yet she sort of had it right. If Veronica were to do something like this, she wouldn't want it to drag out for months on end. And she was fairly certain she'd know within a few minutes if she'd found someone she clicked with. No need for drinks *and* dinner. She shook her head. "Show me."

Bea took her phone out of her skirt pocket, because of course Bea's skirt had pockets. She pulled up Veronica's profile. "I may have embellished a little bit."

Veronica rolled her eyes. "Did you make me a judge instead of an attorney?"

"No, I made you interesting."

"How am I not supposed to be offended by that?" Veronica skimmed through her profile and looked at Bea. "This looks like my mother wrote it."

"She may have helped."

Veronica held up the phone. "This is high school me. Not thirty-four-year-old me. I don't surf anymore. I don't love board games. I don't, for the love of God, go camping, and I haven't eaten an Eggo waffle since—"

"High school?"

"Bingo!"

"Got it." Bea paused for a moment. With excitement written all over her face, she said, "But you could! Your mom said you were great at all that outdoorsy stuff back in the day, and I still eat Eggo waffles when I'm in a hurry. It's nothing to be ashamed about."

Bea had indeed lost her damned mind. At least she'd picked a good profile pic, one Veronica's mother had no doubt given her. It had been taken on Thanksgiving Day, so yes, her hair was down, and she looked more rested than normal. Thank God the photo wasn't from high school too.

Would it be so bad to find someone this way? On a dating app? Veronica cringed at the thought, then considered her other options. Hanging out in bars wasn't her thing. Asking friends to set her up was a definite no go. Most of her friends had terrible taste in women, especially her straight friends. They acted as if there was nowhere to go but up. Besides, she worked so much, she hardly ever saw them anymore. What was she going to do, call them out of the blue and say *Hey, sorry I'm too busy to do lunch, but do you mind going through your contact list to see if there are any single lesbians in the mix?* God could just kill her now.

Random encounters were also unlikely since they certainly hadn't happened so far. The truth was, she was beyond ready to find a woman she could share her life with; she just wasn't sure this was the best way to go about it.

Bea's phone dinged in Veronica's hand, and a photo of a woman popped up. "That means you have another interested party," Bea said with a wink.

"Don't wink at me."

Bea slouched in her chair. "Fine. If you tap on the pic, her profile will come up."

Veronica followed Bea's instruction and slid the phone back across the desk. "It was wrong of you to go about it this way, conspiring with my mother the way you have."

Bea sank even lower in her chair.

"Having said that, it's not the worst idea ever. Hell, it's not even the worst idea you've ever had. Close, but not the worst. So, here's what I expect from you."

Bea sat up straighter. "Okay, go."

"I don't want to have to look at that app ever again. You'll email the woman's full profile to me an hour before the date. I don't want to get distracted by who I'm meeting that day. Got it?"

"Got it."

"Also, you'll ask each of them what their favorite drink is, and that's what we'll both drink during the appointment."

"Date," Bea said, grabbing her phone off the desk. "These women will think they're going on a date, even if it's a short one." She swiped through the still-open app until she found what she was looking for. "There she is. Lucky Lady Number One." She typed with both thumbs into her phone, muttering softly, "What…is…your…favorite…drink?"

"Fine, we'll call it a date, but these women need to know up front that it's just a drink. No dinner. No hooking up later. Just drinks."

Bea pointed her finger. "Unless you like her."

Veronica cocked her head and smirked. "If I like her, I can manage the rest, okay?"

Bea nodded. "But you'll tell me, right? I mean, I'll go crazy if you don't tell me how it went."

"We'll see." Veronica pulled a file out of her briefcase. "Now, let's get to work."

"Don't you want to know where you'll be meeting these women?"

"Well, Bea, you're actually a very competent assistant when you're not meddling in my personal life, so I'm guessing you picked somewhere close by. Nice, but not too nice. Not too loud, so I can actually carry on a conversation and get to know the person. Am I warm?"

"Very warm. It's this great little place called Monaghan's. It used to be kind of a dive. You know, regulars who'd been there since the place was built. Anyway, the owner died and left it to his daughter. She's transformed it into this modern yet rustic haven. You walk in, and the hustle and bustle of the city and all your troubles just melt away."

"Bea, if I look on their website, what will it say on the homepage?"

Bea gave a sheepish grin. "That it's a modern yet rustic haven where all your troubles melt away."

Veronica rolled her eyes and laughed. "That's what I thought. As much as I look forward to all of my troubles melting away, they're going to multiply if we don't get to work."

Bea stood. "Right. Back to work we go!"

"Hold on." Veronica held up her phone. "It's my mom. You're staying right here."

Bea put her hands over her eyes, leaving a tiny slit between two fingers.

Veronica set the phone down and put it on speaker. "Hi, Mom."

"Hi, sweetheart. Any plans tonight?"

"I know you know, Mom. You don't have to pretend you're innocent in all of this. And really with the Eggo waffles being my favorite food?"

"You loved them so much I couldn't keep the freezer stocked. I had to buy them in bulk. Your father says hello."

"Hi, Dad. Mom, listen."

"What are you going to wear, dear? You must not wear your hair in a bun."

Veronica narrowed her eyes at Bea. "Yes, your little co-conspirator already passed on that information to me."

"You're such a pretty girl, V. Let your hair down, and let your light shine."

Bea added her two cents with a big nod. Veronica shot her a glare. "Okay, gotta get back to work. Bye, Mom."

Bea pointed at the door. "I'm just going to…"

"Good idea." Veronica raised her voice and shouted, "You're lucky you still have a job!"

❖

Oh, for God's sake, her hands were shaking. Veronica couldn't remember the last time she'd been on a real date. Maybe her late twenties? Surely, it hadn't been that long. Truth was, it had probably been longer. She never did count anything with Avery as a real date.

"Monaghan's?" Veronica looked up from her phone and spotted the small sign across the street. "There you are. So far, so good, Bea." The place was only two blocks from her office. It looked quaint. Not big enough for rowdy crowds. She opened the door, and sure enough, the hustle and bustle of the city disappeared when the door shut behind her. She laughed a little to herself about the cheesy website description and how accurate it actually was.

There was nothing about this bar that said *dive*. The industrial lighting made it look sleek, but the dark wood tabletops and chairs brought a warmth to the space. A modern yet rustic haven. Veronica needed a haven if she was going to get her hands to stop shaking. Hell, she needed a ninety-minute massage or, better yet, a Xanax followed by an hour of meditation. Or maybe some of the "float therapy" she'd scoffed at when she read about it in a waiting room. It was sounding better by the minute.

"Veronica?" A woman stepped into the bar behind her. "I hope I'm not late."

Veronica had hoped to get a table and order the drinks before her date arrived so she could take a few sips and calm down a bit. No such luck. She put out her hand. "Eve. It's good to meet you." At least Veronica's hand wasn't sweaty. Unfortunately, her throat was bone dry. She looked around and decided a table by the window would work best. "Let's sit."

They took off their coats and hung them on the chair. Veronica hesitated to sit first. Should she wait until her date sat? What were the rules for lesbians? She stood there awkwardly, but so did Eve. The look on her face told Veronica she wasn't sure what was going on. "Sorry." Veronica sat. "Are there rules of chivalry for lesbians?"

"Rules?" Eve shook her head. "I'm not sure what you mean."

Great. Now Eve knew that Veronica had no clue what she was doing. *Smooth, V. Real smooth.* "Never mind. Should we order drinks?" She turned and saw that the bartender was busy. "I'll just go up and order for us." Maybe she'd calm down if she could stand at the bar for a minute. *Don't trip on the way there.*

The bartender smiled at Veronica as if she knew her. "Hey there!"

But they didn't know each other. Veronica was sure of it. Still, it was nice to be greeted that way in the rudest city on earth. She smiled back. "Hi. Can we get two coffee and Baileys please?"

"So polite," the woman said. "You must be from somewhere else."

"Nope. Born and raised on the Upper West Side. Besides, you started it."

The woman laughed. "I guess I did. I'll bring the drinks to your table. No need to wait here."

Veronica wished waiting was required. She'd much rather stand at the bar and talk to the friendly woman with curly hair than go back to

Eve. Not that Eve didn't seem nice. She was pretty too. Short dark hair. High cheekbones. Veronica glanced back at her. Yeah, long legs too.

"Go get to know her."

Veronica turned back to the bartender. "What?"

"I can spot a first date a mile away. Trust me, she's just as nervous as you are."

"You think so?" Veronica wasn't so sure about that.

The bartender leaned in close. "I'll be right behind you with the drinks. Talk about the weather until I get there."

That was quite possibly the worst advice Veronica had ever heard, but she nodded. "Okay."

Eve smiled at her as she approached the table and sat. "It's a chilly night," she said. "I'm really glad this bar isn't cold and drafty."

Yes! Veronica didn't have to be the one to bring up the weather. "Are you okay by the window? We could move closer to the bar." Eve had on a chunky black sweater, but Veronica thought it would be polite to offer.

"I'm fine." Eve tugged at the neck of her sweater. "That thing you said about lesbian rules. I guess I don't know about those because I'm not one actually."

"One what?"

"A lesbian," Eve whispered.

"Okay. Um…" Veronica wasn't sure what to say next.

"I'm…well, I don't really know what I am at the moment."

"I'm not sure what you're trying to tell me. Your profile said you're interested in women only."

"It also said I'm single. I'm not that either. Not yet anyway."

"Oh."

"I'm not trying to deceive anyone," Eve said.

"All evidence to the contrary."

"I just didn't think a woman would go out with me unless I implied I have a little more experience than I do. But you seem like a very nice person, Veronica. In fact, you're exactly the kind of woman I'd love to…"

"Experiment with?" All of the air seemed to leave the room as Veronica said the words. The bartender set the cups of coffee on the table. From the concerned look on her face, Veronica was fairly certain she'd heard the last of the conversation. "Thank you." Veronica got her wallet and pulled out a twenty. She set it on the bartender's tray. "That'll be all for us tonight." She gave her a smile and said, "Keep the change."

"I chose coffee because I knew it would be cold tonight, but right now, I feel so flushed with embarrassment, I think I might burn up if I take a sip."

Veronica wasn't sure how to respond. Eve's profile had obviously been a complete lie. "Maybe you could tell me something that's true. Are you really a manager at Macy's?"

Eve laughed nervously. "God. Are we really going to do this?"

"We don't have to," Veronica said. "But I can tell you we certainly aren't going to do anything else."

"There's a woman I like there. She's a manager in the handbag section." Eve pulled her sweater up over her mouth. "It's so *Carol*, isn't it? I've probably seen that movie twenty times."

Veronica didn't have time for this. Hell, she didn't even have time to date *actual* lesbians, let alone someone who had made up an entirely fake profile based on some woman she had a crush on and a movie she liked. "Is your husband getting sick of you filling the closet with designer bags?"

"Ha! You have no idea."

Okay, so Eve wasn't even separated from her husband. Veronica sighed. "I'm sorry, I just don't have time for games."

Eve's expression sobered. "Oh. I really didn't mean any harm. You're my first date. With a woman, I mean."

Veronica felt frustrated that she'd been misled, but she also understood that Eve was probably questioning her sexuality. "Eve, I'm sure there are women out there who would be totally fine with what you have to offer, as long as you're up front about it. Unfortunately, I'm not one of them."

Eve stood and put her coat on. "Please forget you ever met me."

Veronica picked up her cup and held it with both hands. "I already have."

❖

"So? How did it go?"

Veronica glanced at the clock on her monitor. Bea was twenty minutes early and sporting a huge smile, which was so far from normal, Veronica wanted to laugh. "You're never early."

"I could hardly sleep." Bea crossed her fingers. "Please tell me it went well."

"Shut the door."

Bea's smile faded. She backed up and pushed the door shut. "You're twirling your pen. That's never a good sign."

Veronica set the pen down. "Perhaps I wasn't clear about my 'type' when we spoke earlier." She used finger quotes. "You get points for style. Eve is well put together. She's well-spoken, and no one would argue that she isn't beautiful."

Bea shook her head. "I don't understand. What's the problem exactly?"

"Well, you see, Bea, what I apparently failed to make clear is that I am looking for an *actual lesbian*."

Bea threw a hand over her mouth. "Oh God. No."

"Now, I can't discount the possibility that Eve is an actual lesbian—and keep in mind bisexual is great too—but it was a little hard to tell because I couldn't quite get past the fact that she has a husband."

Bea threw both hands over her eyes. "What have I done?"

"We're not giving up."

Bea uncovered her eyes. "We're not?"

Veronica had given it some thought. There was only so much information Bea could glean from the profiles these women created. It was up to Veronica to get to know who they really were. She liked the bar Bea had chosen. She liked the bartender with the pretty curly hair that seemed to have a life of its own. Why give up after only one date? "We move on from the experimenter and hope for better future results."

"The experi…" Bea waved a hand. "Never mind. I don't want to know." She stood and put a fist in the air. "Onward and upward!"

CHAPTER TWO

Rachel rushed into the bar her cousin owned. Monaghan's was already busy with the after-work crowd, and she was late. "Sorry!" she shouted as she ran into the service area. She stopped short when she realized her cousin hadn't even noticed her. Charlotte seemed mesmerized by two women sitting at a small table by the window. Three of the bar patrons appeared to join her in gawking.

She went into the back room and threw her satchel and leather jacket in a locker. She grabbed an apron and tied it around her waist, then joined Charlotte behind the bar. She leaned on her elbows and threw a few beer nuts in her mouth. "What are we looking at?"

Charlotte, who seemingly chose that very moment to start being subtle, leaned in and whispered, "First date."

Rachel took a closer look at the women. They were seated against the window, so she could only see their profiles, but she could tell that the blonde in the tailored charcoal power suit was a total knockout. Nice legs. Long, slender fingers. Rachel always noticed the fingers.

The redhead was cute too but not really Rachel's type. Too cutesy. Too giggly. Was Power Suit really that funny, or was Cutesy just nervous? Power Suit glanced over at them, and the entire group immediately tried to look busy. One man took a sudden interest in a bowl of pretzels. Another swirled his beer as if it were a fine wine. The lone female patron found herself with an urgent need to rifle through her purse.

Charlotte's way of looking busy was to wipe down the bar. She gave Rachel a sly grin as she worked. "I know which one you like. You have a type, Rachel Monaghan."

Rachel threw another nut in her mouth and grinned back. "I like *all* women."

Charlotte lowered her voice and leaned in close. "That's true, but I know how much you love the power suit type. Overworked and undersexed. Isn't that what you said?"

Rachel sighed. "I would never say something so crass."

"Like hell you wouldn't." Charlotte pointed at Power Suit. "But that nice lady is looking for love, not a quickie with some burned-out wedding photographer who thinks real, lasting love isn't even a thing."

"I am not burned out!"

Charlotte raised her eyebrows. "Okay, fine. I'll give you that one back. But we both know the rest of it is true."

So maybe Rachel had become cynical over the years. So what? Her current routine suited her just fine. Three dates, max. It was enough to have some fun and possibly some great sex, but not enough to ever get attached to one person ever again. It worked. And she wasn't changing anytime soon.

Charlotte kissed Rachel on the cheek. "Thanks for covering for me. I won't be more than a couple of hours." She went to walk away but turned back. "Promise me, Rach." She motioned with her head toward Power Suit.

Rachel waved her away. "Yeah, yeah. Go, or you'll be late."

Once Charlotte was out of sight, Rachel glanced at the couple again. Cutesy girl was still giggling. Power Suit was sporting a tight smile. This would never work. Rachel knew it and so did Power Suit. Rachel's attention turned to the customers sitting at the bar. She worked her way over to the threesome, now in a deep discussion. She wiped the bar as she went, leaning in as she got closer to the customers.

"This is the one," the woman whispered. "There will be a second date. I'd put money on it."

"This is only the fourth lady she's seen. She has twenty-six more to go. Don't go marrying her off yet."

Rachel glanced at the elderly couple. At least, she assumed they were a couple since the woman had just pushed the bowl of nuts away from the man. The other man sitting next to the couple smiled at her. "Hello, pipsqueak."

Rachel peered at the man. "Harry, is that you?" She hadn't seen her uncle John's old friend since his funeral. A Yankees cap that sat low on his head obscured her view.

"In the flesh." Harry took off his cap and set in on the bar. "Probably didn't recognize me with the facial hair. My son and I are having a beard-growing contest. Guess who's winning?"

Rachel couldn't believe it was Harry. She remembered him always being clean-shaven and wearing a suit and tie. Now he sported a full beard that was mostly gray. "Keep it up and they'll have you playing Santa at Macy's next year," she said.

Harry shrugged. "Not a bad gig for an old guy like me. These are my new friends, Carol and Joe."

She gave them a quick wave. "Nice to meet you both. I'm Rachel." They seemed like your typical retired couple. Rachel guessed they were in their early seventies and probably halfway to Boca Raton already. Carol wasn't letting her short hair go gray, though. It was a pretty shade of blond, and her pink lipstick matched the color on her fingernails.

Joe was bald. If he had any hair left, he shaved it regularly. He had bright blue eyes and a friendly smile. He reached across the bar for Rachel's hand. "Nice to meet you, Rachel. I'll have another—" He stopped when Carol put her hand on his arm. "Oh, all right. Make it a Diet Coke."

Rachel took the empty beer glass away and poured him the soda. This was exactly the kind of thing she was avoiding. If she stayed single, no one would ever tell her what she could and couldn't drink. Or eat. Or buy. No one would remind her of her faults or write honey-do lists or tell her to bathe every day. Okay, that last one wasn't an issue, but still, these were the things couples argued about. She didn't need that in her life.

"Haven't seen you in a while," Harry said. "What brings you back to the bar?"

"Just covering for Charlotte. She has a lot on her plate right now."

"She sure does. You're a good kid, Rachel."

"Hey, it's family. I'll help whenever I can." Rachel leaned in closer. "So, I heard you all talking about the fourth date, but Charlotte said it's a first date, so what's the deal?" She motioned with her head toward the two women.

"Don't know much," Harry whispered. "Just what Charlotte tells us."

Carol also leaned in. "The pretty one in the fancy suit, her name is Veronica," Carol said. "She's on a mission to find the one. Thirty dates, just as fast as her assistant can set them up."

Rachel scrunched up her face. "Oh, come on. You're telling me that perfectly put-together woman came in here and spilled her guts to Charlotte?"

"Heavens no, not at all," Joe exclaimed. "We can't even figure out what drink she likes!"

Carol continued. "Her assistant came in and explained things to Charlotte. Char said she's the cutest little thing too. Her name's Bea. I guess she wanted to make sure Charlotte didn't spill the beans from one date to another."

"Or even worse, that Charlotte might think she was a hooker!" Harry interjected.

Rachel raised an eyebrow, and Carol gave him an elbow in the side.

"What?" he tried to defend himself. "She's here every night. Someone could make that assumption."

Joe leaned in and whispered, "She seems like a nice gal. I hope she finds what she's looking for."

Rachel rested her chin in her hand and took a longer look at the women. So, Power Suit was looking for "the one." She had to disagree with Carol. Cutesy girl was definitely not the one. Power Suit looked bored out of her mind. She smiled every now and then, but she was about to pass out from boredom. Rachel could change that. She winked at Harry and her new friends and said, "I'll be right back."

If only Veronica felt as giddy about the evening as her date did. It seemed as if the response to everything she said was a giggle. And while Veronica thought herself slightly snarky, she wasn't exactly doing standup at that moment. To make matters worse, she kept having to remind herself of the woman's name. She quickly glanced at the dossier Bea had put on her phone. *That's right. Penelope Jones.* "Are you nervous, Penelope? Would you like another—"

"Let me guess. Two more Shirley Temples?" A tall brunette stood at the edge of their table with her hands behind her back and a twinkle in her eye. She wasn't Charlotte, the regular bartender. Veronica looked past her to see where Charlotte had gone. "Looking for the owner?" Veronica nodded.

"She had to step out for a bit. I'm covering for her. I'm her cousin." Rachel extended her hand. "Rachel."

"Oh." Veronica didn't feel the need to introduce herself or her date to the new bartender. This Rachel person was sporting a grin the size of Texas. Great. Just what Veronica needed—another happy soul to remind her she should probably smile more. Let her hair down. Let her freaking light shine. How disappointed would her mother be that she'd left her hair in a bun this time? She'd never have to know. Besides, Shirley Temple didn't seem to care. All she could do was giggle. Heh. Shirley Temple. The name suited Penelope better than Penelope did.

Now, the bartender—did she say her name was Rachel? Her smile was naturally wide. Veronica shouldn't knock her for that. She was just being friendly. Besides, she was very easy to look at with those warm brown eyes and kissable lips. And she was still waiting for an answer. Veronica cleared her throat. "Penelope, would you like another…" She had to force the next two words out of her mouth. "Shirley Temple?"

"Yes!" Penelope said it with a giggle, of course. "I don't drink alcohol, and the only thing I know how to order in a bar is a Shirley Temple. I've been drinking them since I was a kid. My parents were alcoholics, and they took me to bars when I was pretty young. I would sit in the corner and make up stories about everyone. That's why I'm a writer now. I have lots of stories in my head that just have to come out."

"Wow," Rachel said. "What kind of stories do you write?"

"Horror, mostly." Penelope made a slashing motion across her neck with her hand. "Heads coming off and stuff." Her eyes rolled into the back of her head, and her body slumped as if she'd died. Veronica and Rachel looked at each other, then Penelope came back to life and laughed. "Gotcha!"

"Two Shirley Temples coming right up." Rachel winked at Veronica before she walked away. She wasn't sure what that meant, but she took a long look at her backside until Penelope drew her attention back to the table. Penelope Jones, the extremely fast talker who, with boundless energy and a dark imagination, was a mystery Veronica had no desire to solve. But she was kind of stuck there until her phone vibrated, indicating her thirty minutes was up.

The wink had meant vodka. Veronica's second Shirley Temple was no virgin. She sucked half of it down and gave the new bartender a grateful smile. She didn't need to ask Penelope any more questions, so she let her talk about her books. The second her phone vibrated, she put some cash on the table and stood. "It was a pleasure meeting you, Penelope. I wish you all the best in your future endeavors."

It was a blow-off of epic proportions, but Penelope seemed to take it well enough. She shook Veronica's hand and said, "You too. Being a lawyer and whatever."

And that was that. Date number four was in the books, and it certainly wasn't anything to write home about. Neither were one, two, or three. Not that they weren't pleasant women. They all had traits that Veronica liked, and Bea certainly knew how to find some lookers, but there wasn't that thing. She wanted that magnetic force to pull her in. Or at the very least, she wanted to find someone she could wake up next to and not be annoyed by. She glanced over at the bartender as Shirley Temple left the restaurant. She wondered if Rachel was gay or straight. She never did have good gaydar. It didn't matter anyway. Bartenders worked nights, and Veronica wanted someone to spend her evenings with. Someone to cook dinner with and snuggle on the sofa with while they watched a movie. She wanted *that* life—the life she'd put off for far too long.

❖

Veronica looked at her watch. "Bea!"

"Sorry!" Bea rushed into the office and pushed a few buttons on her phone. "Okay, sent!" She sat. "Are you going to tell me how last night's date went?"

"Two words. Shirley Temple."

"Yeah," Bea said. "The drink choice concerned me too. Isn't that something kids usually order?"

Between the drinks and the constant giggling, Penelope did seem rather childlike. "Let's just say she's a very young thirty-one. But it's not worth rehashing." So far, none of the dates had been worth telling Bea or her mother about. She'd managed to blow off their constant queries so far.

Veronica pulled up the just-sent email and perused the profile of tonight's date. "Oh, she's pretty." She was breaking her own rule. So far, Veronica had been good about not opening the emails until just before date time. All bets were off after Shirley Temple. She needed to know tonight's date was a bona fide grown-up. Veronica leaned on her elbows and expanded the profile photo. "Very pretty."

"Who is?" Veronica's ex-lover, Avery, sauntered into the office. She never just walked. She sauntered.

Bea stood and made a quick exit. "I'll close the door behind me."

Avery sat. "Why does your assistant hate me?"

Veronica pulled her eyes away from her phone. "Because you're unlikeable."

"That's not what you said when I had you up against—"

"Not here." Veronica put her phone down. "Please, Avery."

"Yes. That's exactly what you said when I had you up against that wall over there."

Avery Hunt was a pretentious, arrogant, sexy-as-hell tax attorney with a full roster of downright shady clients. Avery and Veronica had been in a relationship, if you could call it that, for all of three months. A relationship that had been kept quiet for the most part. Veronica hadn't even told her own mother about it. Why bother when she knew what the outcome would be before they even had their first kiss?

Avery had joined the firm the previous year. She'd brought with her those shady clients and a pair of legs that Veronica had been caught staring at more than once. Avery made her move one night in Veronica's office when they were both working late. And from that moment on, Avery never let Veronica forget how easy it had been to seduce her. They'd barely spoken at all except for a few hellos in the hallway. And yet, a few sexy words whispered in her ear, and Veronica was there for the taking.

"Oh God. *Please*, Avery." Avery leaned back in the chair and giggled at her own joke. Veronica didn't laugh. "I'm just teasing you, V. Now, tell me. Who's the lucky girl that's caught your eye?"

"Promise not to laugh?"

"Why would I laugh?"

"Because you're kind of bitchy." Veronica sighed. "Fine. I'm on Ryder."

Avery's eyes widened in surprise. "No way."

"Way."

"Wow. You really *are* serious about that white picket fence."

That white picket fence was exactly why Veronica had broken it off with Avery. The sex had been great, but it wasn't enough. And when someone is always the first to leave the bed, it was telling. Veronica knew because she'd been that person too—not wanting to get so wrapped in a woman that her priorities would change. Her career came first, and she didn't begrudge Avery for feeling the same way. "I'm also serious about making partner. So, please, Avery."

Avery sat forward and put an arm on the desk. "Oh, the begging again. You know what that does to me."

Veronica rolled her eyes. "God, you're something else."

Avery grinned. "I am. And so are you, Veronica Welch." She reached across the desk and ran her finger over Veronica's arm. "Forget whoever's in your phone. Let me take you to dinner. We could go to that place you love so much, with the tiramisu. We'll get it to go, and I'll lick it off your amazing body at my place. What do you say?"

It was tempting. Avery, with her perfect auburn hair and that little dent in her chin. God, it was tempting. But they were in different places, and Veronica didn't want to waste her time or, even worse, get her heart broken. "I appreciate the offer, Ave. I really do. But I have a date tonight with," Veronica looked at her phone, "Randi."

Avery stood and leaned on the desk, giving Veronica a peek down her silk blouse. The bra was pink today, which meant the panties were as well. She tried not to think about how good it would feel to slide her fingers into those panties and find bare skin. She looked away, but it was too late. Avery knew where her mind had gone.

"Yeah," Avery said in her sexiest voice. "I was thinking the same thing." She straightened and put her hands on her curvy hips. Veronica made eye contact again. Avery bit her lip, then winked. "Have fun tonight."

Veronica knew that wasn't what Avery wanted to say, but it was sweet of her to voice the sentiment. "Thanks, Avery. See you tomorrow."

❖

Randi was the perfect distraction from Avery and her lovely offer to smear tiramisu all over her body and then lick it off. She was curvy in all the right places and wore her blond hair in a cute bob that she tucked behind her ears. She was talkative but not overly talkative the way Shirley Temple was. And she definitely seemed interested in Veronica. Her eyes had roamed over her body several times already. They were off to a good start, and that was a relief.

"I've never been here before. It's nice," Randi said.

"It is nice. I've been here a few times." Five, to be exact. Veronica had to admit that Bea had done well with her choice of bars. These dates could've happened anywhere, but she'd chosen a quaint, intimate place that wasn't too crowded and just happened to be right next door to an Italian restaurant that had great reviews. If things went well with Randi, a dinner table for two was just a few feet away. Veronica found herself hoping that was exactly where they'd end up. She could picture herself asking about Randi's family over a medium rare filet. Or a bowl of bolognese. Anything, really. She'd skipped lunch, and the small bowl of nuts on the table wasn't cutting it. Maybe she should just make the reservation right now. Why wait until the designated thirty minutes was up? *Just go ahead and ask her to dinner.*

"Do you live close by?"

"I work close by," Veronica said.

"I do too. Maybe we could do lunch sometime."

"Or dinner." Veronica picked up her phone. "Do you like Italian? The restaurant next door has excellent reviews."

Randi glanced at her purse sitting on the floor. "You mean now?"

"Well, we can finish our drinks first." Veronica picked up the large glass and put it to her lips.

Randi looked at her purse again and said, "I have a pet boa constrictor."

Veronica choked on her piña colada. She put her napkin over her mouth and sputtered into it, then held up a finger, indicating she needed a second. She needed more than a second. How was this information not in the profile? Randi looked concerned, so Veronica managed to blurt out, "I'm fine," then covered her mouth again and proceeded to cough up her right lung.

Randi's look of worry turned into one of determination. She grabbed both of their purses and took Veronica's arm. "Stand up. I'm taking you to the restroom."

It was for the best. Veronica didn't want to get banned from the bar for spewing rum and pineapple juice on the other customers, especially since she still had twenty-five more dates scheduled there. Also, what was it with these cute girls and their questionable drink choices? Had no one heard of a simple vodka tonic? Or a glass of red?

In the restroom, Randi wet down a paper towel and gave it to Veronica. "Just breathe."

That was proving difficult. Veronica bent over and coughed as hard as she could a few more times. It seemed to help settle things. She straightened back up and leaned against the wall. "Sorry."

Randi had a nice smile. Genuine. Her touch was nice too. She gently wiped the leftover tears from Veronica's cheeks with a tissue. "It's okay. I take it you don't love snakes."

Does anyone? Veronica noticed the small cage sitting on the sink next to Randi's massive handbag. Oh, God. Was that a live mouse? How had she not noticed Randi carrying that when she walked into the bar? "Is that…" *Snake food?* She leaned against the counter and tried not to faint.

"I probably should've put Vicki in my profile."

"Vicki?" Veronica put her hand over her mouth and coughed a few more times.

"That's her name. My pet boa constrictor. Sorry, but the pet store was closing. I had to get Vicki's dinner before I came here."

Veronica glanced at the mouse again. Was this really happening? Randi stepped closer and pushed a lock of hair behind Veronica's ear. "Don't hold it against me. Not yet. I think you're beautiful, Veronica, and if we weren't in a bathroom, and you weren't choking, I'd kiss you right now."

Veronica noticed part of a tattoo peeking out from under Randi's scoop-neck blouse. It looked like the tip of a forked tongue was licking her breast. She had to know. "Is that Vicki?"

Randi's eyes lit up. She pulled her blouse to the side and revealed a coiled-up snake squeezing the life out of a human heart. "Vicki, meet Veronica."

Veronica wanted to jump up onto the counter so the imaginary snakes that were now covering the floor couldn't get to her. She was truly freaking out on the inside, but she managed to push herself up and sit on the counter. "I'm sorry, Randi, but I don't do snakes. They terrify me."

Randi's smile faded. "Oh." She covered the tattoo with her blouse.

"I'm sorry. I wasn't thinking." She looked at Veronica's shaking hands. "Wow, they really do freak you out."

"It was my childhood nightmare, waking up and seeing snakes slithering all over the floor. I blame Indiana Jones." The mouse squeaked in its little cage. Veronica covered her eyes and tried to block the images of a snake devouring the poor little guy. "I think it's best if we just call it a day. I'm too freaked out to be good company right now."

"Sure." Randi grabbed the mouse cage and tucked it behind her purse. "I'm really sorry about this."

Veronica felt like such a fool for reacting the way she had. She put up her hands. "It's okay. Really."

"Okay, then." Randi backed toward the door. She was kind enough to make sure the mouse stayed hidden. "Good to meet you, Veronica."

"Good to meet you too." Veronica gave her a little wave. When the door closed, she took a deep breath and shook her head at herself. She slipped off the counter and turned to look in the mirror. Her mascara wasn't too bad. Just a couple of smudges from the coughing attack. She cleaned up a little, ran her fingers through her hair, grabbed her purse, and headed for the door, running smack into Rachel, the hot bartender. "Oh! Sorry."

Rachel put her hands on Veronica's shoulders. "Are you okay? We saw what happened."

We? Who's we? Did the whole bar witness her choke on a damned piña colada? "Yeah, um…I'm fine."

"How about some water?"

Veronica's throat felt rough. Water sounded good. She gave Rachel a nod and followed her to the bar.

"She's fine. Just needs a little water," Rachel said.

Veronica watched in confusion as three customers sitting on the short side of the bar nodded their understanding. Charlotte, the regular bartender, was there too. She opened a small bottle of water and slid it across the bar. "Here you go."

"Thanks." Veronica set her purse on the bar and sat on a stool. She could feel everyone's eyes on her as she took the first sip. Even Rachel was leaning against the back of the bar with her arms folded, still looking concerned. She wasn't wearing an apron this time. Just a T-shirt and jeans with a cool leather belt. The silver buckle looked like a camera lens or something. Veronica wanted to squint to get a better look, but she'd embarrassed herself enough already. She'd leave appearing to squint at another woman's crotch for a different day.

"She seemed nice, the woman with the pet mouse," Charlotte said.

Veronica watched the three customers nod in what appeared to be a unanimous vote. "It wasn't a pet. It was dinner." They all looked horrified. Good. At least Veronica wasn't alone in that. "For her pet boa constrictor."

Again, more horrified looks. But not from Rachel. She was snickering. *Yeah, laugh it up, beautiful.*

The older woman sitting between two men said, "We had high hopes for this one."

Rachel threw her hands in the air. "She ordered a piña colada! Do you see a beach anywhere nearby? Or even the sun?"

Charlotte shrugged. "It was an interesting choice."

Veronica didn't know what to think. These people, whoever they were, had obviously been watching the shit show that was her current dating life. Her first instinct was to run out of there and never go back. Bea could find a different location. A big bar where no one insinuated themselves into another person's business. But a part of her felt comfortable right where she was. They all had kind faces, these nosy people. What would it hurt to get to know them a little better? She kind of liked the idea of having a few kind strangers in her corner. "I'm Veronica."

"Yes, we know, dear. We've seen your profile on Ryder," the woman said. "I'm Carol, and this is my husband, Joe, and our friend, Harry."

"It feels like we've met, but I'm glad to do it formally." Charlotte pointed at her name tag. "Charlotte. I own the bar. And this is my cousin, Rachel."

They were cousins? Had Rachel said that to her earlier? Veronica thought back. Shit. She had, but Veronica had been blinded by Rachel's...well, everything really. Charlotte was on the short side with thick, curly red hair. Rachel was taller, and her hair was dark and straight. They couldn't have been more different, appearance-wise. Rachel pushed off from the back of the bar and offered her hand. "It's a pleasure, Veronica. Can I pour you a real drink?"

Rachel's low-timbred voice seemed to reverberate through

Veronica's body. She found herself not wanting to let go of her warm hand, but with several pairs of eyes focused on her, she gave it a firm shake. "The water is fine." She looked around, and those same eyes seemed to be filled with disappointment at her drink choice. Oh. Had they been watching this whole time hoping to find out Veronica's drink of choice? She'd save that little tidbit of information for a later date if they were still interested. In the meantime, she had a question for them. "If you've been watching my dates, who have you liked for me?"

The man with the blue eyes spoke up first. "I liked Appletini."

"Oh, Joe," Carol said. "You've always been a sucker for a girl with a big smile."

"Well, that's true," Joe said. "It's the first thing I noticed about you."

It was Veronica's second date who had ordered appletinis. Nice woman but zero chemistry. While Joe and Carol cooed at one another, she turned her attention to Harry. "What about you?"

Harry shrugged. "Doesn't matter what I think, but can I give you some advice?"

It was hard to see who Harry really was. The baseball cap cast a shadow over his eyes, and his face was covered in a rather thick beard. Veronica glanced at his hand and said, "You're not wearing a wedding ring. Should I trust the advice of a single man when it comes to love?"

Harry tilted his head and smiled. "You have a point. But I was married to a lovely woman for forty years. I'd still have the ring on, but she insisted I bury her with it. Till death do us part and all that."

"I'm sorry," Veronica said.

"Don't be. Like I said, I had forty great years with her. But I wouldn't have had any of that if I hadn't followed my gut. So, that's my advice. Follow your gut."

It wasn't bad advice. Veronica had followed her gut when it came to Avery. She remembered waking up one morning with a feeling of dread because she knew she had to end it. Avery wasn't her future. Her gut had told her that.

Rachel leaned on the bar and looked Veronica right in the eye. "I think you're going about this all wrong."

Veronica found Rachel's intense look unnerving, but she tried not to show it. "Last I checked, it wasn't up to you." She looked at Rachel's ring finger and continued, "Besides, you're not married, either."

"*No*. Definitely not."

Veronica wasn't sure why seeing a wedding ring on someone's finger mattered so much. She knew there were people who were completely committed to one another but had never taken any vows. Who was she to judge these people? "Okay, fine. How am I doing it wrong?"

Rachel smiled. She seemed grateful for the opportunity to share her wisdom. "You can't force fate any more than you can force someone to fall in love with you. It has to be organic. A thing that just happens."

Really? That was her big, important advice? "Organic?" Veronica said the word in a mocking tone and rolled her eyes. "I don't have time to hang out in the park or the pet store or a club or wherever the hell lesbians hang out and wait for someone to notice me from across the room."

"You don't hang out in pet stores? What kind of lesbian are you?"

Rachel was obviously mocking her. Lesbians didn't really hang out in pet stores, did they? Veronica wasn't even sure why she'd said it. Maybe it was because her first four dates had all talked about their pets. "The busy kind."

"You could notice them *first*, these women who might or might not notice you from across the room," Rachel said.

"Or here's a novel idea," Veronica said. "I could set up dates with women who I know are gay and buy them a drink."

"Yeah, about those drinks." Rachel raised her eyebrows and let out a slow whistle.

"Okay." Veronica was so over this conversation. She just needed to go home and sink into her favorite chair with a glass of something ice cold. With her feet up on the ottoman, of course, because snakes. She shivered at her own thought and checked the floor. Nope. No snakes.

"I have a question," Rachel said. "If you don't have time to really get to know a woman, how do you expect anyone to believe that would suddenly change once you married her?"

Who was this woman to judge? She had no idea how hard Veronica had worked to get where she was. How many hours she'd put in every week. It wasn't all for nothing. Once she made partner, she'd be able to relax a little bit. Take the weekend off a few times a month. Of course she'd have time for another person. She'd make time! "You don't know what you're talking about." Veronica held her stare. "When I find a wife, I'll have time for her *and* a damn dog. Because I want it all. I've worked too hard to not have it all. In fact, I'd even have time for Appletini *and* her petting zoo!"

Rachel laughed. "You don't remember her name, do you?"

She couldn't for the life of her remember her second date's name. Just that she helped run her family's mobile petting zoo business. Goddamnit, what was her name? The timer went off on her phone, causing it to vibrate.

"I think that means the date is over," Rachel said.

Carol reached over and patted Veronica's hand. "I don't think you've met her yet, but don't stop trying. You're a real catch."

Veronica looked at Rachel, who was still smirking as if she had some big secret. Man, that look pissed her off. "I'm not a quitter, Carol. See you tomorrow."

Chapter Three

C ould you maybe not be so hard on a regular customer?"
Rachel stopped counting cases of wine and set her clipboard
down. "It's ridiculous, Charlotte. *She's* ridiculous."

"Maybe she is. Or maybe she reminds you of someone you used
to love."

"She reminds me why it's better to keep it simple. And who's
choosing these women for her anyway? I could do a better job by
blindfolding myself and pointing at someone in my contact list."

"You've slept with everyone in your contact list. Besides, I doubt
Veronica would give you the time of day after the way you spoke to her
tonight."

"I'm just saying, no one finds the love of their life this way."

"Now you're an expert on love?" Charlotte stepped behind Rachel
and wrapped her arms around her. "Sorry. I didn't mean that the way it
sounded. I know it wasn't anything you did."

The last thing Rachel wanted to think about was her last failed
relationship. She patted Charlotte's hand. "You should go. You'll be
late."

"My mom's not going anywhere. Not yet, anyway. And I'm
worried about you. What's wrong with you?"

"You've got bigger things to worry about."

Charlotte let go and sat on a step stool. "When my mom goes, and
don't try to convince me she'll beat the cancer this time because we
both know she won't, when she goes, you're all I'll have left, Rach.
You and this bar. So, I'll worry about you as much as I damn well
please."

Rachel adored her cousin. Charlotte was a few years older, and she'd always been there for her. She stepped closer and cupped Charlotte's cheeks with her hands. "I'm fine. Really. Now, go be with your mom. Tell her I'll stop by soon. I have that wedding this weekend, but I promise I'll stop by soon. Can you tell her that?"

"Bring your camera?"

"Of course. She won't like it much, but I'll make sure I sneak in a few good shots."

"Thanks, Rach. I need all the photos I can get of her." Charlotte gave her a hug and left the storage room.

Rachel really wasn't sure why this whole "thirty dates" thing bothered her so much. Veronica seemed like a smart woman. At the top of her game, even. And then her date would walk in. The second her date arrived, Veronica seemed to lose her confidence. It was as if she had no idea what she was actually looking for in a woman. But how could someone so put together be so insecure about love? It certainly wasn't for a lack of confidence in who she was—and Rachel knew exactly who Veronica was. She'd looked her up online. Veronica was a business litigator for a major law firm. She represented large corporations in things like intellectual property disputes. Top of her class at Columbia, Law Review, some fancy clerkship, blah, blah, blah. And this amazing woman couldn't even order her own drink! She always ordered the same thing as her date, no matter how juvenile or ridiculous the drink was.

Rachel found herself wanting to scream at Veronica, *What's your fucking deal?* And yet, when she saw her choke on that piña colada, she felt more concern than she'd ever admit. Maybe that was just concern for her cousin more than Veronica. The last thing Charlotte needed was for an attorney to choke to death on the premises. The lawsuit would be never-ending. Yes, that was it.

Charlotte's father left the bar to her when he'd passed away several years ago. She'd been sinking all of her money into it ever since, and it was paying off. The neighborhood had improved in the last couple of years, and Monaghan's was well positioned on a good block. Rachel had worked nights in the bar for her uncle John while she was building her photography business. These days, she covered for Charlotte whenever she could. She no longer had to, but she wanted to. Charlotte needed the help more and more now that her mother was ill.

Besides, Rachel and Charlotte were like sisters, so no request was too big or too small. Rachel knew Charlotte's time with her mom would be short-lived. She'd be there every night if she could. For now, that was manageable since it wasn't wedding season yet. She still had a month before she'd be booked solid every week. She loved that she could put Charlotte first. Unfortunately, that also meant she'd have to continue to watch the hot lawyer awkwardly navigate those stupid dates. If only Veronica wasn't looking for true love. Rachel would show her how fun a good one-night stand could be.

❖

"A snake."

Bea stopped mid-stride and lifted one foot. "Oh God! Where?"

"Not here," Veronica said. "I'm talking about Piña Colada."

Bea dropped her foot and sat in the chair across from Veronica. "Maybe it's the way I ask the question. Instead of asking what their favorite drink is, maybe I should ask what they drink on the regular."

"Scotch and soda." Avery walked in and sat in the chair next to Bea. "Buy me a drink, Bea?"

Bea seemed to wilt under Avery's cool stare. Veronica could've saved her by breaking in, but she kind of wanted to hear Bea's answer.

Bea coughed. "Well...um...sure."

Avery giggled and slapped Bea's knee. "At least you didn't run out of the room the second I came in." She turned her attention to Veronica. "Tell me about your date last night. I'm dying to hear all of the gory details."

Veronica rolled her eyes. "It involved a mouse, a snake tattoo, and me choking—"

"Oh my God!" Avery leaned forward. "You didn't tell me you were into kinky shit."

Bea looked horrified. She swallowed hard and raised her hand. "Did it hurt? The tattoo. I've thought about getting a unicorn on my... anyway, I'm afraid it will hurt."

Veronica gasped. "You think I got a tattoo of a snake? *Me?* Who hates snakes with a burning passion?"

"I love it when you talk dirty," Avery said. "Tell me more."

"I didn't get a tattoo of a snake or anything else. Piña Colada had the tattoo." Veronica shooed them away with her hand. "Never mind. It didn't work out."

"Well, of course not," Avery said. "Her name is Piña Colada. What were you thinking?"

"No," Bea said. "Her name is Randi. Her favorite drink is a piña colada."

Avery shrugged. "I'll ask again. This time the question is directed to both of you. What were you thinking?"

"There will be some misses," Veronica said. "All I need is one good one. Bea, there was no way for you to know that Randi has a pet boa constrictor named Vicki. Keep doing your thing. And if you can find a way to casually determine reptile ownership status, maybe on Facebook or something, please do so."

Avery looked at Bea. She mouthed the name *Vicki?*

Veronica turned her attention back to her computer screen. "Working on a summary judgment here, ladies. Do you mind?"

Avery stood. "I expect more details later." She smiled at Bea as she left. "See you later, Bea."

Once Avery was gone, Bea waved a hand in front of her face. "I can't breathe around her."

Veronica raised an eyebrow. "Why is that?"

"She's so intimidating. I feel like she can see right through my clothes to my Supergirl underwear."

"Hers are black silk, just like the bra she wants all of us to get a look at." Veronica rolled her eyes.

Bea shook her head. "Black silk…That doesn't help."

Veronica laughed. "No, I'm sure it doesn't. Look, she's not so bad. She just likes everyone to think she'd eat their spleen for dinner."

"Hey, sounds like a great candidate for date number six. Spleen eating could be a step up!"

"I'm not so sure about that." Veronica wasn't about to admit just how horrible the date had been, with the coughing and the mouse, and the jumping up on the bathroom counter. "Last night was thirty minutes I can never get back, but not the end of the world."

Bea stood. "Let's hope for better things tonight. I'm just waiting on the drink order, and then I'll send her profile."

❖

Veronica rushed into the bar and looked around. Her usual table was empty, so she sat and looked at her phone one last time. She didn't recognize the drink her date had requested. Charlotte stepped up and set two bar napkins on the table. "I can't wait to see what you'll be drinking tonight."

"Yeah, me too. A Jägerbomb?" She said it with a hard *J*. "I've never heard of it."

Charlotte looked surprised. "Well, this should be interesting."

"Haven't had a boring drink yet." Veronica waved at the three regulars sitting at the bar. They all lifted their glass to her and smiled. She watched Charlotte put two glasses on the bar and report the drink order to them. It was met with raised eyebrows and a chuckle from Harry. He said something to the other two and held his glass up for a toast. Great. Just great. Whatever a Jägerbomb was, it couldn't be good.

Veronica's phone vibrated. It was a text from a number she didn't recognize. Bea had given all of the dates Veronica's cell number in case there was a problem with the meeting time or place. She hoped it wasn't Jägerbomb canceling on her. She opened the text, and there was a huge emoji. It was the poop emoji. The one from the commercials. Veronica couldn't fathom a more appalling introduction to her date for the evening.

And then the poop started talking.

> *Hey, gurrrl! It's me, Cameron, but everyone calls me Cam. Bitchy day all around, but can't wait to get wasted with you. Don't bail on me. I'll be there soonish. Like, five minutes tops. Had to go home and freshen up the armpits, but you'll thank me for that later. Okay, babe-eh-liscious. Cam out! (Kissing noises)*

A talking poop. Veronica set the phone on the table and folded her arms. She and Bea would need to have a serious talk about this one. She picked the phone back up and looked at Jägerbomb's profile again. Thirty years old. Sous chef. Loved adventure of any kind. Lived in Paris for a year. She seemed normal enough, so long as she didn't own a snake. The test would be whether or not she knew what five minutes was. Veronica switched over to her email. Never one to waste time, she'd use the four and a half minutes she had left to catch up on work.

Not more than two minutes later, a woman walked in and shouted, "Dude!" She rushed over to Veronica's table. "So sorry I'm late." She sat at the table and offered her hand. "I'm Cam."

"Veronica."

"Cool. Cool. But do you have a nickname, because that's, like, three syllables too long for me."

A woman of few syllables. That was something new. "You can call me V."

"*Vee*. I like it. It's like I'm breathing a sigh of relief when I say your name. Or, like, if I say it lower, it's kinda sexy. Know what I mean, *Vee*?"

Veronica really needed a sip of that Jägerbomb right about now. She saw Charlotte approach with two pint glasses and two shot glasses. She set one of each in front of Veronica and then Cam. "Enjoy," she said with a wink.

"Dude, I need this so bad." Cam dropped the shot glass into the larger pint glass and gulped half of it down.

Veronica should've googled it. Why didn't she google it? "Can I ask what I'm drinking here?"

"Oh! You'll love it. It's Red Bull and Jägermeister." Cam dropped Veronica's shot glass into the pint. "I never feel drunk when I drink JBs, but a good time is always had, know what I mean?"

"Uh-huh. Sure." The drink was surely an acquired taste—if cough syrup was something one could acquire a taste for.

"So, you're a lawyer." Cam stated it matter-of-factly with a big bob of her head.

"I am. Business litigation."

"Cool. Cool." Cam downed the other half of her drink and waved the bartender over. "But a lawyer is a lawyer, right? Like, say, if someone had a super-minor weed charge hanging over their head. Yeah, two more," she said to Charlotte.

Veronica put up her hand. "I'm good."

"No, dude. You gotta have two. One barely takes the edge off. Two makes the world go round. Know what I'm sayin'?" Cam gave her a big wink and laughed.

Veronica looked at Charlotte. "Two more." She probably wouldn't drink the second one, but she really didn't want to argue the point. She glanced at the regulars. Carol didn't look pleased. She pursed her lips together and gave Veronica a mom look that said, *Don't you dare bring that girl into my house.*

"So, about the weed charge thing," Cam said. "It's actually me. I made a super-stupid move, and I just need it to go away, so I'm thinking maybe you could help me."

Maybe one more sip of the JB, as Cam called it, wouldn't hurt. After taking the sip, Veronica dabbed the corners of her mouth with a napkin and hoped her eyes wouldn't water. It really was the most disgusting drink she'd ever had. She put on a fake smile and said, "Cam, if someone stole your intellectual property, I'd be your girl. But weed is a whole different area of the law."

"My intellectual what? No, it's not that complicated. I don't usually buy it off the street, but this one night—"

"Tell me about your job," Veronica said, interrupting her. "I'd love to hear what the life of a sous chef is like." Even as Veronica asked the question, her attention was stolen by the woman who'd just walked in. Rachel looked hotter than ever in her low-cut jeans and what looked like motorcycle boots. Her T-shirt was tighter today too, which didn't hurt. She smiled at Veronica, then eyed the drinks that were on Charlotte's tray as she passed by. She raised an eyebrow and continued on her way to the back.

"Oh, she's hot," Cam said.

"Yeah." Veronica watched until Rachel disappeared. She couldn't blame Cam for appreciating Rachel too. The woman was a knockout but smarmy as hell every time she opened her mouth. It was a frustrating combination.

"This time you're chugging it," Cam said.

Veronica hadn't heard that word since college. And she certainly hadn't chugged anything alcoholic since then either. "I don't think that's a good idea. I have to go back to work later."

"No, dude. Don't tell me that. I thought we'd party tonight. Get to know each other at your place. Maybe…" Cam put two fingers up to her mouth and did a quick inhale as if she was smoking a joint. Veronica hoped Carol wasn't watching from across the bar. She took a quick look, and sure enough, Carol was shaking her head.

Veronica imagined not many women had ever kicked Cam out of

bed. She had beautiful blue eyes and long, straight dark hair. Her voice had a husky, sexy tone to it. In many ways, she reminded Veronica of Demi Moore. And who wouldn't want to take Demi Moore home and get to know her better?

But if sex was all Veronica was after, she could get that from Avery. Unfortunately, something told her Cam had only accepted this date in hopes of getting some free help from an attorney regarding her "minor weed charge."

Cam held the Jägerbomb in front of Veronica and urged her to take it. She glanced over at the bar again. Everyone, including Rachel, was watching her. She appreciated the others' concern, but Rachel's disapproving look just pissed her off. Judgy McJudgerson, that's what she'd call her from now on. She took the drink from Cam's hand and gulped down most of it, then wiped her mouth with the back of her hand. It tasted so bad a shiver ran through her body, but she shook it off and threw a fist in the air.

"That's what I'm talkin' 'bout!" Cam clapped dramatically, then downed half of her second drink.

It didn't take long for the alcohol to kick in. Veronica giggled so hard she snorted. It felt kind of good to let go, even though she knew she'd regret it in the morning. Cam told good jokes. Or maybe they were only funny because Veronica was tipsy. No, drunk. She was definitely drunk.

Two glasses of water were set on the table. "Dude, you read my mind," Cam said to Rachel.

Veronica held up the glass in a toast-like fashion. "Yeah, dude. Mind. Read."

She expected Rachel to move on, but she stayed at the table and folded her arms. "Anything else, or can I bring the bill?"

"I really need to pee." Cam stood and bounced on both feet until Rachel threw a thumb behind her, pointing out the way, then she jogged to the restroom.

"Perfect timing," Rachel said. "She leaves when the bill is brought up."

"Listen, Judgy." Veronica's words came out slurred. She tried again. "Listen, Sexy. I mean, Rachel. I'm paying like I always do." She handed Rachel her entire purse.

"The Amex?" Rachel took the purse and pulled out the wallet.

Veronica gave her a nod. "Yeah, dude."

"Drink that water while I run this."

Veronica gave her another nod and watched her walk away. Rachel, the snarky, rude, hot bartender, made her feel warm inside. "Warm," she shouted. Luckily, Rachel didn't turn around.

CHAPTER FOUR

The dress didn't fit right. Two adjustments with the tailor, and it still gaped open at her cleavage. Veronica tugged on the coral satin, but her bra was still visible. The dark circles under her eyes were ridiculous. What was she thinking, drinking two Jägerbombs the night before her cousin's wedding? "I don't have to be in the wedding party," she said. "Seriously, Tiff. Just leave me out. I'm a disaster."

"Bullshit, V. Here!" Her cousin, Tiffany, threw her a bra. "It's a push-up. Your boobs will look fantastic, and really, what else matters?"

"Says the straight girl."

"Oh, please. You're telling me lesbians don't appreciate a pushed-up set of tits in some silk?"

"It doesn't hurt, but it's not a deal breaker."

"Just put on the damn bra, V. I'm not getting married without you."

Veronica looked at the padded bra and sighed. "Fine." She went into the bathroom and put it on, then looked in the mirror. Tiff was right. Her boobs looked great in the deep V-neck dress. It was more cleavage than she was used to showing off, and she'd probably hate Tiff's wedding photos for the rest of her life, but she didn't have any other options. Today, she'd have to be *boob girl*.

The bridal room had filled with people by the time she stepped out of the bathroom. Her fellow bridesmaids were all there, along with other female family members. Veronica's mom spotted her and walked over. "Stand still, V. Let me look at you."

No matter how old or successful Veronica became, she knew she'd always be sixteen in Karen Welch's eyes. An insecure teenager who needed her mother's advice and direction. Her mom scrutinized her closely. She swiped a hand over her hair to smooth it down. "Your hair looks great, but you need more concealer under your eyes." She pulled several tubes out of her purse that were mostly lipstick, then chose one and threw the rest back in. "Look up. Good, now tell me why you're showing off everything God gave you."

"Not everything. Just my fabulous, sky-high boobies."

Her mom pulled back and inspected her work. "That's much better." She glanced at Veronica's chest and pursed her lips together.

"I know," Veronica whispered. "It's too low, but I can't do anything about it now."

"No, I don't suppose you can. Just make sure you stand tall. No slouching, or there will be gapping." Her mom turned and took Veronica's arm. "Now, doesn't your cousin look gorgeous?"

"She looks amazing." They stood there admiring Tiffany in her wedding dress. Her blond hair had been styled in an updo that perfectly complimented her long veil. It reminded Veronica of when they were young and played dress-up. Tiffany always wanted to be a princess, and today, she looked like one.

For the last several months, this wedding was all Veronica's mother could talk about. The whole family was thrilled when Tiffany's fiancé proposed to her on Christmas Eve. It was a storybook romance. Two people meeting and knowing in an instant that they'd spend their lives together. Veronica was so happy for Tiffany but also slightly jealous. Would she ever have a storybook romance?

Veronica was starting to think she'd waited too long to look for love. *Real love.* The kind that knocked you off your feet at first but then grounded you in a way nothing else could. The kind that gave you a home, no matter where you were. Tiffany had found it with Eric, and Veronica couldn't have been happier for her.

"Oh, honey." Her mother took a tissue out of her sleeve and dabbed Veronica's tears away. "Why are you crying? You'll ruin your makeup."

"I just feel emotional today, I guess. I don't know why."

"We all do. Your father always cries at weddings. Look at the ceiling."

Veronica tried not to blink while her mom dabbed under her eyes. Maybe it was the hangover that was making her so emotional. Maybe it was seeing Tiffany in her princess wedding dress. Or maybe it was because her boobs were on display for the whole world to see.

"There. All done. You look gorgeous."

Veronica didn't feel gorgeous, but she gave her mom a smile. "Do you think this will ever happen for me?"

"You only just took your head out of those legal briefs long enough to start looking," her mom said. "Of course it will happen. She's out there."

Veronica nodded. And then it hit her, why she felt so emotional. She wanted this. She wanted it even more than she'd let herself realize. She'd always looked at it as a box to check. School, then career, then family. Simple as that. But after years of focusing on nothing but her career, her heart longed for the warmth of another person in her bed. Not just any person. Someone who loved her with their whole heart. Someone who couldn't live without her. Someone she felt lost without. Someone who...

Veronica's attention lapsed. She watched in shock as Rachel walked in the room. Rachel, the snarky, impossibly beautiful bartender Rachel. She took Tiffany's hand and kissed it, then kept hold of it and took a step back to look at her dress. "Wait. What? Who?" Veronica stuttered.

"The photographer," her mom exclaimed. "They're old college friends." She lowered her voice. "I'd love to book her for your wedding one day, but this is strictly a favor for Tiffany. Apparently, she's highly sought after by New York's elite crowd, celebrities and such."

"Wait. Rachel is the photographer?" Veronica was confused. This person wasn't supposed to be in this room with these people. She belonged in the bar, with Charlotte and Harry and Joe and Carol and Piña Colada and whoever else happened by.

Her mom rambled on. "Tiffany is so lucky. Her friend's work has even been featured in *Town and Country*. Oh, and *Vogue*!"

"Rachel," Veronica whispered.

Her mom turned to her. "Do you know her?"

"What? No. I mean, not really." Veronica's eyes fluttered closed as the memories of the previous evening came rushing forward. The memories she had anyway. She was so drunk, Rachel and Jägerbomb had to call an Uber and physically put her in the car. Then Rachel placed what looked like a small office trash can on her lap and said,

"Don't mess up this nice man's car." Veronica cringed at the thought. Should she find a way to inform Rachel that she hadn't needed to avail herself of the trash can? Or maybe she should just pretend it never happened. What were the odds of dying in this very moment? They felt higher than normal, and Veronica thought maybe it wouldn't be the worst thing. Good God. Was there a way to disappear into oblivion? Or if nothing else, cover up this cleavage?

"V!" Tiffany waved her over.

Rachel turned. When their eyes met, Rachel furrowed her brow, then she got that annoying little smile that bugged Veronica so much. God, this day would go down in history as the most humiliating ever, she was sure of it. Okay. Maybe it was tied with the night before.

"We'll start in here," Rachel said. "The light is great right now, and everyone looks gorgeous, by the way."

Rachel had looked right at Veronica when she'd said that last part and let her eyes wander down her dress and back up. Thank God she turned her attention back to Tiffany because Veronica was sure her chest had turned several shades of red.

She watched with interest as Rachel directed the show. First, she had Tiffany stand by the window. The light almost made a halo effect around her, and Veronica had to hold back the tears again. Tiffany looked angelic and so very happy. At times, Veronica found herself so riveted she actually forgot about her intense desire to run screaming out into the streets of Manhattan.

Rachel and a young man Veronica assumed was her assistant saw to every detail. They made sure there wasn't a hair out of place or a poorly placed flower in Tiffany's bouquet. Faces were powdered, shoulders straightened, angles adjusted, chins tilted just so. Veronica found herself mesmerized by Rachel's every move. The clicking of the camera and Rachel's gentle direction almost put her in a trance-like state.

"I need you now." Rachel offered her hand to Veronica. "You okay?" she whispered.

"Fine. I'm fine."

Rachel led her to a spot at Tiffany's side. She kept hold of her hand and looked at the two of them, then squeezed Veronica's hand and said, "Come forward just a smidge. Perfect."

Veronica found it hard to focus on the camera. Rachel had on that cool belt with the camera lens again, which made total sense now. She had on black jeans that fit her body like a glove, a black T-shirt, and a short-waisted black jacket. It was subtle, so she wouldn't stand out in the wedding crowd, Veronica assumed. But she did stand out, and Veronica couldn't take her eyes off her.

"Up here," Rachel said, pointing at the lens.

"Right." Veronica put on a smile, but it faded when Rachel walked toward her with a look of concern. "What's wrong?"

"May I?" Rachel pointed at her chest. "It's just gapping a little bit."

Veronica hadn't ever had the chance to look closely enough at Rachel to know she had hazel eyes. She'd never noticed the tiny mole under her right eye, either. Or the little scar on her chin that must've been from a childhood fall. But it was Rachel's lips that thrust Veronica into a parallel universe. So pink. So smooth. And close enough to kiss. Tiffany nudged Veronica back into reality. She cleared her throat and said, "Right! Um, do what you have to do."

Rachel gave the dress a gentle tug. Her index finger grazed the top of Veronica's breast. "There. That's better. Relax, okay?"

Veronica didn't realize she'd stopped breathing. Tiffany placed a hand on her back. "You okay, V? You look a little flushed."

"Yeah. I'm fine. Good. We're good to go." She wasn't fine at all. Rachel had taken her breath away, and she was having a hard time hiding it. She forced a smile and glanced around the room. Their mothers were looking on with pride. The three other bridesmaids were fussing over themselves in the mirror. And then there was Rachel. Sexy without even trying Rachel. Bartender slash photographer Rachel. You make my heart skip a beat Rachel. Good Lord. Veronica knew she needed to get a grip. And fast.

Veronica thought back to when she'd woken up that morning. She honestly thought she'd never drink alcohol again. How quickly things changed. As a waiter passed by with a tray of champagne, she grabbed a glass for herself and one for her mother. "Bottoms up, Mom."

"You seem very anxious, dear." Her mom held up the glass with raised eyebrows. "Is there something I don't know about? Or perhaps, someone? Maybe a love interest?"

"What? No. I told you, none of the dates have worked out so far."

"I'm not talking about the dates." Her mother pointed across the room. "I'm talking about the photographer you claimed you didn't know but haven't taken your eyes off all night."

Veronica resisted the urge to look at Rachel. She was on the other side of the ballroom, waiting for the first dance to happen. "I don't know what you're talking about."

"She's been looking at you too, you know."

"She has?" Veronica tried to play it cool, but the lilt in her voice completely betrayed her.

"She has indeed."

If Rachel had been looking at her, Veronica certainly hadn't noticed it. Sure, their eyes had met a few times, but Rachel was busy doing her job. She didn't have time to—and then it happened. Rachel looked right at her and smiled. It wasn't the smirk she usually had; it was a genuine smile. And it was a beautiful smile. The kind only Rachel could give. Veronica handed her glass to her mother. "I have to do something."

What that something was, Veronica wasn't sure. But she wasn't going to waste another second not talking to Rachel. She worked her way through the crowd of waiters and guests. She didn't have much time before the music started, and Rachel would be busy again. She walked right up to her and said, "Hey."

"Hey." Rachel looked her up and down again. Her eyes landed on Veronica's very visible cleavage. "You clean up good."

Of course she'd say something sarcastic. "I wear a suit every day. How is that not clean?"

Rachel leaned in and whispered, "You're welcome for saving your ass last night."

"Yeah, about that. I looked at my Uber account this morning, and there wasn't a charge. Did you pay for it?"

"Well, you can be damn sure Jägerbomb didn't pay for it."

That's what Veronica assumed had happened. Rachel might be snarky and sarcastic, but she had a caring side to her as well. "Thank you. Really, Rachel. Thank you, for everything you did last night."

Rachel stared at her for a few seconds and said, "You're welcome. It really wasn't a big deal. I've called many an Uber for our customers."

"And paid for their ride?"

Rachel shrugged. "A few." She smiled at Veronica and asked, "Who gets the first dance?"

"My uncle David. His wife passed away when I was twelve. Ever since, he and I have found each other at weddings to dance the first dance together."

"That's very sweet," Rachel said. "And I think Uncle David is headed your way."

Veronica turned, and sure enough, there he was. She looked at Rachel again. "See you around."

"Hey, V?"

For some reason, Veronica liked hearing Rachel use her nickname. She must've heard Tiffany use it earlier. Or maybe Jägerbomb the night before. "Yeah?"

"Who gets the last dance?"

Rachel had said it in a flirty way, so Veronica decided to flirt back. "Isn't it tradition somewhere that a bridesmaid gives the photographer the last dance?"

Rachel grinned. "If it isn't, it should be."

"Agreed." Veronica took her uncle's arm. "See you later."

There would be far too many photos of Veronica Welch on Rachel's camera. Candid shots taken when she was unaware she was even being photographed. Rachel took those kinds of shots all the time at weddings, but never so many of the same person. She couldn't help herself.

She also couldn't help feeling protective of Veronica the night before. Rachel basically grew up in her uncle's bar. She could spot bad intentions a mile away. And when Jägerbomb insisted on getting in the Uber and going home with Veronica because she felt responsible for getting her drunk, Rachel knew it was a lie. Whatever Jägerbomb had in mind for the rest of the evening wasn't going to happen when Veronica's decision-making abilities were compromised. Rachel laughed out loud at the choice of words in her head. Compromised. More like, her decision-making had gone to complete shit.

It wasn't an Uber Rachel had called. It was her friend Mike. He often worked the same weddings as Rachel did. Of course, most weddings—including Tiffany's—didn't require a security detail, but Rachel didn't shoot most weddings. She worked for the rich, ultra-rich, and sometimes famous, where security was a must-have. Mike, being a hulk of a man, often worked the front lines. He was the sweetest guy Rachel knew, often keeping an eye out for her when drunk, entitled assholes would take a special interest in the photographer. She trusted him to get Veronica home safely. He'd insist it wasn't necessary, but she already knew she'd be sending over a nice bottle of bourbon for his troubles.

When she had walked into the bridal room a few hours earlier, Rachel had been shocked to find Veronica there. Judging from the look on her face and the awkward-looking conversation that ensued with her mother, Veronica appeared just as surprised. The unexpected run-in was one thing. Rachel could manage that. But she certainly wasn't ready for how beautiful Veronica looked in that dress. The power suits she wore every day were hot, but that dress? Rachel had seen some ugly bridesmaid's dresses in her day. She often wondered if the brides purposely had their friends wear hideous styles just so they wouldn't outshine them, but that wasn't how Tiffany operated. She might not run in the same social circle as Rachel's typical clients, but Tiffany was all class. She wanted everyone to look their best on her big day. And Veronica looked absolutely stunning. The dress hugged every curve perfectly. And that plunging neckline? At one point, she considered sending Tiffany a thank-you card. It took all of her willpower to not stare endlessly.

"Someone's looking for you." Justin, her assistant, put a bag on the table and started loading up their gear. The bride and groom were on their way to the airport—destination unknown until they posted photos on Instagram, and then everyone had to guess where they'd gone on their honeymoon. Rachel had shot weddings just about everywhere. It wouldn't take her long to figure it out.

"Who?"

"That bridesmaid you've been shooting all night."

"What bridesmaid? I have not!"

"Yeah, okay, Miss Stalky Pants. Either way, she's looking for you. Something about the last dance."

Apparently, Rachel hadn't been very subtle with her camera. And why she'd asked Veronica who got the last dance was a question she'd been asking herself all night. She never danced at a wedding she was shooting. It just didn't happen. And it wouldn't happen tonight, either. She'd chalk it up to being busy until the very end. No big deal.

"I'll get this," Justin said. "Go find her."

That wasn't going to happen. Charlotte had warned Rachel to stay away from Veronica. She was looking for *real* love, Charlotte had said. She'd never hear the end of it if she slept with Veronica. And a dance would probably lead to more. Rachel was self-aware. She knew if she touched Veronica in an intimate way—and dancing could certainly be intimate—she'd want more. She'd want all of her. She'd want to devour Veronica Welch and then devour her again.

"Rach, I think you've missed something." Justin gave her a little shove. "A hot chick is looking for you. Why the hell are you still standing here?"

If it were anyone else, Rachel would have Veronica's number by now. She didn't make a habit of sleeping with bridesmaids on the night of the wedding, but she wasn't against getting a number for a later date. But Justin was right. A beautiful woman was looking for her, and she couldn't very well leave her hanging. That would just be rude. "Okay, pack up the gear and take it to my loft. I'll get a cab home."

"Good luck," Justin shouted.

"I won't need it," Rachel shouted over her shoulder.

Rachel made a habit of thanking the mother of the bride before she left. Most of her business came from word of mouth, so being gracious to the mothers was an important step to getting future business. Even though it wasn't as critical in this case, she'd known Tiffany's family for years and wanted to give them the same service everyone else got. When she walked back into the ballroom, the band was already breaking down their equipment. A group of people, including Tiffany's parents, sat at a large table, having what she assumed was a final glass of champagne.

"Rachel!" Tiffany's mother stood.

"Janice." Rachel kissed her cheek. "I don't want to interrupt."

"Nonsense. Have you met everyone? This is my sister, Karen Welch."

The woman stood and shook Rachel's hand. "Pleasure to meet you, Rachel. I believe you met my daughter, Veronica? She's an attorney at Belden and Snow. Very successful and very single. She'll make partner this year—"

"Oh, stop, Karen," Janice interrupted. "V doesn't need you trying to set her up. She's quite capable of finding a fantastic woman on her own."

Rachel held in her laughter. From what she'd seen, Veronica wasn't exactly batting a thousand when it came to finding a *fantastic woman*. "Yes, we've met. Veronica looked lovely today." She turned her attention back to Janice. "Give me a few days to sort through all of the photos, and then I'll send them to you and Tiffany."

"Excellent. Thank you, Rachel. I'm sure they'll be magnificent."

Rachel glanced over Janice's shoulder and noticed Veronica backing out of the ballroom. She'd changed into street clothes—really nice street clothes but street clothes nonetheless. Rachel guessed she was coming in to say good-bye to her family but saw Rachel there and changed her mind. Rachel said a quick good-bye to everyone and rushed to the door. "Veronica!" She was in the elevator when Rachel caught up to her. "Hey, wait a minute!"

"I was just leaving," Veronica said.

"Before saying good-bye?" Rachel held the elevator door open. She should've just let it go, but she couldn't. She felt bad that she'd brought up the last dance and then made sure she wouldn't be found when it happened. Veronica's tone was flat, and her expression was just this side of pissed off, so Rachel knew her feelings were hurt. "Look, I'm sorry about the dance. I stayed busy right up until the very end."

"What dance?"

So, she was going to pretend the conversation had never happened? Rachel stepped into the elevator. "Look, it's been a long day, and I could really use a drink. Would you like to join me?"

Veronica pushed the button for the lobby. "I could use a drink too, but I think I already spend too much time at your cousin's bar."

"I was thinking my place. It's closer. And I have this great bottle of wine I brought back from Italy. Do you like wine?"

"It sounds nice, but…"

"No buts," Rachel said. "One glass of the best wine you'll ever taste to make up for the dance we never had."

Veronica seemed to contemplate the idea. "I do like wine."

Rachel turned and stood next to her so they were both facing the door. "I'll have to tell Carol and Joe. They're dying to know what your favorite drink is."

"I never said wine is my favorite drink. It was just the only thing you offered."

"So, you're going to continue to drink whatever your dates order? Even after choking on a piña colada and suffering through that Jägerbomb?"

"My grandpa once told me that a person's drink can tell you a lot about them."

"Okay. But that doesn't mean you have to drink it too."

"Doesn't it?"

Rachel sighed. "I'm never going to know what your favorite drink is, am I?"

Veronica exited the elevator. "You could try to guess."

Rachel followed behind. "I accept that challenge."

CHAPTER FIVE

Veronica didn't have an artistic bone in her body. She'd failed art and aced calculus, both in the seventh grade. If someone asked her what her personal style was, she wouldn't have a clue how to describe it, except maybe as the stuffy lawyer type. Even now, she'd "dressed down" into jeans, a white blouse, and a navy suit jacket. She took the jacket off so she wouldn't look so stuffy.

Just because Veronica wasn't artistic didn't mean she couldn't appreciate Rachel's very cool aesthetic. She scanned the walls of the loft apartment. They were covered in travel photos and small works of art—she guessed Rachel had brought them home in suitcases. The leather furniture was well worn. There were colorful woven blankets folded over each end of the sofa, and several photography magazines were spread out on the coffee table. It was like a photographer's waiting room, if that was a thing.

One corner of the large living space was a makeshift office. The desk appeared to be a large door supported by two metal sawhorses. Veronica had never seen anything like it, but somehow, it worked in the eclectic space. She desperately wanted to say something clever. What came out was, "Very cool apartment."

"Thanks," Rachel said. "It's a work in progress. I just moved in a year ago." She pointed at the high ceiling. "See that spot? Right after I returned the tall ladder I'd rented, I realized I'd missed it with the second coat of paint."

Veronica could see the spot where the bright white paint hadn't quite covered up the old yellow paint, but she squinted. "I can't see it. Maybe I'm looking in the wrong place?"

"It's right—" Rachel dropped her hand. A look of realization crossed her face. "You're a nicer person than I thought you were."

Veronica gasped. "You didn't think I was nice?"

Rachel went to the kitchen and pulled a bottle of wine off the rack. "You're a sassy drunk. Anyway, after painting the place, I couldn't get used to climbing a ladder every day, so the first thing I did was put that in." She pointed to a spiral staircase that led up to the sleeping area.

Veronica craned her neck to look. "You had to climb a ladder to get up there?"

"I did. It was a nightmare. The staircase made my life so much easier."

Veronica did the math in her head. "Taking into account you might need to use the bathroom in the middle of the night, that's one thousand four hundred and sixty trips up and down a ladder per year."

Rachel's mouth hung open. "Wow. You just did that in your head?"

"I needed to redeem myself. I'm trying to impress you with multiplication so we can banish the sassy drunk thing from your mind."

Rachel held up a finger. "Did I say sassy? I meant sexy."

Veronica sat on a barstool at the butcher block kitchen island and watched Rachel uncork the wine like an expert, then pour a small amount in a glass. She put her nose to the glass and took in the aroma, then took a sip. "I think you'll like this," she said. "It's a favorite of mine. Brunello di Montalcino from Tuscany."

Veronica was more interested in the way Rachel moved than she was in knowing where the grapes were grown. She always moved with such confidence, whether she was pouring drinks or taking photographs or even just walking. She seemed to move through the world with an ease Veronica hadn't often seen.

Rachel rounded the island and sat on the stool next to Veronica. She held up her glass. "Cheers."

"Cheers." Veronica took a sip. "Wow, that's good."

"I'll give you a bottle. I brought back two on this last trip."

"You don't have to do that."

"I'm there a few times a year," Rachel said. "It's no big deal."

"A few times a year?"

"Italy is a popular place for destination weddings."

"Ah. Well, my mom did say that you're highly sought-after."

Rachel grinned. "Did she now?"

Veronica gave her a playful shove and clarified, "As a wedding photographer."

"I do okay," Rachel said. "And your mother told me you're a very successful attorney."

"She didn't." Veronica felt slightly horrified but not the least bit surprised.

"She did."

Veronica shrugged. "I do okay."

"Making partner seems huge."

"Oh my God, what didn't she tell you?"

"Aw, she's just proud. And really, it seems like she should be."

"Well, I've worked my ass off to get it. Put everything else on the back burner for it."

"Everything else?"

"Love. Marriage. Kids." Veronica sighed. "The stuff that makes getting old worth it."

"And you think you'll find that in a bar?"

"That's the plan," Veronica said. "Thirty dates in thirty days. Except it won't be exactly thirty days because things like my cousin's wedding come up."

"You could've brought her to the wedding."

"Who?"

"Jägerbomb? Piña Colada? Shirley Temple?"

Veronica covered her eyes with one hand and laughed. "Oh God. No. Definitely not." She took another sip of wine. "Although, I did think about bringing someone from work. A friend of mine. Well, a friend with benefits. But everyone would've dogpiled on her and asked when we were getting married."

"I take it she's not marriage material?"

Veronica had to think about that one. If given the opportunity to have a long-term relationship with Avery, would she? She didn't think so. "Avery is very married to her job."

"Like you," Rachel said.

"Like me. But that's changing. I need balance in my life. I need—"

"Love?"

"Doesn't everyone? In the end, isn't that what matters?"

Rachel set her glass down. "I suppose everyone is looking for that dream relationship, except apparently your friend." She paused. "With benefits."

Veronica thought she heard a tinge of annoyance or perhaps jealousy in Rachel's tone. Then again, maybe Judgy McJudgerson was on the loose again. "And while everyone else chases after the dream, you've got a front row seat being a wedding photographer."

"I guess. I help them craft the fairy tale."

Veronica shook her head. "I don't need a fairy tale. For the right girl, I'd get married at the courthouse, but my mother would kill me."

Rachel smiled. "So, you're a practical girl."

"Not always. I splurge on things."

"What things?"

"I have to look my best, so I splurge on clothes."

"I've noticed." Rachel reached over and touched the collar of Veronica's blouse. "Gucci?"

Their eyes met for a moment, and Veronica felt a tug in her stomach. Rachel hadn't touched her skin, just the collar of her blouse, yet she felt the heat between them. She set her glass down and said, "You know your designers."

"I know just enough to get by with my higher-end clients."

Veronica was close enough to see that sexy little mole under Rachel's eye again. Her throat tightened up, and her heart beat faster. "I like your belt buckle. That couldn't have been cheap."

"No, it wasn't," Rachel said. "An artist friend made it for me, so, I guess I splurge on clothing too."

With every passing second, Veronica found it harder and harder to breathe. She either needed to get away from Rachel's seductive stare or do something about it. She broke the connection by lowering her gaze. "You definitely splurge on your footwear." She could tell from the intricate stitching on the boots that they were high quality.

"Yeah, the trips to Italy have definitely fed a shoe addiction. Well, leather in general. Not to mention, wine, prosecco, cheese. God, I love that place."

"We Americans are heathens."

Rachel laughed. "We can be."

Veronica held Rachel's stare. It wasn't easy, seeing as how most of the oxygen had been sucked out of the room by some unseen force. "Rachel."

"Yes?" Rachel's knee grazed Veronica's. She didn't think it was an accident.

"I want to kiss you." She couldn't believe she'd said the words out loud. She quickly added, "But I'm terrible at making the first move."

"I find that hard to believe." Rachel leaned forward and made little circles on Veronica's knee with her finger. "Surely, a seasoned attorney such as yourself would be used to tense situations."

Butterflies had come to life in Veronica's stomach with only a single finger touching her body. What would happen if they actually kissed? "I do okay in the courtroom," she said. "But when it comes to a beautiful woman, I stumble and fall and make a fool of myself."

Rachel grinned. "Sounds sexy."

"Oh, it's so sexy. Would you like to see?"

"Does it involve choking on a piña colada?"

Veronica slapped her forehead. "Oh God." She was grateful for the comic relief. She needed to breathe.

"I'm kidding. Try me."

"Okay, but don't laugh if it's not sexy."

Rachel crossed her heart. "Promise."

Veronica was dead serious about what she'd said. The courtroom didn't scare her at all. She thrived in the courtroom. She relished it when she got the judge wrapped around her little finger. But trying to seduce a woman turned her into an anxiety-ridden mess. She took a breath and said, "I've been watching you all day. Is that creepy?"

"I've been taking pictures of you all day. Is that creepy?"

That made Veronica smile. "No, but only because you're a photographer."

"Oh, good. Please, go on."

"I wanted that dance tonight." That almost felt like too much honesty, but Veronica took another deep breath. "I looked for you."

"I'm sorry I wasn't there."

"Me too. Is this working?"

"It's working," Rachel said. "Keep going."

The air between them felt thick. Veronica found it increasingly hard to breathe and felt grateful she was sitting. But if she wanted that kiss, she needed to be brave, so she stood and moved closer. She rested a hand on Rachel's thigh to steady herself. "I've been attracted to you from day one." She felt like such a dork saying that out loud that she wanted to cover her eyes, then she felt Rachel's hand on her hip.

"Your bridesmaid's dress today? My God," Rachel said.

Veronica needed to touch Rachel somewhere. Anywhere. She needed to feel her skin. With a feather-light touch, she put her hand on Rachel's arm, just below the sleeve of her T-shirt. "You liked that dress?"

"Stunning. The sexiest bridesmaid's dress I've ever seen. I think Tiffany is a saint for letting you wear it."

It had never been like this for Veronica before. She'd certainly experienced the excitement of something new and even raw lust from time to time. Granted, not many times, but she wasn't counting. Especially not now. What was happening with Rachel felt like more than that. She caressed Rachel's arm with her thumb. "Am I close to getting a kiss?"

"Very. But you have to initiate it. That's the deal."

"Really? I have to?" Veronica was close enough to see the little gold flecks in Rachel's hazel eyes. She wouldn't have to lean in far for that kiss.

"Yes, you do," Rachel said. "It sounds like you could use the practice."

"You're right. I haven't had to initiate much."

"That doesn't surprise me," Rachel said.

Veronica wondered if she'd turned bright red with how hot she felt. Rachel's voice was low and sexy, her touch gentle but firm. She imagined where Rachel's hands would go. Since she was slightly taller than Rachel in this position, she imagined how good it would feel for Rachel to slide her hands around her hips and pull her closer.

And those lips. Veronica desperately needed to taste those perfect lips. "I can't really breathe right now, but I'm going to kiss you anyway."

"I'll breathe for both of us."

Veronica held her stare. That statement, even though it was probably just a line Rachel would use with anyone, touched her. "You might have to." She leaned in, and their lips met in a tender kiss. And then another. And nothing had ever felt so perfect.

It didn't take long for tender kisses to turn into an explosion of heat and desire. Rachel pulled back just long enough to say, "You take my breath away too."

Veronica wasn't sure if this kiss would kill her or make her fly. Either way, she knew she'd never be the same. She worked her way over to Rachel's ear and whispered, "God, you feel good," while she tried to steady herself. Rachel opened her legs and did just what Veronica had imagined; she pulled her closer.

Rachel kissed Veronica's neck and worked her way down her chest until her blouse got in the way. "Fucking Gucci," Rachel whispered.

Veronica needed more, and apparently, so did Rachel. She needed Rachel to go wherever she wanted, unimpeded by clothing. She unbuttoned her top button and then another. Rachel pushed the blouse aside and kissed Veronica's chest. She worked her way back up to the neck. Her kisses were soft and tender until she reached a spot just below Veronica's ear where she sucked a little harder.

Veronica ran her fingers into Rachel's hair and pulled her away. She needed that tongue in her mouth again. As their lips collided, Veronica felt a jolt of electricity pulse through her body. This was uncharted territory for her. She wasn't quite sure what to do with these sensations—how good Rachel felt to her, how much she turned her on.

Veronica reveled in the knowledge that Rachel was just as turned on as she was. The shallow breaths and Rachel's hands told the story. They were roaming her backside with abandon, from her shoulders down to her thighs. She wanted the same access to Rachel's body, so she took Rachel's hand and stepped back.

Rachel stood and pulled Veronica back to her. With their bodies pressed together and Rachel's hands finding skin under her blouse, just above her jeans, it felt even more right to Veronica. It probably wasn't fair to compare Rachel to her last lover, but she couldn't help it because there really was no comparison. She'd felt more in the last few minutes with just Rachel's kiss than she'd ever felt with anyone else during sex.

"You're so beautiful," Rachel whispered against her neck. "So sexy." She ran the tip of her tongue over Veronica's ear. "And you smell like heaven."

It sent shivers through Veronica's body, and a moan escaped her mouth. "Oh my God, you're good at that." She tugged on Rachel's

T-shirt and pulled it out of her jeans. She found skin and held firm while Rachel devoured her neck.

Veronica couldn't help but wonder who the last person was who had the pleasure of removing the belt Rachel wore so well. She moved her hands down a bit and ran them along the black leather that encircled Rachel's hips. God, she wanted to be the next person to undo the buckle and slowly pull the belt from its loops. She wanted to unzip those jeans and slide her fingers into hot, wet folds. She wanted to get on her knees and take Rachel into her mouth. She wanted to hear her cry out in ecstasy and hold her while she came down from it.

Rachel moved her hands from Veronica's waist to the third button on her blouse and then the fourth. She pushed it aside and whispered, "Oh my God." It was only then that Veronica realized she hadn't given Tiffany her push-up bra back.

Their eyes met, and Veronica whispered, "I want you." Her entire body was aching with need. She wanted to strip their clothes off and fall in bed together and stay there until they were both too tired to move. She wanted skin and sweat and tongues and profanities whispered and shouted.

She wanted early Sunday morning and everything she imagined that would entail. They'd wake up in each other's arms and talk for a while. Rachel would make coffee and toast with jam. They'd talk more and laugh and kiss and maybe shower together, then go out for brunch and walk hand in hand, going nowhere in particular.

Eventually, Veronica would have to hail a cab. She'd hang on to Rachel until the driver yelled at her to get in or lose the ride. They'd kiss one more time and make plans for the following weekend. And Veronica wouldn't have to suffer through another bad date ever again.

The spiral staircase was only a few feet away. She took Rachel's hand and led her to them. She was four steps up before she realized Rachel hadn't followed her. "What's wrong?" Rachel's gaze fell to the floor. "Rachel?" She didn't answer. Veronica waited.

Rachel finally raised her head and said, "It's not you."

With a heavy step, Veronica went back down to the main floor. The euphoria was gone. Then tension in the room morphed into an awkward silence. She wasn't sure what had happened or even what to say. The look on Rachel's face said it all. She wasn't into this. Veronica buttoned up her blouse. "Sorry, that was a bit presumptuous of me. I guess maybe I took the initiative a bit too far."

"Not at all." Rachel took her hand. "I want to take you upstairs, but…"

"But?" This was going nowhere good. Veronica fully expected the next words out of Rachel's mouth to be *I'm just not that into you.*

"I think it's only fair for you to know up front that I can't offer you anything more than tonight. If you're good with that, then so am I."

Veronica furrowed her brow in confusion. "Is there someone else?"

"No. It's not that."

"Then what is it?" Rachel couldn't seem to look her in the eye. "Rachel?"

"I'm not interested in the life you want," Rachel blurted out. "I can give you right now, but I can't give you what I know you're really looking for."

Veronica shook her head. "I don't understand. I mean, why bring me here if you weren't interested?"

"I'm interested. In tonight. And maybe tomorrow. But I won't allow myself to…" Rachel looked away again.

"To what? I don't understand."

Rachel took a few steps away and put a hand on her hip. She scratched her head and said, "It's not real, V. This dream you have of falling in love and living happily ever after, it's not real."

Veronica had no idea where this was coming from. "Of course it's real. People do it all the time."

"Mostly, they don't," Rachel said. "I can tell within five minutes if a newly engaged couple is going to make it or if I'll be back in a few years to shoot round two. Nine times out of ten, I'm dead right. I figure the other one is just running behind."

Veronica tried her best to interpret what Rachel was trying to tell her, but it didn't make any sense. "So, you don't want to get involved with me because some of your clients get divorced?"

"I'd rather not get caught up in the fantasy of it all. I let my clients do that. It's my job to help them do that, even create a record of it to help them believe the lie, but it's not my reality. And you and me, we're just in different places."

"Different places?" Veronica raised her voice a bit. "A minute ago, your tongue was in my mouth. It fucking felt like we were in the same place then."

"I know. I'm sorry."

Rachel reached for her, but Veronica shrugged her off. A feeling of anger and embarrassment bubbled to the surface. "If you knew you felt this way, why did you let me say those things to you? Why did you let me admit my attraction to you?" She grabbed her jacket off the chair and put it on. "Was this all just an ego play? You didn't actually want to sleep with me? You just wanted to see if I would?"

Rachel shook her head. "No. God no."

That answer wasn't good enough. Veronica grabbed her purse and opened the apartment door. She waited for a split second in the hope that Rachel would stop her. Maybe come up with a better explanation so they didn't have to leave it like this. But Rachel didn't move. She didn't say anything at all.

As much as Veronica wanted to step back inside and take her jacket back off, she couldn't. Rachel had encouraged her to initiate something only to crush her. Had she just been laughing at her on the inside? Had she been pretending that she was into it? Her confusion, along with her broken ego, kept her hand on the door. She stepped into the hall and shut the door behind her. She wouldn't let herself cry in the hall. Or in the cab. She'd hold it all in until she got home. Only then would she let it all out and lick her wounds.

Chapter Six

The New Mrs. Spear—capital 'N' in 'New,' please—would like you to take twenty pounds off her body using your amazing Photoshop skills." Justin set a cup of coffee on Rachel's desk. "And yes, that's how the former Katie Schmidt signed her email. At least she won't have to change her monogram."

"Oh my God," Rachel said. "She dieted so hard before the wedding, the tailor had to take her dress in five minutes before she walked down the aisle. There's no way I'm manipulating those photos. Mrs. Spear will just have to be okay with her size-six figure." She took a sip of coffee. "Thank you, Justin. You're a godsend."

"I'll tell her you'll do your best."

"You're catching on quick."

"I'm a quick study." Justin tilted his head. "I'm also very observant, and you are not yourself today. Woman troubles?"

"No. Why would you think that?" Rachel minimized the photo of Veronica she had up on one of her three computer screens.

"Because I've been your assistant for six months, and I've never seen you photograph one bridesmaid like you did the other night. Jesus, for a minute, I was worried you didn't get enough of the bride and groom. So, spill it. Who is she?"

"She's Tiffany's cousin. She's a lawyer at some big firm downtown, and she's absolutely not an option for me."

"A hot lawyer. Yeah, I can see how that isn't appealing at all."

"I need simple," Rachel said. "Veronica Welch is not simple. She comes with all kinds of complications. Things like feelings and expectations."

Justin nodded. "Right. I get it. A hot lawyer with feelings for you wants more than a one-night stand. That would *suck*. I sure hope that never happens to me."

Justin was a kid in college who, by his own admission, knew nothing about women. Besides, Rachel didn't need him nosing into her personal life right now. "Okay, back to work. The New Mrs. Spear is waiting for a reply."

"Oh, I almost forgot. She also said she'd like a bit more arch on her eyebrow if it isn't too much trouble. Just the right one."

"Jerk! She did not." Rachel grabbed a hacky-sack/stress ball thing that was sitting on her desk and threw it at him.

"Mmm-hmm." Justin didn't even look up from his keyboard.

Rachel clicked her mouse and brought Veronica's picture back up on her screen. Of all the shots she'd taken, this one was her favorite. In most of the shots, Veronica was all smiles, her excitement and joy for her cousin written all over her face. But in this particular shot, she looked introspective, staring off into the distance. Rachel couldn't help but wonder what she had been thinking about in that moment.

She felt bad about what had happened between them. Or, more specifically, she felt bad about what had *not* happened between them. On the surface, it probably looked as if she was trying to protect Veronica from future heartache. If that's what she thought, it wasn't a bad thing. It just wasn't the truth. Stopping what would surely be a night of incredible sex was purely a selfish move on Rachel's part. It was her own heart she was protecting, not Veronica's. Rachel knew that feeling well—the one where a first kiss was so full of emotion, it opened up a world of possibilities, and you started to believe that God dropped this person into your life for a reason. "Everything happens for a reason," she whispered, mimicking her mother. It was bullshit on a colossal scale, and she wouldn't buy into that philosophy ever again.

Rachel repeated her story to herself more than once. "You're protecting yourself," and "You promised you wouldn't let this happen again." But every time she let her mind wander to Veronica, she saw the crestfallen look on that gorgeous face when she realized Rachel wasn't following her to the stairs. God. She hated being the cause of that look. It made her sick. Guilt-stricken and heartbroken and nauseated at the same time. She couldn't...wouldn't...hurt her again. Rachel didn't believe in fate or destiny or whatever, but she suddenly found herself sure of one thing: She was absolutely not meant to hurt Veronica Welch. Not ever.

❖

Rachel had hoped Veronica's date would be over by the time she walked into the bar. She'd waited until the very last moment, not going in even a minute before Charlotte needed her there. Their eyes met as she'd walked by, but Veronica had looked away before Rachel could acknowledge her.

She tied an apron around her waist and took a deep breath. She needed to get the images of Veronica's open blouse out of her head before she went back out into the bar. "You can do this," she whispered to herself.

Charlotte gave her a nod. "Hey, Rach. How was Tiffany's wedding?"

"Beautiful. I got some really great shots of her and Eric."

Carol waved Rachel over to the end of the bar. She looked excited to share some sort of news that Rachel was sure she had absolutely no interest in, but she forced a smile and said, "Hey, how's it going? Need another beer, Harry?"

"Thank you, baby girl, but one is enough for me."

Harry had been Charlotte's dad's best friend. Rachel couldn't help but think he still came around most days because he missed his buddy.

"This one might be a keeper," Carol whispered. She pointed at Veronica and her date. "She ordered a nice pinot noir. Very classy."

"Go see if they need a refill," Charlotte said.

Rachel didn't move. Veronica looked as gorgeous as ever. She wasn't wearing her usual power suit and heels. She had on a sweater and jeans. She still wore the white nail polish from the wedding, and Rachel followed her every move as she lifted the wine glass to her mouth and took a sip. It appeared that Veronica was enjoying this drink. The glass was almost empty. That never happened. Veronica glanced over at her, but again, she looked away before Rachel could acknowledge the look with a smile or a nod.

"Rach?"

"Yeah." Rachel cleared her throat. "Yeah, um…would you mind making sure they're good before you leave?" Everyone just stared at her. Rachel turned away from them and busied herself by stacking clean glasses.

Charlotte took a glass from Rachel's hand and set it down. "Come with me." She pulled her to the other end of the bar and whispered, "What did you do?"

"Nothing. Almost nothing. It didn't happen."

"Oh God." Charlotte shook her head. "Rachel, we talked about this! You promised."

Rachel put up her hands in defense. "It's not that bad, but it turns out she's Tiffany's cousin. She was a bridesmaid at the wedding."

"Oh God."

"Stop saying that, Char. And please just go make sure Classy Pinot is taken care of before you leave."

Charlotte clasped her hands together in front of her mouth. "Please tell me you didn't do exactly what I asked you not to do."

"You asked me not to sleep with her, and I didn't. I stopped it before it got that far."

"What the hell, Rach? You know she's looking for the one thing you swore off four years ago."

"I had good reason to swear it off, and you know it," Rachel whispered.

"I disagree. Seems to me you're letting the past dictate your future. And you're being a total bitch about it too." Charlotte glanced at Veronica and motioned with her head. "Did she make the first move, or did you?"

Rachel sighed. "I did. And then I changed my mind. Then I saw her again, and she's just so beautiful, you know?"

"She is. And she'd be great for you, but I can't say the same about you for her, so keep it in your pants, Rach."

Charlotte's words stung, but Rachel knew she was right. "Hey, Charlotte!" Rachel caught her before she went into the back. "Stay with your mom tonight. I'll close up for you."

Charlotte pulled the key to the front door out of her pocket. "I take back everything I just said. Anyone would be lucky to have you, Rach. If you weren't my cousin…"

Rachel made a face. "Gross, Char."

Charlotte gave her a hug. "I know. That came out wrong. But I adore you for closing up. See you tomorrow."

The beauty of family. One minute you were a bitch, and the next you were a hero. Rachel tried to look busy while keeping an eye on Veronica and her date. It seemed to be going well. Better than any of the other dates Rachel had seen her with. Classy Pinot looked like a ballet dancer. Tall, lanky, perfect posture, long brown hair. Yep, a dancer. Rachel would put money on it.

Rachel found herself hoping that Classy Pinot was actually Smoker Pinot and that Veronica would be turned off by this. The foundation for this wish was having slept with two dancers in college. Both were smokers, which of course, meant that Classy Pinot must surely be a smoker too. If she was a dancer, that is.

A group of rowdy twentysomething guys walked in. They pushed two tables together and sat close to Veronica and Classy Pinot. Rachel could tell by their hand gestures that they were egging each other on to hit on them. She walked over. "Hey, guys. A couple of pitchers?"

"Whatever's cheap," one of them said. "And something for the ladies."

Rachel bent down. "So, here's the thing, guys. They're on a date. With each other. So, how 'bout I just get the pitchers?" Their reactions were all different. There were fist bumps and looks of shock along with a few whispered words. As Rachel walked away, Classy Pinot caught her eye and mouthed a thank you. Rachel smiled and gave her a nod.

Once she'd finished serving the group and refilling a few drinks of other customers, Rachel went over to the regulars and leaned on the bar. In a low voice, she said, "What do we know?"

Joe chuckled. "She's not Jägerbomb. Isn't that all we need to know?"

"Good point."

Harry leaned in. "Truth be told, this is the craziest thing I've ever seen. How can sparks fly when everything about this screams job interview?"

"Because just like a job interview," Carol whispered, "she only needs one good one. The odds are in her favor, in my opinion. And look how she's getting on with this one. I can feel their electric energy from all the way over here."

"Carol, you always think it's the one. And electric energy? Seriously?" Carol was delusional as far as Rachel was concerned. Sparks were definitely not flying between Classy Pinot and Lovely Veronica. Rachel knew what sparks with Veronica looked like, and this wasn't it. Veronica wasn't unbuttoning her own blouse, revealing soft, supple cleavage that Rachel so badly wanted to get lost in. Her eyes weren't dark with hunger, and her tongue wasn't exploring Classy Pinot's mouth with a skill Rachel had rarely encountered. Carol didn't know what she was talking about.

Veronica stood, and Carol whispered, "Look busy." All three of them picked up their phones. Joe put his phone to his ear and nodded as if he was listening to someone. Rachel turned away and snickered.

"Hey."

Rachel turned back around and found Veronica standing there. "Hey."

Veronica gave her and the regulars a suspicious look. "What's so funny?"

Rachel tried to wipe the smile from her face. "Nothing." She grabbed the bottle of pinot. "Need a refill?"

"No, just run my card for me." She gave the regulars a wave. "Hey, guys. You can stop trying to look busy now. And, Joe, I know no one's on the other end of that phone."

"How's it going?" Carol whispered.

"Good. We're going to have dinner next door."

Carol gave her husband's hand a friendly slap. "See, Joe? What did I say?"

"Good for you," Harry said. "Is she as good-hearted as she is pretty?"

Rachel swiped the card and looked over her shoulder at Veronica. She was staring right back at her. "She seems honest," Veronica said. "Sincere. What you see is what you get kind of a girl."

"That's a good start," Joe said. He cupped a hand next to his mouth and whispered, "What about the fire?"

Rachel set the receipt and a pen in front of Veronica. She couldn't wait to hear the answer. Veronica scribbled her signature and said, "Look at those legs, Joe. I mean, come on."

All of their heads turned in unison to check out Classy Pinot's long legs. Veronica glared at Rachel and walked away.

"V!" Rachel shouted. "Your card."

Veronica grabbed the card from Rachel's hand and said, "Don't call me that."

❖

Pinot Noir was attractive and confident in her sexuality, seemed to be on a good career track, and was definitely worth pursuing. Surely that was reason enough to ask her to dinner.

Veronica perused the menu. "What looks good to you, Michelle?"

"Are you okay? You seemed a little worked up when we left the bar."

Great. She'd noticed the growling Veronica had done under her breath. "Oh, I'm fine. That bartender just makes me a little crazy."

"The one with the curly hair?"

"No, the other one. Rachel What's-her-name. God, she can be snarky and arrogant."

"Oh." Michelle looked at her menu. "So, you go there often?"

"Every day." Veronica shook her head. "That sounds bad. I'm not a heavy drinker."

"Not judging." Michelle set her menu on the table. "I think I'll have the chicken piccata."

"Me too." Veronica slapped her menu shut. "The truth is, I've been on a few dates in that bar lately, but you're the first woman I've asked to dinner."

Michelle smiled and reached across the table for Veronica's hand. "I like you too."

Veronica glanced at the open hand. Long, slender fingers awaited her touch. She looked into Michelle's eyes and saw warmth and gentleness. She should take her hand. There was no reason not to. Except she knew everything she wouldn't feel. No spark. No excitement for what could be. *Oh, for God's sake, just take her hand.*

Michelle caressed Veronica's fingers with her thumb. It felt nice. Her hand was soft and warm. "I thought you might have done this before," she said. "You seemed to have all of those preliminary questions down pat."

"That's the lawyer in me, I guess. I hope it didn't feel like I was interrogating you."

Michelle's expression turned dark, and her grip on Veronica's hand tightened. "You can interrogate me anytime you like."

Oh God. Veronica was in no mood to flirt back. She waved the server over. "I think we should order."

Michelle let go of her hand and sat back in her chair. Her stare was unnerving. "Can I ask you a question?"

"Sure. Hold on." Veronica looked at the waiter. "We'd both like the chicken piccata and a bottle of your best pinot noir." She turned her attention back to Michelle. "Okay, shoot."

"Do you two have a history?"

"Who?"

"You and the bartender. You seemed to want to bolt the second she walked in."

"Nope, no history. I barely know her." Veronica took a keen interest in the ice in her water glass.

"Okay. I was just making sure. The last thing I need is to date a woman who's hooked on someone else. I've been the rebound woman before, and it's no fun."

"No rebounding here," Veronica said. "Nope. The only history we have is her history of being a bit of a jackass."

Michelle shrugged and said, "That's cool. I'm just trying to avoid baggage."

"Then it's a good thing you're not on a date with Rachel, because she's got plenty of it."

"Right." Michelle drew out the word ever so slightly.

Veronica put her arms on the table and leaned in. "Michelle, *what* are you really looking for?"

"I'm looking for stability," Michelle said. "Someone who's loyal and reliable. Someone who enjoys art exhibits and Broadway shows, and on the nights when we stay in, someone who will rub my feet while I knit them a scarf."

"And what about that indescribable thing? That burning attraction. But it's not just attraction, it's also wanting to know someone's soul. What makes their heart beat faster? What makes their eyes light up? What their insecurities are so you can take them all away."

"In my experience, it's best to be careful with that kind of love," Michelle said. "If the fire is too hot, the attraction too strong, it can burn out, and what are you left with?"

Michelle's words made sense, but Veronica didn't agree with them. She wanted more than a companion. She wanted her heart to soar and her stomach to ache and her knees to buckle. She wanted what she saw in her parents and other people she'd met along the way who couldn't seem to get enough of each other, and whose fire would never burn out.

CHAPTER SEVEN

W e need to talk about second dates."
Veronica didn't look up from her laptop. "No, Bea. We don't."

"You've been on nine dates now. Surely, one of them is worth another look. What about," Bea looked at her tablet, "Pinot Noir? You even had dinner with her. Don't you want to see her again?"

Pinot Noir was three dates ago. Since then, Veronica had seen Bloody Mary, the nurse, and Cosmopolitan, the actress. Life would not be fun with either of them due to Bloody Mary's love for working the graveyard shift and Cosmo's ego, which as far as Veronica could tell, fell somewhere between "is she for real" and "downright unbearable."

As for Pinot, they'd had a nice dinner. The conversation was pleasant. There weren't any red flags. There also wasn't a spark. Not even the hope of a spark. "I'm looking for that thing," Veronica said.

"What thing?"

"That thing, Bea. You know, when you look at someone and wish you knew what their dreams were so you could make them come true?"

"Wow," Bea said in awe. "I thought you just wanted a wife."

"Very funny."

Bea plopped down in a chair. "I feel like I'm failing both you and your mother. She calls every day, wanting to hear good news about the date, and I just don't have any for her."

"Yeah, well, that is a burden of your own making. I don't even feel bad for asking her to bug you about it instead of me. I don't have time for her fifty questions. 'What did she smell like? What color were her eyes? Did she have good manners?' It goes on forever, Bea, so please know what I lack in sympathy, I make up for in gratitude."

"She just wants you to be happy."

Veronica sighed. "I know she does. But I haven't made partner yet, so work still has to come first."

Bea stood. "And that's my cue to get back to work." She turned back around when she got to the door. "Don't give up, V. She's out there. And when you find her, she's going to be the luckiest girl in the world."

Veronica had her doubts about that, on both counts. Would she find someone she connected with? And would that person be understanding when she was in the middle of a big case and had to work long hours? It was starting to feel like an unattainable goal, but she gave Bea a smile. "No giving up. We push on, right?"

Bea threw her fists in the air. "Right!"

Rachel set the glass on the small table with some force.

Date number ten looked at the glass and then at Rachel. "I'm good, thanks. Unless that's something V ordered? Bourbon neat isn't for everyone."

Rachel had been keeping her eye on this one. Something about her didn't seem quite right. She was a striking woman, Rachel couldn't deny that. Veronica's assistant definitely seemed to have a direct line to the Hot Lady Factory. But her moves seemed too practiced. Too smooth. No one was that relaxed on a first date. And the way she kept reaching across the table to touch Veronica's hand looked like a trick she'd used on men, not women. And then Veronica had excused herself to use the restroom. That's when Rachel took the diet soda she'd just poured for herself and marched over to their table.

The casual use of Veronica's nickname was interesting. It was all part of the game, Rachel decided. Get familiar enough with the mark so they let their guard down. Well, that wasn't going to happen. Not in Charlotte's bar. And certainly not to someone Rachel cared about. She pushed the drink toward the woman. "I thought maybe you'd like something a little stronger. It's called, 'put the cash back in Veronica's purse before I call the cops, bitch.'" She paused for effect. "On the rocks."

The woman rolled her eyes and pulled the wad of cash, along with Veronica's driver's license and Amex card, from her bra as smoothly as she'd tucked it there. She stood and straightened her tight dress. "Tell V sorry, I had to run."

Rachel held out her hand, palm up. "Yeah, I won't be relaying any messages on your behalf." The woman put the cash in her hand and sauntered out of the bar.

Rachel picked up her diet soda and took a long sip. She couldn't imagine this would go well with V since they'd hardly spoken in several days. But what was she supposed to do? Just watch that woman steal from her? Unfortunately, Harry wasn't there, or she would've had him do the dirty work.

Veronica came out of the restroom and looked around. "What's going on?"

Veronica's tone was filled with irritation, but damn, she looked good. The same white Gucci blouse that Rachel had so carefully unbuttoned only a week ago was tucked into a tight black skirt.

"Yeah, it's the same shirt," Veronica said. "Now, where did Dusty go?"

Rachel didn't realize she'd been staring right at Veronica's chest. "Dusty? That's the name she gave you? I seriously can't take this anymore."

Veronica looked around the bar. "Take what? Where's my date?"

"I can't watch you go on another ridiculous date with women who are so wrong for you it would be funny if it wasn't so sad. I mean, does your assistant even know you?"

"Bea? She's worked for me for going on four years. Of course she knows me."

Rachel shook her head. "Then she must not like you. Not at all."

Veronica put her hands on her hips. "Where did Dusty go? Did you say something to her? I happen to really like her. She's interesting."

"Ha! I'm sure she is, setting that ridiculous name aside." She placed a wad of stolen items on the table. "That woman is a con artist who tried to steal from you."

"What? That can't be. Dusty?"

Rachel shook her head in disgust. "Her name should've been

the first clue. How many women do you know that actually have that name?"

Veronica grabbed her phone. "The name on her profile is Dusty. Dusty Springfield."

Was Veronica really this naïve? Rachel softened her tone. "V, Dusty Springfield was a singer. 'Son of a Preacher Man'? Ring any bells?"

Veronica tossed her phone on the table. "Damnit, Bea."

"You need help."

"I beg your pardon?"

"If you're madly in love with being madly in love, then you need help. I can do better than Bea. I can get on Ryder with you and find exactly what you're looking for. Let me help you, V."

Veronica sat back down and folded her arms across her chest. "You don't even believe in love."

"This isn't about me. It's about you. Let me help you."

"Absolutely not. You'll set me up with God knows who."

"No," Rachel said. "Bea is the one setting you up with God knows who. I know a lot of women. Women I can vouch for. We wouldn't even have to use Ryder."

"Women you've dated? Slept with and then dumped? That's your MO, isn't it? Seduce women and then quietly slip away when they get too close? I know your type, Rachel, and there's no way—"

"Tell me what you're looking for," Rachel said, interrupting her. She took a pen and small notepad out of her apron.

"Are you nuts? I'm not doing this with you. I'm not dating one of your conquests. And stop standing there like you're ready to take my damn order."

"One thing." Rachel wrote the number "1" on the pad. "Just tell me one thing you're looking for, and I promise it won't be anyone I've dated."

"Forthrightness."

That answer had come a little too quickly for Rachel's liking. And she knew it was directed right at her. She didn't write it down. "I really didn't mean to hurt your feelings."

"So, how would you like me to feel about what happened?"

"Optimistic," Rachel said.

"Excuse me?"

Veronica's expression was anything but friendly. Rachel tried to ignore it and keep her tone even. She didn't want to argue in the bar, even though she probably deserved whatever harsh words Veronica flung at her. "I'd like you to remember that spark, that attraction we have. And I'd like for it to give you some hope that you can feel that with someone who's actually capable of giving you what you're looking for."

Veronica leaned forward. "Tell me the honest truth about something, and I'll try to feel a little less repulsed and more 'optimistic' about our moments together." She used finger quotes around the word *optimistic*.

"Repulsed?" Rachel was shocked by the use of that word. "You couldn't possibly feel repulsed. It was hot. And also, on top of the fact that it was hot, it was hot!"

"The truth."

"Fine," Rachel said. "About what?"

"You said you're able to predict which of the couples you photograph will stay together and which won't."

"And I'm almost always right." Who could look down their nose at a ninety-five percent accuracy rate? No one, that was who. And that word Veronica had just used. *Repulsed? Really?*

"My cousin, Tiffany, was your college roommate, right?"

"Yes." Oh, shit. That was where she was going with this? Rachel's pride in her accuracy rate dissipated.

"Will she and Eric stay together?"

She shook her head. "I can't."

"But you're an expert on spotting true love."

"She's my friend."

"And she's *my* cousin. So, just tell me what your Spidey sense told you."

Rachel hesitated. Should she reveal her prediction for Tiffany and Eric? Veronica stared at her, waiting for an answer. "I'm going to have to give you a non-answer."

"You're pleading the fifth?"

Rachel nodded. Veronica held her stare for a moment and said, "But my family thinks the world of Eric. They couldn't stop talking about how perfect they are for each other. And now you're telling me he's going to cheat on her? Or one day dump her for a younger woman?

And why the hell didn't you warn her? Some friend you are, Rachel Monaghan."

"What makes you think Eric is the problem?" Rachel regretted the words the second they left her mouth.

Veronica gasped. "Tiffany would never!"

"Look, I'm probably wrong about them."

"Damn right you are. I've never seen Tiffany happier. Your Spidey sense, or whatever you call it, sucks."

Rachel sighed. Her predictions were usually accurate, but she'd have to let it go if she wanted to help Veronica. "Can we get back to you? I need one thing to go on if I'm going to find your next date."

"Since you're so smart, you tell me. What am I looking for?"

It hit Rachel like a brick to the head. She shouldn't have been surprised by it, considering the wide range of women Bea had chosen. Along with their drink choices, those women seemed to be all over the map, personality wise. "You don't know what you want, do you?"

Veronica looked away. "Don't be ridiculous."

"Did you give Bea any parameters? Any requirements?"

"Of course I did. Do you think I'd date just any old lesbian?"

Rachel snickered. "I'm not sure if you're referring to their age or their employment status."

"Both," Veronica said. "I'd like them to be employed and close to me in age."

"Okay. That's something. How old are you?"

"Use your Spidey sense."

"You just told me it sucks."

Veronica leaned forward and said, "Prove me wrong."

"Hmm." Rachel took the opportunity to really look at Veronica while she tapped her pen on her chin. She was so pretty, and this feisty mood she seemed to be in was kind of a turn-on. She focused on Veronica's lips for a moment, remembering what they tasted like. There was a hint of something sweet. Maybe a fruit-flavored lip gloss. God, she'd tasted good. And the scent she'd inhaled when she'd kissed her chest—there was a slight hint of it in the air right now. She found herself wanting to push the small table out of the way and pull Veronica into her arms so she could taste her again. Devour her this time. No stopping.

They could go in the back room. Rachel could push that tight black skirt up Veronica's legs. Unbutton her blouse all the way this time. Push the bra to the side and take a nipple into her mouth. Caress the heat between her legs. Kiss her with abandon until she was flushed and out of breath. Hear her say things she only said to her lover. Rachel was almost her lover. Almost.

"Well? How old am I?"

"Right." Rachel tried to focus, but in her mind, she was sucking on Veronica's tongue while she kneaded her ass with both hands. "Um." She cleared her throat. "You're about to make partner at your law firm, so I'm going to guess that takes a while, which means you're not twenty-five."

Veronica smirked at her. "Compliments will get you nowhere."

"When we kissed, you tasted like thirty-three." Rachel wasn't sure why she'd had the number thirty-three in her head that night. It should've been sixty-nine, obviously.

"Ha! Your Spidey sense, and your lips, apparently, are off by two years. And nice try at getting me to think about that kiss, as if it was something worth remembering."

Rachel could tell by the way Veronica's eyes had momentarily dropped to her lips that her words didn't match what was going on inside her head. "Oh, but it was, V. You know it was."

"And where does that get me, knowing that we have chemistry?" Veronica turned away for a moment. "It certainly doesn't get me any closer to my goal."

There it was, the reason Rachel had stopped them from going any further the other night. The reason she'd never fulfill her little fantasy of taking Veronica to the back room for a quick romp amongst the boxes of beer and wine, no matter how strong their chemistry was. And good Lord, it was strong. Rachel needed to wipe that thought from her mind forever and focus on the task at hand. "You want a wife." It seemed to help calm her libido to say it out loud, even though it didn't need to be. They were both very aware of Veronica's wants and needs.

"A future," Veronica said. "A family. One day seeing my own kids reach their goals. I know love isn't perfect. I get that some people don't stay together forever, but that doesn't mean you don't try."

"So, give me one thing you're looking for," Rachel said. "Just one."

Veronica took a moment to answer. "It's intangible. It's not a physical trait or a personality trait." She unfolded her arms and leaned forward. "I'll tell you what I just told Bea. It's that thing. You know, when you look at someone and you wish you knew what their dreams were so you could make them come true?"

"Yeah, I do."

She tapped Rachel's notebook. "That's number one."

"There aren't any search words for that."

"No. I guess not." Veronica stood and grabbed her jacket and purse. "But thanks for thinking of me."

Feeling foolish and defeated, Rachel leaned back in the chair. Out of the corner of her eye, she saw a customer wave at her. "Yeah, I'll be right there!"

"Mom?" Veronica shut the door to her parent's Upper West Side apartment. "I'm here!" She kicked off her heels and took off her suit jacket. "Where are you?"

"Back here, dear!"

Their bedroom smelled like the old liniment cream her grandmother and mother swore by if you'd injured yourself. She put her hands on her hips and said, "Oh, Dad."

Stanley Welch was propped up in bed with his right foot elevated on several pillows. "Your mother exaggerates," he said. "She just wanted to get you here so she could ask about all of these dates you've been going on. You're not shaming the family name by sleeping with all of them, are you?"

"Oh my God. Dad, we are not going there. Not ever." Veronica sat on the bed and pushed her dad's graying hair off his forehead. "Besides, you and Mom had a shotgun wedding because of me. I don't think the family name is in much jeopardy."

"Oh, right. I forgot we told you about that. Karen, why did we tell our daughter she was an illegitimate child?"

"Because she had a right to know. Plus, she was too damn smart for her own good. One look at her birth certificate and she would have done the math. And then she would have asked why we'd lied to her all of these years."

"I knew we would have been better off having a dumb kid." Her dad shook his head. "But you're what we got. Now, about these women you may or may not have been sleeping with."

"Not," Veronica said firmly. "Most of the time, it's just a thirty-minute date." She examined her dad's foot a little more closely. The ankle was badly bruised. "You should stop playing against the pro. Choose someone your own age so you're not diving for tennis balls."

"This is your advice to me? After trudging through the snow for all of those ballet classes that winter? After suffering through your high school years with the acne and the questioning your sexuality and the not eating enough vegetables to please your mother? This is what I get? Play with someone your own age? You should be encouraging me to buy a Ferrari because I deserve it."

Veronica laughed. "You were, and are, a great dad. And I guess fifty-six isn't so old."

"That's better. Now, tell us about these dates. Have any of them lit a fire in your heart?"

Her dad winked at her mom when he said it. They were still so in love after all this time. Veronica wanted that. She wanted someone who would look at her that way, not just on their wedding day, but every day. She moved next to her dad and rested her head on his shoulder. "I feel like I'm failing at this, and you know how much I hate to fail."

Her dad kissed her head. "Why does it feel like that?"

"Because I can see the beauty in all of these women, but I can't feel them. I can't connect with them, and the one woman I *can* feel isn't available."

"Who?" Her mom sat on the bed with them. "Who's this one woman you connect with?"

"She's a bartender at Monaghan's, the place where I meet the dates Bea sets up for me." Veronica covered her eyes with her hand. "It's so ridiculous."

"So, you're on a date with a pretty woman," her dad said. "And you can't stop looking at the bartender?" He started to giggle, and then her mom joined in.

"What's so funny?"

"You know this story, honey." Her dad wrapped his arm around her. "It's *our* story. We've told you at least a hundred times."

"I don't see how you and mom meeting in an arcade is the same thing."

"Bowling alley," her mom corrected. "Your dad just happened to be addicted to *Ms. Pac-Man* at the time."

"I worked there during college. Your mother was in a bowling league with her boyfriend. Some jackass named Chuck."

"Nice guy," her mom said. "But there was something about the blond guy behind the counter. As you said, honey, I could feel him."

"I caught her staring at me more than once," her dad said.

Veronica's mom took her hand. "Does she ever stare at you from behind the bar?"

"It doesn't matter. She doesn't believe in love."

"I didn't either," her dad said. "Who would with the example your grandparents set? I assumed the unhappy home I had was normal, and I was having no part of that. I wanted to be free and live my life how I saw fit. That was, until your mother came along."

"You called it a shotgun wedding," her mom said. "But no one forced your father to marry me. He couldn't wait to be my husband and your father."

Tears came to Veronica's eyes. "I hope I can find this someday."

"You will, honey." Her dad kissed her head again. "I have no doubt about that."

❖

Rachel adjusted her aunt Jenny's oxygen cannula. "There we go."

"Take it off," Aunt Jenny said, her voice so weak Rachel could barely hear her. "If you plan on snapping a photo of me, take the damn thing off."

Rachel removed it from her nose and behind her ears. "Just for a minute."

Aunt Jenny gripped Rachel's arm. "I'm only doing this for Charlotte."

"I know. You look like hell, but for some strange reason, your daughter wants to remember you as the bald, brave, skinny woman you are."

Aunt Jenny huffed out a weak laugh. "Thank you for not lying to me. Everyone thinks I want to hear that I haven't changed a bit. It's bullshit."

"No bullshit from me." Rachel stepped back and positioned her camera. "And you don't have to smile. In fact, I insist you don't. Not even a hint of a smile."

Jenny rolled her eyes. "Reverse psychology. Good one, Rach. Do you use that one on the women too?"

"Yeah, I tried that one last week on a beautiful blonde." Rachel took several shots, zooming in on a few.

"She must be a dumb blonde if she fell for it."

"She didn't." Rachel lowered her camera. "And really, with the stereotypes?"

"Don't go trying to make me a better person now. It's too goddamned late."

"Fine." Rachel looked through the camera lens again. "I'll make you a deal. Give me your best smile, and I promise to Photoshop these pictures."

"What are you going to do, give me bigger boobs?"

"No, I'll just put them back where they belong."

Aunt Jenny's smile popped out as she shook with laughter. Rachel got a couple of great shots. "See? That wasn't so hard."

"Are we done?"

Rachel set her camera down and sat on the edge of the bed. "All done." She put the oxygen cannula back on and straightened the pink beanie on Jenny's head. "Can I get you anything?"

"You can promise me something."

"Anything," Rachel said. "But you already know I'll be there for Charlotte. Whatever she needs, I'm there."

Jenny nodded. "I know. This is about you." She closed her eyes and took in some oxygen, then opened them again. "Don't waste time, Rach. It's over before you know it. So live, and love with all your heart, and don't ever forget who gave you your first camera."

"I still have it, the camera you gave me."

"Promise me, Rachel Monaghan."

Rachel took a deep breath. "I'm not getting out of here without making that promise, am I?"

Jenny gave her a weak slap on her arm. "Only you would deny a woman her dying wish."

"Was that reverse psychology, Aunt Jenny?"

"Did it work?"

Rachel laughed and leaned in. "I promise." She kissed Jenny's cheek and whispered, "You will always be my favorite aunt."

"And the other part? You have to get over her, Rach. We don't know what's on the other side. Maybe this life is all we've got."

Rachel gasped. "Why, Jenny Monaghan. What would Father Michael think if he heard you say that?"

"Don't throw that Catholic guilt on me, Rachel Monaghan. I'm dying. I can say whatever the hell I want." Jenny turned and looked at the wooden cross that hung on the wall. "I pray John is out there somewhere, waiting for me. I pray I'll have the chance to show him how much I loved him."

"He knows, Aunt Jenny."

"We were arguing a lot before he died. We kept it behind closed doors for Charlotte's sake, but somehow, we'd lost sight of what was really important—each other."

Rachel felt a pang in her stomach. Uncle John's death had been sudden. She had no idea Aunt Jenny had been living with so much guilt. She took her hand. It felt cold and bony. The realization that there wasn't much life left in Jenny's tired body brought tears to Rachel's eyes. "Uncle John is out there, and he knows. He probably feels horrible about it too. He probably can't wait for you to join him in heaven so he can pick you up and twirl you around like he used to do, remember?"

Jenny smiled. "Thank you, Rach. I'm going to hold that thought in my heart today." She pressed her hand to Rachel's chest. "And you hold what I've said in yours."

"I will, Aunt Jenny. I will."

CHAPTER EIGHT

Watching three people in their seventies debate the finer points of online dating was an exercise in patience. Rachel had enlisted the help of Harry, Joe, and Carol in her search for Veronica's one true love by having them download the Ryder app on their phones. That took more time than four of Veronica's dates combined.

"Life moves fast now, Joe. It's all about information," Harry said.

"Where's the mystery? If you know all about the person before you even meet them, what do you have left to talk about?"

"They say these dating apps are efficient," Carol said. "You filter out the people you have nothing in common with. Imagine how much time you'd save. Back in our day, if you wanted to find the one, you had to go on at least—"

"Thirty dates?" Joe turned to her, laughing. "We had absolutely nothing in common. I was from the wrong side of the tracks. Your mother, God rest her soul, hated me. I'd hate to think where I'd be today if you had used a filter."

"Well, that's true," Carol said. "I had to defy my parents to be with you, but there was no stopping me." She grabbed his face and turned him toward Rachel. "Could you resist these gorgeous blue eyes?"

Rachel took a good look at Joe. Carol had a grip on his face that caused his lips to pucker up like a fish. "Put those eyes and lips on a woman, and I'm a goner."

"Well, then, I'd be my sister," Joe said. "She's a little too old for you, Rachel, but I like your good taste."

"Thanks, Joe." Rachel looked at her watch. Veronica would be walking in at any moment. Rachel's faith in her team was waning. No,

Veronica didn't want her help, but that wasn't going to stop her. In the meantime, they'd all have to suffer through more of Bea's choices. And yes, Rachel had said she didn't need Ryder, that her circle of friends included many eligible lesbians who were not among Rachel's "conquests," as Veronica had put it. Once Rachel scrolled through her contacts, she realized this was not entirely true. Not that she had slept with all of them. She most certainly hadn't. It was just that most were either taken or just entirely wrong for Veronica. It was funny how many of Rachel's smart, successful friends simply were not a good fit for Veronica. "Keep scrolling, people. I want at least one good option before she gets here."

Joe picked up his phone. "Ooh, she's pretty."

Carol leaned over and looked at the profile pic. "That's Piña Colada, the snake lady. Put your glasses on, Joe."

Harry peered over his reading glasses at Rachel. "Who are you dating these days, pipsqueak?"

Rachel uncapped a bottle of beer and slid it down the bar to another customer. The question surprised her, but she could tell by the expectant look on all three of their faces they weren't going to let it go. "Whoever I want."

"What the hell does that mean?" The tone in Harry's voice told her he wasn't impressed by her answer.

"It means I keep it simple. Play the field."

"One of the players just walked onto the field," Carol said. She motioned with her head at the door, then gave Rachel a wink. Harry and Joe looked at Veronica, then at Rachel. Both of them wagged their bushy eyebrows at her. Great. Because what she needed right now was those three scrutinizing her every interaction with Veronica, as if there wasn't enough tension already.

"Hey, everyone. It's cold out there." Veronica took off her coat and set it on a barstool along with her purse.

All eyes were on Rachel. The three regulars were obviously watching with bated breath for her reaction to Veronica. If they insisted on staring, maybe she'd give them a show. "Hi, V. What'll it be today? Sex on the beach? That should warm you up."

Veronica's mouth gaped open. "Um."

"A buttery nipple?" Rachel tried like hell to not glance down at Veronica's tight sweater. "How about a redheaded slut?"

With confusion written all over her face, Veronica turned to the regulars. "What's happening right now?"

"They're drinks, honey." Carol shot Rachel a mom glare, then smiled at Veronica. "Who are you seeing tonight?"

"Her name is Mack. I think it's short for MacKenzie."

Rachel leaned on the bar. "So, what'll it be? A screaming orgasm?"

Harry laughed. Veronica looked at him, and he put up his hands. "Sorry. It's just been a long time since someone offered me one of those."

Joe started to say something, but Carol nudged him. "Don't you dare say a thing."

Veronica turned back to Rachel. "Mack likes dirty drinks but not that dirty."

"A dirty martini, then?"

Veronica held her stare. "Extra dirty."

"Whatever the lady wants, but don't discount the deliciousness of a redheaded slut." Unfortunately, Rachel's sarcasm couldn't hide the heated blush that started the second Veronica walked through the door. Why didn't she choose a T-shirt that had a high neckline? Or better yet, a turtleneck? And why was Veronica still there? "I'll bring them to your table."

"I love that mole under your eye," Veronica said.

The words stopped Rachel's movements for a brief moment. She recovered and kept working. "Two extra-dirty martinis coming right up."

Veronica finally moved to her regular table. Rachel poured olive juice into a shaker. "I can feel you staring at me," she said in a loud whisper. She didn't get a reply, so she stopped what she was doing and put a hand on her hip. "What?"

Harry tossed his phone on the bar and took off his glasses. "We don't need to look any further than right here, behind this bar."

Carol set her phone down as well. "What Harry said."

Joe shrugged. "I was having fun on Ryder." He set his phone down too.

Rachel shook her head. "Never gonna happen."

"She likes you!" Carol said in a loud whisper.

"I like her too, but we want different things." The front door swung open, and in walked a woman who Rachel could only assume was Mack. "I have drinks to make, people. Stop harassing me."

Rachel kept her eyes on Veronica and her latest date while she made the drinks. Mack was tall and handsome, which was sort of a surprise. So far, all of Veronica's dates had been femmes, but Mack was not quite that. She had a quiff haircut and wore an untucked men's dress shirt. Her high cheekbones and hip black glasses probably got her no shortage of attention. If Veronica had a type, Rachel had no idea what it was. She poked two skewers into the bowl of olives and put them in the drinks.

"Behave," Harry whispered.

Rachel looked at him. "Behave? What did I do?"

"You started pulling on her pigtails the minute she walked in the door."

Rachel rolled her eyes and groaned at him. Of course, she knew he was right. She picked up the glasses and walked them over to the table. "Two dirty martinis." She folded her arms and waited for an introduction. Up close, she found Mack to be disarmingly handsome. Strong jaw, and the gray-blue eyes behind those glasses were intense. Smelled nice too.

Veronica took a sip of her drink. She didn't seem to hate it, but she did raise an eyebrow at Rachel.

"Right. Okay, enjoy your drinks."

What was she thinking, standing there like an idiot? Of course Veronica wouldn't feel the need to introduce them. It wasn't as if they'd said they were friends. They barely even knew each other. Besides the fact that she was Tiffany's cousin and a lawyer and she could kiss like there was no tomorrow, what did Rachel really know about Veronica?

"I found her." Carol handed Rachel her phone with Mack's profile open. "She's a professor at NYU. English literature. Her pronouns are she/her. Seems like she could give smarty-pants over there a run for her money."

Rachel looked over the profile. It seemed like a good match, except for all of the outdoorsy stuff. Hiking the Appalachian Trail didn't seem like something Veronica would be into. She probably didn't even own a pair of hiking boots. Avid reader? Veronica had to read contracts and briefs and whatever else lawyers read all day. She wouldn't go home at night and double down on the reading. No, definitely not. Or would she? Maybe she longed to read for pleasure. Even so, if there was a second date, Rachel would eat her leather belt. She gave Carol her phone and with a smile said, "They're perfect for each other."

❖

"You put in your Ryder profile that you enjoy camping," Mack said. "Do you like hiking too?"

"What? Oh, that was something I used to do before law school. Back in the day, you know?" Veronica couldn't focus. Rachel saying words like sex and nipple and slut had her thinking about other things. She'd imagined how it would go if they'd climbed that spiral staircase. Clothes torn off. Naked bodies writhing against one another. Whispered promises of more. Except Rachel couldn't make that promise. Or wouldn't. She turned back to Mack and said, "I'd love to go hiking with you sometime."

Mack had a cute smile, and it came out in full force. "Great!"

Veronica took another sip of the martini. Mack had an engaging personality, but Veronica didn't find herself wanting to tear the professor's clothes off. Still, she could envision them enjoying each other's company. If nothing else, they could be friends, and maybe that would turn into something more down the road.

Sometimes attraction was instant, and sometimes a person had to grow on you. Both ways worked. She knew people who'd been friends for years before they'd dated. Mack was a good soul. She knew that the moment they shook hands. If she excused herself to use the restroom, Mack would protect her purse, not rifle through it.

"Mack, do you have any pets?" Veronica wanted to ask if she had any *weird* pets, but she thought that might be rude.

"I have a little dog. He goes to work with me and stays in a crate when I'm in the classroom. Everyone loves him. You would too, I think."

"So, you don't have any snakes or lizards or rodents?"

Mack chuckled. "I take it you've met some interesting people on Ryder?"

"Piña Colada had a snake. And a tattoo of said snake on her..." Veronica patted her chest. "Well, right here. Oh, and a mouse that she was going to feed to the snake." She shivered. "But I can't talk about it, or I'll have to jump up on the table, and that would be embarrassing."

Mack smiled. "I get it. My little sister is terrified of snakes." She leaned in and lowered her voice. "Can I ask why the bartender is staring at me like I've done something wrong?"

Veronica looked over at the bar. Rachel quickly turned her attention to another customer. "Oh, that's nothing. She caught my last date stealing from me when I went to the restroom. She's probably just keeping an eye on me."

Mack looked concerned. "Someone you met on Ryder? You should report that."

"I did. They took her profile down, but she'll probably be back with some other singer's name. She went by Dusty Springfield." Veronica shook her head. "I should've known."

"Hey, don't beat yourself up about it. I've had some interesting dates too."

"Any snakes or con artists?"

Mack laughed. "No. And I haven't met a woman named Piña Colada either."

Damnit. Veronica had called her by her drink name. What was her real name again? All she could remember was— "Her boa constrictor's name is Vicki," she exclaimed.

Mack laughed harder. Veronica joined in. It was the first time she'd really laughed with one of her dates. It felt good.

At the thirty-minute mark, Veronica gave Mack her business card, and they said their good-byes, agreeing that there would be a hiking date when their schedules allowed it. After Mack left, Veronica grabbed her coat, purse, and what was left of her martini and went over to the bar. She sat near the regulars and said, "Do I have it all wrong?"

Carol perked up. "What, dear?"

"I thought love needed to hit you in the face, but after going on all of these dates, I think I might be wrong about that. I mean, most of them have been really nice women, minus the con artist. So, why am I not getting to know them better? Why don't I want to give them a chance? It seems silly now to have such high expectations. I mean, who do I think I am?"

"Sometimes you have to date a lot of lady frogs to find your princess," Carol said.

"But that's just it. I'm not really dating any of them. I'm giving them a few minutes of my time, asking them a few questions, and then on to the next one."

Harry cleared his throat. Veronica took that as an indication he wanted to add his two cents. "Yes, Harry?"

"What does your gut tell you about Dirty Martini?"

Veronica thought about it for a moment. "Good heart, I guess."

"That's important," Joe said. "For the long haul, she has to have a good heart like my Carol, here. Of course, a nice rack never hurts."

Rachel walked over to them. "How'd it go with Mack?"

"She noticed you were staring at her," Veronica said.

All eyes went to Rachel. She threw her hands in the air. "Do you expect me to ignore you after what happened with Dusty Springfield? I mean, who knows what kind of maniac Bea found for you this time."

"Well, thanks for wanting to protect me, but Mack is really nice. We're going hiking sometime soon."

"Ooh," Carol said. "That sounds like fun."

"Watch for blisters," Joe added.

Veronica looked at Harry because surely, he had some advice for her as well. He just shrugged. "Don't let this rugged beard fool you. I'm a city boy."

She turned to Rachel. "And you? What do you have to say about this?"

"Do you even own a pair of hiking boots?"

Veronica narrowed her eyes at Rachel. "I used to be outdoorsy, thank you very much."

Rachel put up her hands. "Okay. You just seem more like the resort spa type."

"I'm not like your hoity-toity clients. Just because I wear nice clothes doesn't mean I spend all of my free time, which isn't even a thing, getting facials and salt scrubs."

"And yet you know what a salt scrub is," Rachel said with a smirk.

"Everyone knows what a salt scrub is." Veronica looked at the regulars. They all shrugged. "Fine. Whatever." She took a sip of her drink and grimaced. "I can't drink any more of this. It's too salty for me."

Rachel rubbed her hands together. "Okay, let's hear it. What is Veronica Welch's favorite drink?"

"Yes, we're dying to know, dear," Carol said. "What's your favorite alcoholic beverage?"

Veronica looked at their drinks. Carol had a full cup of coffee, Joe had what looked like a diet soda, and Harry had an empty beer mug. "I'll have whatever Harry's having."

Rachel rolled her eyes. "So stubborn." She grabbed a mug from the freezer and poured a Sam Adams. "Here you go."

Harry chuckled. "I'm both shocked and impressed, but something tells me that's not your favorite drink."

Veronica pushed the drink over to Harry. "This one's on me, Harry." She grabbed her wallet and put a credit card on the bar. She watched Rachel serve a couple of people who had just walked in. She was no amateur at bartending. Her movements were smooth and practiced. She never had to search for a certain bottle on the lighted shelf behind the bar. In fact, sometimes, she didn't even need to turn to look at it. She knew right where everything was.

Watching Rachel photograph Tiffany's wedding was even more impressive. She exuded confidence and made everyone feel at ease while she adjusted clothing, hair, and positions. But really, who was Veronica kidding? Rachel Monaghan oozed confidence 24/7. Veronica found herself wishing these people could see her in the courtroom or in a deposition. That was her element, her comfort zone. That's where she shined. Instead, they got to see her interact with women she might possibly have a romantic interest in. In other words, the worst possible situation where she felt nervous and fumbled over her words and turned several shades of red every night. God. Why did Rachel always have to see her like that?

Rachel glanced over at her and noticed the credit card sitting on the bar. She said something to the other patrons and then walked back over to her.

"I could've waited," Veronica said.

"I never keep a pretty lady waiting."

Rachel gave her a genuine smile this time, minus the smirk. Veronica turned to the regulars and said, "She confounds me."

Harry leaned in. "What does your gut tell you about her?"

"Ha! My gut tells me she's a smart-aleck and nothing but trouble." Technically, she wasn't lying, but Veronica couldn't say out loud what her gut told her about Rachel. The three regulars—straight regulars—

didn't want to hear her thoughts on what she imagined it would feel like to make love to Rachel. It wouldn't just be sex, not even the first time. It would be all-consuming. It would be a dance. And Veronica would fall fast and hard.

It was different for her to feel this way. She'd always played it safe and careful with women. Even with Avery, she didn't let her feelings get out of control. She kept her guard up because, in her heart, she knew they wouldn't be anything more than friends with benefits, minus the friends part. She found herself wondering if she really had the self-control to keep her feelings in check as she always assumed. Or maybe she was able to keep them in check because they weren't all that strong to begin with.

It wasn't like Veronica to frantically run around a wedding looking for a certain person to dance with, either. She felt a little bit embarrassed that she'd done that. It was a silly move. Something a teenager would do, not a thirty-four-year-old woman. What her gut really told her was to run as fast as she could because Rachel could break her heart into a million pieces, given the chance. But there she sat, watching Rachel's every move.

"I've known her since she was a teenager. She's special," Harry whispered.

Rachel looked over her shoulder and shouted to the end of the bar where Veronica sat with the regulars. "Sorry, the credit card machine is slow today."

Veronica didn't care. She could sit there all day and stare at Rachel's backside. Her shirt had worked its way over the apron strings, exposing a little bit of skin above her jeans. Veronica wanted to run her lips over that skin. Maybe work her way down one leg and back up the other.

It would be easier if they'd never kissed—if Rachel's hands had never been on Veronica's body. It was terrible, but she'd already forgotten Dirty Martini's name. What was it? Oh yeah, MacKenzie.

She'd never been bad with names before. Why was she now? Was it just because there were so many of them? She alternated between watching Rachel and trying not to watch Rachel.

Carol leaned toward her and spoke softly. "Dear, has it ever occurred to you that maybe the reason you can't connect with your dates is because your attention is focused elsewhere?"

Veronica stared at her. Oh God. It was so obvious. Or at least it was once Carol said it. Her problem was the fact that Rachel was in the bar. That had to be it. She was too distracted and couldn't focus on her task at hand. God, why hadn't she figured this out sooner?

Clearly, Veronica needed a change of scenery. A different venue. Bea would have to find a new location for any future dates. It would be a relief, actually. A new start. And she'd give everyone her full attention instead of always being distracted by the damned bartender.

"Sorry it took so long." Rachel set the receipt and pen on the bar and leaned on her elbows so they were eye to eye. "So, you like Dirty Martini? The person, not the drink."

"Her name is Mack." Veronica signed the receipt and left a hefty tip like she always did. She knew it all went to Charlotte, who'd probably need it given her mother's medical bills. "She's smart. Genuine. We even laughed."

"You can do better."

Veronica set the pen down and pushed it and the receipt back to Rachel. "Don't be so judgy. She's a nice person."

"I'm just saying, keep your options open. I haven't found anyone for you yet, but I'm still looking."

"Don't do me any favors." Veronica slid off the stool and put on her coat.

"See you tomorrow," Rachel said. "Same time, same place, different lesbian."

Rachel's smirk was back. God, how it pissed Veronica off when she looked at her that way—as if she was the only one in the whole world who had a brain in her head, and everyone else was a one-celled mud dweller. "Don't count on it." Veronica grabbed her purse and left.

CHAPTER NINE

Everyone had been looking at their watches for the last ten minutes. Rachel had blown it. She wasn't quite sure how, but it was pretty clear Veronica had changed the venue for her dates. Or maybe she just had a work event. She'd said before that it wouldn't be exactly thirty dates in thirty days. Sometimes things came up. Rachel knew it wasn't true, though. She kept hearing Veronica's parting words from the evening before. "Don't count on it," she had said. The regulars were giving her not-so-subtle looks of disappointment. She couldn't take it anymore. "What?" she shouted. "What did I do?"

"You pulled on her pigtails," Harry said.

"That doesn't even work in grade school. Trust me, I know," Joe added.

"I'm not interested in starting anything up with her," Rachel said.

"But you like her." Carol narrowed her stare and gave her a nod.

Rachel imagined when Carol gave that look to her kids, they knew not to argue back. Well, Rachel wasn't her child. "So what?"

"So, grow up and get a pair," Harry said. "That girl's a catch. Hell, she's a whole season of fully loaded pots."

Rachel suppressed a grin. "Harry, what the hell does that even mean?"

"It's from *Deadliest Catch*. Like when they catch a lot of crabs."

"Right." Joe slapped his friend on the back. "Because that's what everyone's looking for."

"My point, if any of you wise guys would care to listen, is that Rachel is letting a good thing get away." Harry took off his cap, giving everyone a good look at his stern-looking face. "I'd give anything to have just one extra day with the love of my life, so when I see you throwing away your chance at love, it makes me sick."

Carol slid off her stool and walked over to put her arm around Harry. She spoke to Rachel. "Look, we all want you to be happy. And frankly, we'd like to see Veronica back in here."

They all missed her. Rachel felt terrible about it. Veronica and her dates, even the train wrecks, had become a bright spot in their lives. A daily dose of something fascinating, beautiful, and hopeful. Even Charlotte, who was dealing with so much pain at the moment with her mom dying, seemed happy when Veronica would walk in the door. And Rachel had blown it by trying to disguise her attraction with those stupid drink names and snarky replies. Harry was right. She needed to grow up.

Rachel looked at the clock again. "I need some air." She went out onto the sidewalk and took in a deep breath, even though she hadn't actually gone out there for air. She hoped she'd see Veronica walking as fast as she could in her fancy heels, but the sidewalk was crowded with commuters rushing to catch trains and buses.

Just as she turned to go back inside, she saw Veronica standing at the crosswalk on the other side of the street, looking at her phone. Rachel grinned and went back inside before Veronica saw her.

It was what it was. Veronica had been ambushed the minute she'd walked into the office that morning. The opposing counsel for a case she'd been working had filed a last-minute motion that kept her busy all day. Telling Bea to change the venue on her next date was something she'd forgotten to do, and now it was too late. On top of that, she was fifteen minutes late. Fortunately, she had a habit of arriving fifteen minutes early for her thirty-minute date.

She walked in and stopped dead in her tracks when Harry let out a loud whoop. Joe fist-bumped the air, and Carol clapped with such excitement, Veronica had to look behind her to see if the Publishers Clearing House people had walked in holding balloons and a big check. Harry got off his stool and gave her a hug. "Well, aren't you a sight for sore eyes," he said.

Veronica accepted hugs from Carol and Joe as well. They all sat back down in their regular spots on the short side of the bar and smiled like giddy fools. Charlotte was chatting with someone at the other end of the bar, but even she stopped long enough to give her a wave. This was a much better ambush than she'd experienced that morning at work, even if she wasn't sure why it was happening.

Rachel had her hair pulled up in a ponytail, which left her long, very kissable neck on full display. Veronica could *not* let herself get distracted. She looked around the bar. There were a few people sitting at the tables, but a single woman waiting for her date wasn't one of them. "She's not here yet?" She looked at her watch. "I'm fifteen minutes late, which means she should be arriving now."

"Longest fifteen minutes of our lives," Rachel said with a grin. "What will you and your date be drinking tonight?"

Veronica glanced at the profile her phone. "This one likes greyhounds."

"I make a great greyhound." Rachel put two lowball glasses on the bar.

"That's my drink!" Carol said. "Oh, I can't wait to meet this one. I mean, I won't actually meet her, but I'll *see* her."

Maybe that wasn't such a bad idea. Why not have this date at the bar? The regulars could help carry the conversation, and Veronica could relax a little bit. Maybe if she was more relaxed, she'd enjoy getting to know Jordan St. Pierre. It was a fancy name. She wondered if the woman would match her name in fanciness.

Rachel set two pink drinks on the bar. "Have a taste. I think you'll like it."

Veronica took a sip. "Oh, that's delicious. What is it?"

"Grapefruit juice, vodka, and a little something extra." Rachel looked over Veronica's shoulder. "I think Greyhound just walked in. Oh my God. She's…"

Veronica turned around. "Fancy."

Jordan St. Pierre looked like the Queen of Jordan. Not in the proverbial way but in the literal way. She bore a striking resemblance to Queen Rania, who was stunning, as queens went. Jordan's long, flowing hair bounced as she walked, and Veronica knew her kelly-green suit was surely bespoke. Her makeup was flawless. Because of course it was. Veronica wanted to dig herself a hole and hide in it. She couldn't possibly date this perfect specimen of a woman, let alone talk to her.

"Veronica. Pleasure to make your acquaintance."

A sexy British accent? Was someone kidding with this? Veronica took her hand. "Yes, hi." She looked at Rachel with wide eyes. Rachel winked at her and walked away.

Jordan put her Balenciaga purse on the bar and sat on a stool. "You have no idea how much I need this drink. God, what a day."

In her profile, Jordan had indicated she worked in government affairs but hadn't really elaborated on it. Veronica glanced at the regulars. Harry and Joe were practically salivating, and Carol looked giddy.

"Sorry I'm late," Jordan said. "Just a bugger of a day at the UN, but I'm all yours." She looked Veronica up and down before continuing. "For the rest of the evening."

Veronica felt a blush crawl up her chest. "Jordan, these are my friends, Harry, Joe, and Carol."

"Friends? It's like *Cheers*! I do love an all-American experience." Jordan held up her glass. "Hello, friends."

Rachel walked in with a pile of clean bar towels in her arms. "And this is Rachel," Veronica said.

Jordan offered her hand. "Jordan St. Pierre."

Rachel set the towels down and shook her hand. "We've met."

"We have? I don't recall."

"The Lancaster wedding in Italy."

Jordan stared at her for a second, then pointed a finger. "You're the photog! Oh my God, those photos were incredible. I saw the spread in *T&C*. Just amazing work. Rachel, is it? I must book you for my sister's wedding next year. But why on earth are you tending bar? Surely, business can't be that slow."

"It's her cousin's bar," Veronica interjected. She wasn't sure why she felt the need to weigh in, even if the way Jordan phrased the question did seem a bit rude.

"My aunt Jenny is ill," Rachel said. "I cover for Charlotte when I can."

"Well, I think it's wonderful what you're doing for your family." Jordan smiled and appeared well prepared to shoot a teeth-whitening commercial at that very moment. "Although I do hope you like the cold. Astrid wants to get married in Alaska, of all the bloody places."

Rachel laughed. "Have camera, will travel. Even to Alaska."

"We couldn't be more different, Astrid and I. We both love the color green but for completely different reasons. She loves trees, and I love money. Do you have a business card, Rachel? I can't let this opportunity slip by."

Rachel pulled a card out of her back pocket. "Tell her to call me soon. My summer schedule starts filling up two years out."

Jordan kissed the card. "Brilliant! Astrid will owe me forever if I make this happen for her, even though she's marrying a total dick who calls himself an *explorer*, but really he just likes to wander the earth on someone else's dime." She turned to Veronica. "Do you have any idea who is serving your drinks? This is the best wedding photog in the business, and if I ever get married on a hilltop in Scotland, which is my mother's dream…well, her real dream is me standing at any wedding altar next to a man, but that's not ever going to happen." She noticed Veronica's drink. "You drink greyhounds as well? This is bloody well meant to be, Veronica Welch. Here's to our future together—however long it's meant to be."

The regulars whispered to each other. Veronica wasn't sure if their appraisal of Jordan St. Pierre was positive or negative. She lifted her glass. "Long or short, I'm sure it'll be memorable." She glanced at Rachel as she took a sip of her drink. Rachel raised an eyebrow at her, then put a drink on a tray and carried it to a customer sitting at a table.

Jordan leaned in and whispered, "Since I suspect you'll hear about it later, I should probably tell you I'd had a few too many greyhounds at the Lancaster wedding. I believe I may have made a terrible pass at your bartender. Failed miserably and woke up alone the next morning with a well-deserved headache." She glanced over at Rachel. "Such a pity, really."

That didn't quite make sense to Veronica. From everything Rachel had said, a one-night stand with a woman like Jordan was right up her alley. She leaned in and whispered, "She photographed my cousin's wedding. She took me home, but I failed to seal the deal."

"Hey, at least you got a lift home. I had to ask a waiter to take me back to my hotel room. Poor sod got the shock of his life when he realized he wasn't going to score that night. At least, not with the likes of me." Jordan made the shape of an *L* with her hand and pressed it to her forehead. "Lesbian, through and through."

Veronica lifted her glass for another toast. "Yeah, me too."

"Lucky me and every other lesbian who's had the pleasure of your company."

"Speaking of…"

Veronica and Jordan looked behind them to see who had said that. "Ave?" Veronica turned on her stool. "What are you doing here?"

"Yes, Ave. To what do we owe this pleasure?" Jordan gave Avery the once-over, then offered her hand. "Jordan St. Pierre."

Avery took her hand. "Avery Hunt." She waved at Rachel. "I'll have a Glenfiddich. Neat." Then she turned her attention to Veronica. "Bea told me you'd be here. Hope you don't mind."

It was unnerving the way Jordan stared at Avery, but the two of them were a better match than Jordan and Veronica would ever be. Something told Veronica fidelity wasn't one of Jordan's strong suits. She didn't seem like the type who'd want to settle down anytime soon either. Maybe Avery was a godsend, even though she'd have to kill Bea for divulging her whereabouts. Veronica glanced at her phone. "Gosh, it looks like I have an emergency at work." She slipped off the barstool and nudged Avery toward it. "You don't mind entertaining Jordan for a few minutes, do you?"

Avery glanced at Jordan. "No. Not at all."

"Okay, gotta run." She tossed a few bills on the bar. "Pleasure to meet you, Jordan." She rushed out as fast as she could and stopped at the crosswalk to take a few deep breaths of the cool night air. It was a candy-ass move to leave like that in the middle of the date, but why bother anymore? It was all for nothing. She'd never meet a woman who was right for her this way.

"V!"

Veronica turned and saw Rachel jogging her way. "Did I not give you enough money?" She opened her purse.

"No, it's not that." Rachel paused a moment to catch her breath. "Is everything okay? You rushed out so fast, I wasn't sure what happened. And who's that woman flirting with your date?"

"Oh, that's Avery. She's an attorney at my firm. They're perfect for each other, so I thought I'd bail."

Rachel furrowed her brow. "V, what's wrong? You look like you're about to cry."

Veronica tried to blink back the tears. "This whole thing has been a total waste of time, and honestly, I'm worn out. I just want to go home and crawl under a blanket with a bowl of ice cream at night instead of coming to this…" She lowered her gaze. "I don't mean it the way it sounds. Charlotte's bar is great."

Rachel pulled Veronica out of the sidewalk traffic by her coat sleeve. "It's been a lot, but you're not going to give up, are you? This is your dream. You have to fight for it."

"This is my mother's dream." That wasn't really true, but Veronica didn't want to have this conversation with Rachel of all people—the woman who thought true love was an unattainable fantasy. "My dream has always been to make partner at Belden and Snow. That's going to happen very soon, and maybe it's enough. It's what I've lived for, and I've been happy, so maybe I should just keep my focus on work and let the other happen whenever it happens."

"Then why are you crying?"

Veronica didn't realize any tears had fallen. She wiped her cheeks and forced a smile. "It's just stress. Sometimes, you just have to let it out, right?"

"Right." Rachel tucked her hands in her pockets. "As long as you're okay."

Veronica wasn't okay, but she would be. She just needed to get her priorities straight again. "It's cold out here. Get back inside."

Rachel rubbed her arm. "It is. I'll see you around, then."

"Yeah. See you around." Veronica watched her walk away. "Wait!" She took a step closer. "Why did you turn Jordan St. Pierre down at that wedding?"

"I know," Rachel said. "Why would anyone in their right mind turn down a woman who looks like that? Or leave her in a bar to flirt with some other woman?"

"Right," Veronica said. "Well, I don't think she has any intention of settling down anytime soon."

"My money says she'd be perfectly satisfied settling down with a billionaire who doesn't mind how many women she shags on the side," Rachel said. "And believe it or not, that kind of man does exist. In fact, I'm pretty sure I've shot a few of their second and third weddings."

Veronica could feel another lecture coming on about how many marriages failed and how this wasn't a dream worth chasing. "How do you do it? How do you fool your clients into believing you're not the Scrooge of weddings past and future?"

Rachel seemed to cringe at the question, or maybe she was just cold. "V, don't give up on your dream. And don't let women like Jordan St. Pierre or Jägerbomb or that damn con artist deter you. It's a beautiful dream. Truly."

They were nice words, but Veronica knew Rachel didn't really believe what she was saying. "So, that's how you do it. Feign sincerity and say just the right thing. It almost worked." Veronica turned to walk away. She thought Rachel might follow her and try to defend herself. She was glad when she didn't.

❖

"I said I'm done, Bea."

"You can't be done." Bea sat and put her palms flat on Veronica's desk. Her short nails were painted bright pink and perfectly matched her sweater. "Just hear me out."

"Weren't your nails orange yesterday?"

"We've worked together how long, and you're just now noticing I change my nail color at least three times a week?"

"You're right. How is it possible that I haven't focused on issues as important as the color of your nails?" Veronica went back to her paperwork.

"You can't be done, V. The next one is special. I can feel it in my gut."

Veronica rolled her eyes. "You and Harry."

"Who's Harry?"

"Just a guy at the bar who talks about guts and feelings."

Bea blinked. "Okay, well, I think Harry would agree with me about this one."

Veronica scribbled her signature and opened the next folder. "You've thought that about every single date, Bea. Even Dusty Springfield."

"Not true. I've never referenced my gut feeling before, and if you want to be done after this one, I'll be okay with that, but V, I really need you to go on one more date. I'll die of something horrible if you don't."

"Like curiosity? Yeah, that's right up there with dying from a thousand bee stings or being buried up to your neck in the desert and having scorpions chew your eyes out."

"Wow. You kind of have a dark mind. To be honest, I'm a little surprised things didn't go better with the horror writer. What was her name?"

"Shirley Temple. And she had the emotional maturity of an adolescent."

"Okay, well, I promise, no eyes will be chewed out by scorpions." Bea scrunched up her face.

"That's how I feel about going on another date at this point. Who is she?"

"You'll speak the same language," Bea said. "She's an attorney too. And her drink is solid."

"I can't wait to hear what you consider a *solid* drink."

"A lemon drop."

Veronica looked up from her paperwork. "A lemon drop. And in your professional opinion, this is quote, solid?"

"I'm telling you, V. You're going to love both the drink and the woman. Just one more. Please?"

Veronica looked at her watch. "I have a deposition." She grabbed a few files and stood. Bea stared at her with pleading eyes. "Fine. One more. But then I don't ever want to hear another thing about it. We're done, okay?"

"Who's done?" Avery sauntered into the room. "Because I've just started."

Veronica wasn't sure what that meant, but she didn't have time for Avery, and she certainly didn't want to hear how Jordan St. Pierre took her morning coffee. She headed for the door. "Gotta run."

"You're always on the run, V. We need to talk!"

"Another time, Ave!"

❖

Lemon drops. Such a pretty drink, served in a martini glass with a sugar rim. Veronica took a sip. "Wow. That's delicious. Where is everyone?"

"Joe and Carol are at their granddaughter's birthday party," Charlotte said. "I mean, why hang out in a perfectly lovely bar when you can spend your retirement at the American Girl store watching dolls get facials. Harry was a bit cagey about his plans for the evening.

I'm thinking he might have a date." Charlotte smiled. "Anyone else you're wondering about?"

"Nope."

"Well, if you start wondering, she's in the back."

Veronica took another sip of her drink. "Mmm. That's a dangerous drink."

Charlotte smiled. "I'll cut you off after two."

"Let's hope the woman is as special as her drink."

"Good luck, V. Just give me a wave if you need a second round."

"Will do. Hey, Charlotte? Thanks for everything. I'm glad Bea picked this bar. You've all been great, and I'll miss you."

Charlotte stepped back to the table. "This is only date twelve. Is Lemon Drop that promising?"

They were keeping track? Veronica laughed. "Not quite. I'm just tired. And please don't tell me you all are betting on how long I'll last."

"My guess was twenty."

"I appreciate your optimism."

"You'll find her. Who knows, maybe you already have." Charlotte gave her a wink and walked through the swinging doors, which Veronica assumed led to the place where important bar business was conducted.

Veronica had considered asking Bea to change locations for tonight, but it was just one more date that she didn't have high hopes for, so what would it hurt? Also, it would give her an opportunity to say good-bye to the regulars. What a bust it all turned out to be.

Veronica found herself feeling sad about missing the regulars. She would've liked to thank them for their support since she wouldn't have a reason to ever walk into this particular bar again. After tonight, she'd return to her usual routine of staying at the office late, then going home to Netflix and a bowl of her favorite cereal. Currently, it was peanut butter and chocolate-flavored Cheerios.

"Veronica? Hi, I'm Lauren." She scanned the bar, then sat. "I haven't been here in ages. It looks so different."

Lauren seemed more nervous than Veronica was. Somehow, that was comforting. "So, you didn't have any trouble finding it?"

"No." Lauren scanned the bar again. She seemed to be checking the place out thoroughly.

"Everything okay?"

"Fine." Lauren took off her coat and offered her hand. "Hi."

Veronica took her hand. It was warm, and she had a solid grip. "Hi, Lauren. It's nice to meet you."

"You're beautiful." Lauren seemed to blush at her own words. "I'm seriously so happy to be here. Just ignore my nervousness."

Veronica wanted to return the compliment. Lauren's profile photo didn't do her justice. She was beautiful, and more importantly, she had kind eyes. "I'm glad I'm not the only nervous one in the room."

"What if we agreed to be mutually *not* nervous?"

Veronica lifted her glass. "I like it." And maybe years from now, they'd laugh about how nervous they both were. Veronica took a sip of her drink, then turned off the thirty-minute timer on her phone. She had a good feeling about this one.

Rachel heard the office door open. "I know, Char. I'll be right out. Just let me get this email sent." One of her clients had decided to move her wedding date at the last minute and expected everyone involved to shift their schedules as well. Sometimes, working for wealthy, entitled debutantes was more trouble than it was worth.

"Rach, I have to talk to you."

"Give me a minute."

Charlotte leaned on the desk with both hands. "It's important."

Rachel stopped typing. She didn't like the look on Charlotte's face. "Drunk customer?"

"Worse."

Rachel stood. "Oh God. Is it your mom?"

"Mom is…not good, but…"

Charlotte dropped her head. Whatever it was, she didn't want to say it. Rachel put her hand on Charlotte's shoulder. "Just tell me."

"It's Lauren."

No one had uttered that name in Rachel's presence in a long time. It felt like a punch to the gut to hear Charlotte say it. "Lauren? What about Lauren?"

Charlotte tucked her hair behind her ears and folded her arms. "You have to remain calm, Rach. Promise me you'll—"

"What the fuck, Char? Just tell me!"

Charlotte motioned with her thumb behind her. "She's out there. With V."

Rachel's heart sank. No, no, no, this couldn't possibly be happening. "She's V's date?"

"V came in and ordered lemon drops, and I thought 'well, what are the odds?' I mean, it couldn't be, right?" Once she started talking, it seemed Charlotte couldn't stop. "So, I made the drinks, and then I thought, 'Okay, just in case, I'll step in the back and watch the security camera,' and oh shit, Rach. It's her. Rachel, what are we gonna—"

Rachel held her hand up, indicating that Charlotte needed to stop talking. Her eyes fluttered closed. A lemon drop was Lauren's splurge drink. She always ordered it on special occasions. Memories of Lauren sitting across from her, laughing and sipping on her drink, flashed through Rachel's mind. Nine times out of ten, Lauren would spill a little bit on her fingers when they made a toast and then lick her fingers clean. The memories were so vivid in Rachel's mind, she had to do something to free herself of them. She wanted to grab a bottle of whiskey and throw it against the brick wall. She chose to slap her laptop shut. "Kick her out."

"What?" Charlotte's mouth gaped open. "I'm not going to eighty-six Veronica's date."

"We're family, Char. Family comes before your bottom line. Why do you think I'm here every night? I'm here for you. My cousin."

"Just hold on. It's not about a paying customer. It's about Veronica. Maybe they'd be a great match. They're both lawyers."

"They're both lawyers? That's what you've got?" Rachel shook her head in disgust. "Have you forgotten what she did?"

"No. I remember it vividly," Charlotte said. "But I think Lauren is a good person who had a bad moment."

Was she fucking kidding right now? Rachel couldn't believe what Charlotte was suggesting. "A bad moment? That's what we're calling it now? She left me standing at the altar. She ran from our wedding. She humiliated me in front of everyone who's important to me. I will *never* forgive her for that, and neither should you."

Charlotte put her hands up. "Okay. Okay, Rach. It was a terrible choice of words. And it was a terrible thing she did to you. What do you want me to do?"

What did Rachel want her to do? She wanted her to go out there and kick Lauren out on her lying ass, that's what she wanted her to do. Also, throw the damn lemon drop in her face if it wasn't too much to ask. "You have to stop it."

"Stop it? How am I supposed to stop it?"

"I don't care what you do," Rachel shouted. "But you have to stop that date, or I'll go out there and do it myself."

"No!" Charlotte grabbed her by the shoulders. "I'll think of something, but you have to promise me you'll stay here." Charlotte backed toward the door. "Stay here, Rachel. I don't need a scene in my bar."

Rachel's heart raced. Her stomach burned. How dared Lauren think she could just waltz into this bar, of all bars, as if it was nothing? The nerve! Rachel took a breath. "Fine. I'll stay."

Veronica laughed. "I've heard a lot of lawyer jokes, but that one was actually good."

"You have a nice laugh."

Lauren wasn't shy with the compliments. Veronica liked that. She liked her sense of humor too. And her voice. Lauren had a soothing voice. Veronica couldn't see a single red flag. Maybe Bea was actually right about this one.

"Can I see you again, Veronica? Let me take you to dinner this weekend. I know this great place that just opened."

Veronica was about to accept when Charlotte walked up to the table and said, "You have a phone call."

Veronica gave her a quizzical look. "A what?"

"Hi, Charlotte," Lauren said. "It's been a while. The bar looks great."

"Lauren."

Charlotte's greeting didn't seem very friendly. "You two know each other?" Veronica looked to Lauren for a reply.

"Um, yeah. We do." Lauren seemed nervous again.

"You have a call. In the back." Charlotte widened her eyes and motioned with her head.

Veronica had no idea what she was talking about, but she stood. "Um…okay." Lauren's smile had faded. Veronica didn't like seeing that. Whatever this was, she needed to get it over with quickly so she could get back to her date. That thought made her happy, because usually, she wanted to get the date over quickly. This definitely felt different, except for the fact that Charlotte had just made things totally weird. God help her if Charlotte was sabotaging her date as part of the Rachel campaign the whole bar seemed to be working toward.

As they walked to the back, she leaned in and said, "So, where's this phone from 1972?"

"It's the only thing I could think of," Charlotte whispered. "I needed to talk to you."

"You've been watching too many old movies. I mean, seriously. Am I supposed to tell Lauren my mother called the bar looking for me? I'll sound like a drunk. Not to mention the fact that she'll think this is me trying to bail, which is the last thing I want to do because I really, really like her." Veronica stopped short when she saw Rachel standing there. Her chest and face were flushed, and her hands were balled up into fists. This couldn't be good. "What the hell is going on?"

"I'll leave you two to talk this out." Charlotte nudged Veronica into the office and shut the door.

Rachel didn't say anything. She just stared Veronica down. "Well? Why am I here?"

"It's your date," Rachel said. "I strongly advise you to end it before it even begins."

"Why? She hasn't tried to steal anything from me."

"That's your standard now? If they don't steal your purse—"

"No." Veronica folded her arms. "I happen to like her. She's funny and smart and attractive and not full of herself."

"You've known her for what, five minutes?"

Veronica shrugged. "I'm not sure. I turned off the timer."

Rachel turned her back to Veronica and put her hands on her hips. "If you know something about Lauren, spit it out, but I'm not going to end the date just because you tell me to."

"You should just trust me on this one."

"I'll need more than that."

In a huff, Rachel turned around, took her apron off, and threw it on the desk. "You know what? Maybe you two *are* perfect for each other, so do whatever the hell you want." She pushed past Veronica and stormed out the door.

CHAPTER TEN

Veronica couldn't believe she was on another date with Lauren. In the two weeks following their first date in the bar, they'd met for coffee once. Then there was a lunch date. A nice, safe, slow start. They didn't struggle for topics of conversation. Lauren was happy to share stories about work and family, and Veronica felt comfortable doing the same.

Rachel had called a couple of times, but Veronica ignored those calls. Whatever Rachel's agenda was—thinking she could interfere with her dates willy-nilly—Veronica was over it. She was also over Rachel running so hot and cold. One minute, Rachel was offering to help find her someone special, and the next, she was making rude, sarcastic comments about her dates. Talk about confusing.

None of that mattered now. Bea's plan, against all odds, had actually worked. Veronica could definitely see herself spending more time with Lauren.

It was a clear night, so they'd decided to walk off dinner. Veronica let go of Lauren's hand and wrapped her arm around her waist. "Are you warm enough?"

Lauren pulled her closer. "I'd be warmer if you let me kiss you."

"I'm not stopping you."

"True. I guess I'm just waiting for the right moment."

"Yeah," Veronica said. "Make it memorable, would you?"

"Hmm. I guess we could kiss under that light post and then revisit it every year on our first kiss anniversary."

That made Veronica smile, but she didn't want to give away just how invested she was in Lauren. Not after only three dates. "Getting a little ahead of yourself there," she said in a joking tone.

Lauren stopped and turned to her. "Am I? I mean, I haven't felt this way about someone in a long time."

Veronica realized they hadn't really discussed their previous relationships, not that there was much to discuss on her end. "When was the last time?"

"You already know," Lauren said. "And I should thank you for not thinking the worst of me."

Veronica stiffened. "The worst of you?"

"I wasn't ready," Lauren said. "I know that leaving someone at the altar is one of the worst possible things you could do, but I panicked."

"What are you talking about?"

Lauren's expression sobered. "Rachel. I thought Charlotte told you when she dragged you into the back to take a phone call. As if that ever happens. How dumb does she think I am?"

Veronica took a step back. "You…left Rachel at the altar?"

Lauren let out a heavy sigh. "I know, I know. Weddings are her life. She'd planned ours down to the last detail. Everything was perfect. Too perfect."

"What does that mean, too perfect?"

Lauren shook her head. "I don't know. I guess I realized a little too late that I wasn't ready for everything that marriage meant. The commitment. The kids we'd talked about having." She stepped closer and put her hands on Veronica's waist. "You have to believe me when I say that I'm a different person now. I know what I want in life."

It all made sense now. Veronica could envision the moment when Rachel's life blew up. Flowers everywhere. A quartet playing in the background. She must've been devastated. "Did you just not show up?"

"Does it matter?"

"To me it does." Veronica wasn't sure why it mattered. Either way, Rachel was left standing there, with who knew how many people staring at her during the worst moment of her life. For some reason, she still wanted to know.

Lauren turned away and wrapped her arms around herself. "Rachel went down the aisle first. I was halfway there when I froze. My dad urged me to move, but I couldn't." She turned back around. "It was by far my biggest mistake."

"Ya think?"

"V, I've paid for it. I lost friends. I lost the respect of my family, Rachel's family. But most of all, I lost Rachel. I loved her, V, and I lost her. So, yeah. It made me grow up. It took me breaking someone's heart to realize that people's hearts are not something you mess with."

Veronica wasn't sure what to say. Lauren seemed sincere. Heartbroken, almost, at how her actions had hurt the people she loved. Who *hadn't* made mistakes in their lives? Should she hold her past against her? But all she could think about was getting to Rachel as fast as her feet would carry her. She needed to tell her that she got it now. She understood why her view of love was so warped. Who could walk away from a moment like that without some major scars? She wanted to hold Rachel and somehow try to make it better. The thought of Rachel in that kind of pain was more than Veronica could take. "I need to think about this, okay? Just give me some time to work through this."

Lauren's shoulders dropped. "Yeah. Sure."

❖

From across the street, Monaghan's looked dark and empty. That didn't seem right. Veronica looked at her watch. It was only nine o'clock. She could barely make out some sort of sign taped to the door. She waited for traffic to clear and crossed the street. "Closed for a family event." Veronica peered into the window to see if a light was on in the back.

"Haven't seen you here in a while."

She turned to see Harry standing there, dressed in a suit and tie. "Hey, Harry. It says there's a family event?"

"Yeah." Harry loosened his tie. "I never wear a tie anymore. Had to for years." He took the tie off and put it in his jacket pocket. "Walk with me?" He offered his arm.

"Sure." Veronica took his right arm. "That's a nice suit, Harry." It wasn't an off-the-rack suit. It fit Harry's slim body well, and his shoes were shiny and clean. It looked as if he'd had a haircut and trimmed his beard as well.

"Shucks, this old thing?" Harry laughed. "I haven't had a compliment from a lady in quite some time. Let me try that again." He cleared his throat. "Thank you, Veronica. Maybe I should wear it more often."

Veronica smiled. She was pretty sure she'd just made Harry blush. "Where are we going?"

"Can I buy you a coffee?"

"I'd love one."

Harry glanced at her. His expression had turned serious. "Charlotte's mom passed away," he said. "That's why Monaghan's is closed."

"I'm so sorry."

"I thought I'd take the long way home and make sure everything was okay at the bar. Running into you was a nice surprise after a very grim day."

"Is Charlotte okay?" Veronica cringed at her question. Of course Charlotte wasn't okay. She'd just lost her mom. "I mean, how is she holding up?"

Harry sighed. "We all knew it was coming. Another beautiful soul lost to cancer."

"So, you knew her mom?"

Harry glanced at her again. Even though it was dark, she could tell his eyes were bloodshot from crying. "I'm Charlotte's godfather," he said. "I don't know what they were thinking picking me, but I look after her as best I can. I visit the bar every day, as you know. It's my way of letting her know she's not alone. And…" Harry got choked up and put his fist over his mouth. A few seconds later, he said, "It's my way of keeping my promise to her mother. A woman I loved very much."

There was so much Veronica didn't know about the people in Monaghan's. And so much they didn't know about her. But somehow, she still felt close to them.

"It's not as salacious as you're imagining," Harry said. "We didn't have an affair. John, Charlotte's father, and I were best friends. It was only after he died that I saw Jenny through a different lens. A romantic lens, if you will. But she got sick before we could do much about it. That didn't stop me from falling madly in love with her, though."

Veronica leaned in closer and squeezed his arm. "I'm so sorry for your loss. What can I do? How can I help?"

"We kept it from Charlotte, how we felt about each other. Jenny didn't want to cause her any more pain than she was already in, and I understood that." He patted Veronica's hand. "It's nice to have someone I can tell our story to. The whole story." He stopped in front of a small café. "I suddenly have an appetite. They make a great pastrami sandwich here."

Veronica wasn't hungry, but she couldn't leave Harry to eat on his own. "If they make good coffee, I'm in."

❖

Harry talked about Charlotte's mom in between bites of a pastrami and coleslaw sandwich. He talked about the good days when Jenny had enough energy to walk with him to the park. And he talked about the bad days when she was so weak, she couldn't get out of bed. He'd been by her side through all of it.

"We weren't each other's first love," he said. "And by that, I mean that I knew Jenny's heart belonged to her husband, John, even though he isn't here. And my heart will always beat for my wife, the love of my life, my sweet Diane. But we shared something special. She filled an emptiness inside me, and I think I did the same for her."

"It's a beautiful thing," Veronica said. "I'm so glad you had each other, even if it was only for a short time." She hesitated, then said, "Can I ask you something personal, Harry?"

He chuckled. "I've been spilling my guts over here. Can't imagine you'd ask me something I wouldn't answer."

"It's about Rachel."

Harry's eyes lit up. He pushed his plate away and leaned forward, resting his arms on the table. "Great change of subject. Yes, let's talk about Rachel."

Veronica wasn't expecting such a spirited reply. "I was just wondering if you were at her wedding."

"Oh." Harry leaned back in his chair. "What an awful day that was."

"Can you tell me about it? I know the basics. I just wanted your take on what happened."

He looked a bit uncomfortable. "I'm not really sure I'm the one to be asking about that. Shouldn't you be talking to Rachel?"

"I would, but I'm not sure she wants to talk to me. I've been seeing her ex." Harry's eyes widened, and his eyebrows seemed to hit his hairline. Veronica spoke quickly to clarify. "I didn't know, obviously. We were on our third date when I found out. I feel terrible for Rachel, and I certainly don't want to be the source of more hurt. That's why I was hoping to hear more."

"Well, I hadn't seen Rachel since John's funeral. She'd become a very successful photographer and was traveling all over the world. But then I got an invitation in the mail. Rachel Monaghan was marrying Lauren Something-or-other." He pointed at her. "A lawyer, like you."

"Yeah, I know."

"Oh, right. I guess you would, wouldn't you? I was tucked in one of the back rows, but a good two hundred other people and I witnessed what no one ever wants to see."

"I can't imagine."

"Imagine the worst and you'll have it about right. It was awful."

Veronica already had. She knew how painful that moment must've been for Rachel. "Have you ever talked to her about it?"

Harry shook his head. "No. I hadn't seen her again until a few weeks ago. I don't think she even knew I was at the wedding, and I'd rather keep it that way. Why bring up old wounds?"

"No, of course not." Veronica focused on her coffee for a moment. Admitting she was dating Lauren made her feel awful, and not just because Rachel's ex had impacted the lives of so many people she had grown to care about. She felt as if she had betrayed Rachel. Cheated on her in some weird way.

Harry's eyes were kind. He'd been surprised, but he didn't seem to judge her. "So, tell me about this rather unexpected turn of events. How on earth did this happen?"

"I met her on Ryder," Veronica said. "Just like I met all of the other women. I didn't know who she was until tonight. I mean, I told you I just found out about the wedding that wasn't, but I didn't even know she and Rachel had been together."

"Rachel and Charlotte didn't say anything?" He seemed surprised.

"Rachel tried to warn me off her that night in the bar, but she didn't tell me why. We argued about it, actually." Her voice softened almost to a whisper. "I know it sounds arrogant, but I thought she was trying to sabotage my date, you know, because of the thing we have together."

Harry smiled, his eyes twinkling. "Right. The thing."

"So, I kept dating Lauren. She's a lovely person, but she did this horrible thing, and now I'm not sure how I feel."

"So, that's why Rachel's been in such a state. She's been a real pain in the neck, that one." Harry folded his napkin in half and set it on his plate. "I assumed it was because you hadn't been around, but I imagine seeing Lauren again stirred up a lot of feelings for her."

Veronica thought back to that night. After all of Rachel's sarcastic remarks about her dates and their drinks and lasting love not being real, she hadn't taken her angry demeanor seriously. She assumed Rachel was a player and a cranky one at that. Rachel's behavior only reinforced Veronica's assumptions. And the way she'd just taken over and kicked Dusty Springfield out of the bar still bothered her. Rachel should've brought the situation to Veronica's attention so *she* could handle the con artist. And she should've told Veronica the truth about Lauren instead of storming out of the bar. What a mess things were now.

Harry reached across the table for her hand. "I can't tell you what to do, V. All I can tell you is to—"

"Follow my gut. I know, Harry."

"Glad to know you've been listening, kid."

Veronica sent flowers to the bar, extending her condolences to Charlotte. Normally, she would have asked Bea to do it, but this was something she wanted to handle personally. It had been three days since her last date with Lauren, and she still hadn't decided what to do. Should they continue to date? In a lot of ways, they seemed so right for each other. She felt comfortable being in Lauren's presence. They'd walked hand in hand a few times, and Lauren seemed totally comfortable with public affection. That was important to Veronica. She didn't want to ever have to hide her sexuality.

They had similar interests and tastes in food. Both of their families lived in the city, so holidays would be easy. On paper, it looked great. And Rachel once loved Lauren enough to want to marry her, which made Veronica think she had to be a pretty special person in general.

But trust was obviously a big issue. Could she really overlook what Lauren had done to Rachel? Had she really matured since then? And would she ever stop feeling guilty about what she was doing to Rachel? Veronica had a lot to think about.

❖

"Do you like the gold foil? Maybe it looks too much like a wedding invitation. Everyone will open it, get excited, read it, and then feel let down when it's just a party."

"Subtle, Mom. I seriously doubt everyone is waiting by their mailbox for a wedding invitation from me," Veronica said. "If you like the gold, do the gold."

"No," her mom said. "The black print is more professional anyway. We'll go with the black to announce your new partnership with the firm."

Veronica's parents insisted on throwing a party when she made partner. She wanted to tell them to buy a few balloons and a cake and call it good, but that wasn't her mom's style. She'd want a catered event with fancy invitations and speeches. And that would require a sit-down meeting at their kitchen table. She was their only child. What could she do other than be gracious about it? Nothing. She could do nothing. She loved her parents, so whatever her mom wanted, she'd get.

Veronica looked at her watch and then at her dad, who had left this little planning party an hour ago and was watching the sports channel with a beer in his hand. He looked back at her and winked, then chuckled to himself.

Her dad wouldn't plan the party, but he'd picked out whatever piece of jewelry they'd give her. That was his thing, giving Veronica a necklace or bracelet when she hit a new milestone. She still had all of them, even the tiny bracelet he gave her when she'd graduated from kindergarten.

She felt a wave of sadness come over her as she thought about watching her parents get older and eventually losing them like Charlotte had. She'd be lost without them. They were always there for her, through the ups and downs of her life, her schooling, her career. She reached over and grabbed her mom's hand. "Thank you, for wanting to do this for me. I have the best parents."

Her mom gave her hand a pat. "We have the best daughter."

The doorbell rang. Her dad got up. "Expecting company?"
"No," Veronica and her mom answered in unison.

A moment later, Bea came into the kitchen. She was out of breath and looked as if she'd seen a ghost. Veronica stood. "Bea? What are you doing here?"

"I'm sorry for interrupting, but I didn't think this could wait."

Veronica's mom stood. "What's wrong, Bea? You're scaring me."

"I was cc'd on an interoffice email. I don't think I was supposed to see it. They must have cc'd the wrong person. Anyway." Bea wrung her hands together. "I had to tell you in person, V."

"Okay, you're killing us here, Bea. Just tell me what the email said."

Bea hesitated for a moment. "I hate being the one to tell you."

"Bea!"

Bea jumped at the loud request. "Okay! Sorry, I just can't believe this is happening, but it looks like they're making Avery a partner. Not you."

Veronica was stunned. She looked at her dad, who was standing behind Bea, then at her mom. They looked as shocked as she felt. "That can't be. She hasn't even been there a year."

"She brought all those clients with her."

Veronica shook her head in disbelief. "You mean all those super-shady clients?"

"Super-shady clients with lots of shady money. And she landed another big one last week," Bea said. "I think maybe that has something to do with it."

"I don't care who she landed! That partnership was mine!" Veronica put her hands on her hips and shook her head at the ceiling. This couldn't possibly be happening. Seven years of her life she'd given to that firm. Ninety-hour weeks. Some big wins in court. How could they do this to her? Her mom tried to touch her, but she pulled away. "No, Mom. This is a mistake. Bea, you must've read the email wrong."

"I printed a copy." Bea pulled a folded piece of paper out of her purse. "I'm so sorry, V."

Veronica took the paper. It was clear from the first sentence that Bea was absolutely right.

As we discussed yesterday, we are happy to extend an offer of an equity partnership to you as of...

The email was addressed to Avery Hunt. Veronica's hands started to shake. Her dad wrapped an arm around her shoulder. "Can I have a look?" He read the email and gave it back to her, then wrapped both arms around her and kissed her head. "You'll stay here tonight."

CHAPTER ELEVEN

The bar had been busy every night since the funeral. All of Uncle John and Aunt Jenny's friends were stopping by in support of Charlotte. They would sit her down and tell stories about her parents and what an important presence they'd been in the neighborhood. Players from the softball teams they'd sponsored stopped by to reminisce. So did locals who'd celebrated special occasions in her parents' bar. Rachel overheard an older woman relay the story of their wedding. She and her fiancé didn't have the means to do much except buy each other a simple gold band. That was when Uncle John and Aunt Jenny stepped in and offered to host their wedding reception in the bar, free of charge. They even provided a round of champagne for everyone. She'd asked Uncle John why he'd do something like that for them. She said he looked at his wife and said, "Fate's been awfully kind to me. I figure I ought to return the favor."

Rachel had also heard people encouraging Charlotte to be that same kind of presence. Rachel knew she would be. In fact, Charlotte already was. Everyone who walked through that door more than once grew to love both the bar and the owner. Rachel had seen it happen time and again. Carol and Joe were a great example. They didn't come in almost every day because they were hard drinkers. They came in to shoot the breeze with Harry and Charlotte. Eventually, keeping tabs on Veronica was a draw as well.

Charlotte was saying good-bye to a few of those friends when Rachel noticed a new face walk in. She took a closer look and realized she'd seen that face before; she just couldn't place where. As the woman approached, she remembered who it was. Veronica's mother. "Mrs. Welch. It's good to see you again."

"Rachel?" Mrs. Welch looked around the bar. "What on earth are you doing here?"

"This is my cousin's place. I've been filling in for her during a family thing. If you're looking for V, she hasn't been here in a while."

"I'm not really sure what I'm looking for." Mrs. Welch sat on a stool.

Rachel poured a glass of ice water.

"Actually, it's not a *what* I need," Mrs. Welch said. "It's a *who*. A bartender. That's all I know."

"Oh, okay." Rachel set the glass on a napkin in front of Mrs. Welch. "I can get you something stronger if you like."

"No, no. The water is fine." Mrs. Welch took a sip and said, "I can see you're busy, so I'll get right to the point."

Rachel put up a finger. "Give me one second." She poured a beer for another customer, then went back to Mrs. Welch. "Okay. Shoot."

"Things aren't good with Veronica. She stayed in her old bedroom at our place all weekend. She hasn't done that since she was in college, and I know all college students do that, but grown-up lawyers don't."

"Oh, no. Is she sick?"

"No. She just got some horrible news, and it's taken her down. I thought for sure she'd go to work today, but she didn't."

"Oh," Rachel said. She desperately wanted to ask what the news was, but she'd only met Veronica's mother once. How could she pry like that? "That doesn't sound like her."

"No, it's not like her at all."

Mrs. Welch took a sip of water. She wasn't the joyful, smiling woman Rachel had met at Tiffany's wedding. She seemed truly distraught. "How can I help, Mrs. Welch?"

"Well, I asked V if there was anyone I could call. A friend. A confidant. She said no. And then I remembered something she told us a few weeks ago about a bartender. So, I talked to Bea, and she said it must be someone here at Monaghan's."

Rachel was glad Charlotte was still by the front door. She leaned in and lowered her voice. "And what did Veronica tell you about this bartender?"

"That she'd connected with her. That sounded big to me, so here I am, looking for the woman who connected with my V. Because like I said, she's in a bad way."

Okay. Now she needed to know. "Can you tell me what happened?" Rachel prayed it had nothing to do with Lauren. She assumed that since Veronica hadn't been back to the bar, they were still dating.

"Why don't you tell me if I'm talking to the right bartender first?"

Rachel knew it had to be her. Veronica had connected with Charlotte and the regulars on some level, but she hadn't kissed them. And not just a kiss, a hot as hell make-out session. "Yes," she said. "I'm the bartender V was talking about."

Mrs. Welch smiled, but it quickly faded. "Some horrible woman named Avery got my V's partner spot."

"Wait." Rachel had to put this together. Avery was the woman who came into the bar right before Veronica rushed out and left Greyhound there to fend for herself. Which didn't require much fending since Avery was there, ready and willing to flirt her ass off. Rachel wasn't so sure they'd parted ways when they left. It looked as if they'd gotten pretty chummy in a short amount of time. And now, Avery somehow got Veronica's spot in the firm? "That doesn't make sense," she said out loud.

"That woman got some big client and demanded to be made a partner, and those, those, jerks pushed V to the side."

"I'm so sorry, Mrs. Welch. V must be devastated." That was an understatement. She'd worked her ass to get where she was, and to have it taken away from her like that?

"She didn't tell me the bartender was you, Rachel. But why on earth would she say you don't believe in love? That doesn't seem like you at all."

Rachel's shoulders sagged. "It's complicated, but I do care about your daughter, and I'd like to help. What can I do?"

"Come by our place," Mrs. Welch said. "I don't think she's going anywhere tonight."

They were pretty much at max capacity, but Rachel said, "Hold on." She went to the short end of the bar where Harry, Carol, and Joe sat. "Harry, you used to help Uncle John behind the bar, right?"

"I can pour a drink or two," Harry said. "Although I don't know the fancy drinks they serve these days."

Rachel pulled a book out from under the bar. "Everything is in here." She motioned with her head toward Mrs. Welch. That's Veronica's mom. She just told me V didn't make partner."

Carol gasped. "What? Why? I should go talk to her."

"No," Rachel said. "We need to go, but I'd really appreciate it if you and Joe could help Harry and Charlotte while I'm gone."

Joe waved her away. "Go, girl. We'll bus tables if we have to."

"Thanks, Joe. I owe you a drink."

Harry went behind the bar. "Give me your apron." He tipped his baseball cap to Mrs. Welch. "I'll let Charlotte know what's happening."

Rachel kissed his cheek. "You're the best, Harry."

❖

Rachel knocked on the bedroom door, but no one answered. Mrs. Welch motioned for her to go on in. She opened the door a crack. "V?"

"I told you, I'm not hungry, Mom."

Mrs. Welch gave Rachel a knowing look. She had to smile because Veronica did sound like a teenager. "It's Rachel." She stepped into the room and closed the door behind her.

Veronica covered her face with her hands. "Oh God. Why are you here?"

Now she looked like a teenager too. The décor didn't help. The room had pink walls and a canopy bed. Rachel looked around, half hoping to find a pink CD player or an old telephone shaped like lips. No such luck. She did, however, see at least a dozen trophies—physical evidence that Veronica excelled in everything from cheerleading to debate. Rachel turned her attention back to Veronica. She looked at least ten years younger sitting there on that ridiculous bed with her laptop. She didn't have any makeup on, and her hair was a mess. She looked adorable.

Rachel sat on the edge of the bed. "Heard you've had a rough couple of days."

Veronica dropped her hands into her lap. "That's putting it mildly."

"Scoot over." Rachel put a pillow against the wall and joined her on the bed. "Whatcha got going there?" She pointed at the laptop.

"It's a 'Dear Assholes, I quit' letter."

"Good for you." Rachel didn't actually know if it was a good thing, but she figured Veronica needed support at that moment more than she needed career advice.

"I don't know if I'll actually send it, but it felt good to write it." She sighed. "God, if the partners could see me right now, they'd think they made the right decision."

"They might," Rachel said. "But you know better. You may be down, but you're not out."

"You don't even know me."

"I think we both know that's bullshit. I know you. Just like you know me. This stuff here?" She waved her hand between them. "We're just filling in details."

"Rach, I really don't know what to do."

"And I know that's scary for someone like you."

Veronica pulled back and looked at Rachel. "What does that mean? Someone like me?"

"Look at this room. Your life has been planned out since forever. I'm guessing from those debate trophies that you knew in high school what you wanted to be."

"I wanted to be Angie Harmon on *Law and Order*."

Rachel sighed. "Yeah. I wanted to date her. That voice. Those eyes."

"Can we please focus on my plight here? Your life isn't falling apart because you didn't get to screw Angie Harmon."

"Who says I didn't?" Rachel grinned.

Veronica's expression changed. "Wait. Seriously?"

"Sadly, no. And you're absolutely right that my life didn't shatter because of it," Rachel said. "But that's kind of the point, isn't it? You mapped your dreams. You followed the little yellow line you'd made with a highlighter from college to law school to your first job to here. And now that you're here, it doesn't look like it's supposed to look. And that's scary."

"Is this supposed to help me?"

"Honey, if there was something magical I could say to make you feel better in this moment, trust me, I'd be saying it." Rachel put her hand on Veronica's. "But life doesn't work that way, V. There are roadblocks and setbacks and surprises and bricks to the head and things that bring you to your knees."

"You called me honey."

"How's Lauren?" God. Rachel couldn't just address what Veronica had said? She had to be a dick about it?

"She told me about your wedding. I haven't talked to her since, but I need to. She's called several times."

"She's not a terrible person."

"A great kisser."

Rachel bristled at the comment. "Yeah, I can't dispute that. And thanks for letting me know it had gotten that far."

"Not as good as you, though."

Rachel smiled. "Nice save." Veronica stared at her as if she had something else to say. "What is it?"

"We haven't kissed yet. I don't know why I said that. I mean, we were going to, and then you came up. It kind of ruined the mood, hearing what she'd done to you."

"I would apologize for being a mood killer, but I'm not really sorry."

Veronica smirked at her. "No, I'm sure you're not." She closed her laptop and set it aside. "How's the wedding business?"

"Changing the subject?"

"From my failed career and dismal dating life? Yes. Yes, I am."

"Fair enough," Rachel said. "The closer to summer we get, the busier I get."

"And the last couple you photographed, what did your Spidey sense tell you about them? Will they have a long and happy marriage or be miserable and bitter for years to come?"

"It's not a Spidey sense, V. It's how they treat each other in a stressful moment. It's how much they touch each other. It's a number of things, but mostly, it's the look on their faces." Rachel took a deep breath. "Okay, the truth is, I've seen the look of fear before. The look that says, I'm not ready for this. Or am I making the biggest mistake of my life? Lauren had that look on her face on our wedding day, but I ignored it. I thought she was just nervous. And if you want to talk about things that bring people to their knees, let's talk about me in the whole damn year following that awful day."

Veronica put her hand on Rachel's thigh. "I'm so sorry."

Rachel covered Veronica's hand with her own. "You'll get through this. And maybe you'll find that it'll take you down a better path. Maybe there's some other firm out there that will value your intelligence and your work ethic more than these people ever did."

"And maybe someday, someone won't have that look of fear on their face, and they won't leave you standing at the altar, and you'll get your dream of a home and a family and a love that you didn't know even existed."

"I think my scenario for you is more likely," Rachel replied.

"You're stubborn, Rachel Monaghan."

Rachel squeezed her hand. "I'm also your friend. I hope you know that."

"I could use one right now."

Veronica turned her hand over so their palms were touching. Rachel had an unexpected urge to interlock their fingers and hold her hand for a moment, but a knock on the door made her instinctively push Veronica's hand away. She laughed at herself. "Sorry. Sitting in this room, I feel like I'm in high school again."

"Come in, Mom." Veronica leaned in and whispered, "You won't get in trouble for being on my bed. She knows I'm gay."

Mrs. Welch came in with a tray of food. "Are you hungry, Rachel?"

Rachel eyed the tray of sandwiches, chips, and pickle spears. "Starving, actually."

"Good." She set the tray on the bed. "Put some food in V's mouth, will you?" She gave Rachel a wink and left the room, closing the door behind her.

Rachel looked at Veronica. "She wants me to hand-feed you. Does she not know how sexy that is?"

Veronica slapped her leg. "Shut up and give me the ham and cheese."

CHAPTER TWELVE

Veronica had to accept the fact that she'd be neither engaged to a beautiful woman nor made a partner in the firm by her thirty-fifth birthday. This wasn't a brick to the head, like Rachel had said. This was an entire building. She'd given notice to the firm without any prospects for new employment, but she wasn't too worried about it. She had money in the bank and an investment portfolio that she could always cash in if need be. Besides, there was a company in San Francisco that had been courting her for over a year. One phone call, and she'd have a job within the month. Not that she wanted to move so far away from her parents, but it was an option.

She'd considered doing some travel since sitting in her apartment binge-watching Netflix like she'd done for the last several weeks didn't seem healthy. Maybe she'd look into that tonight while finishing up the last few episodes of *The Handmaid's Tale*. What the hell was she thinking starting that show? But she was in it now, for better or worse. It was worse. Definitely worse, considering her current state of mind.

A knock on her door pulled her out of the daze she'd been in for going on twenty minutes. She pushed her chair back from the kitchen table and straightened her oversized sweatshirt on the way to the door. She looked through the peephole and took a step back.

"It's me, V. Please let me talk to you."

Avery was the last person she wanted to talk to. A pound on the door made her flinch.

"Let me in, V, or I'll pound on this door all day."

Veronica opened the door but left the chain lock in place. She peered through the opening. "I have nothing to say to you."

"You don't have to say anything. Just let me talk. Let me explain. I don't want to leave things like this with you."

Veronica tried to hold back her tears. She didn't want to show any weakness in front of Avery. "You knew how much making partner meant to me."

"I know. But if you think I was going to hand them a multimillion-dollar account and stay a junior associate…V, you yourself would've told me to ask for more."

Avery wasn't wrong, but what a slap in the face from someone Veronica had trusted. It was true that Veronica never trusted Avery with her heart. She had no reason to. But professionally, Avery had never seemed like the backstabbing type. "Just go."

"Let me in, V. Let me tell you that this journey could include you. I want it to. I want more."

"What the hell does that mean?"

"Do we have to do this in the hallway?"

Veronica unlocked the chain and opened the door. Avery rushed past her and took off her coat. She went to the fridge and got a bottle of water. "Gee, make yourself at home." Veronica's interest in playing the gracious hostess was nonexistent.

Avery gulped down some water and set the bottle on the kitchen island. "You used to mean that."

Veronica stayed on the other side of the island and folded her arms. "What do you want, Avery?"

"You. I want you, V."

Was Avery insane or just that arrogant? Veronica was sure about the latter. Wanting what she couldn't have. How trite. "After what you did, you think I'm going to sleep with you?"

"It wasn't personal, V. It was business."

"I guess I shouldn't be surprised by the way you conduct business, considering who some of your clients are." Veronica titled her head. "Tell me, Avery. Did you have to sleep with the wife *and* the husband? A threesome, maybe?"

"What are you talking about?"

Avery obviously thought Veronica would never find out who her game-changing client was. But she knew. And it made her ill to think about it. "Greyhound. The woman you met in the bar who looks like the Queen of Jordan. Did you have to sleep with her and the billionaire husband? Hefty retainer too. You must have really given it your all."

Veronica wanted to throw up after hearing the news from Bea. And poor Bea seemed pretty sick to deliver the news too. Veronica would never forget the way her hand shook as she tried to pull up the gossip website on her phone. There was Jordan with her much older, considerably less fit, billionaire husband.

Avery had gone slightly pale. Apparently, it was contagious. "Like I said—"

"I know," Veronica interrupted. "It's just business." She shrugged. "But in some circles, they might call it prostitution."

"Wow," Avery said.

Veronica went to the door and opened it. "I've been saying that same thing to myself for weeks now."

Avery went to the door and stopped. She looked as if she wanted to say something more but changed her mind and left in silence. That was for the best. She couldn't fix this with words.

Veronica walked into the bar and looked around. She wasn't sure why she'd stayed away since it felt just like coming back to an old friend. Carol and Joe were in their usual spots, but Harry was behind the bar, drying a beer mug with a bar towel. He grinned when he saw her. "Well, hello there!"

Veronica stepped up to the bar. "Hi, guys."

"Oh! We've been worried about you, dear." Carol got up and gave her a big hug. "We're so glad you stopped in."

Joe gave her a hug as well. "Good to see you, sweetie. Keep your chin up."

"Thanks, Joe." Veronica sat in Harry's usual spot. "What are you doing back there, Harry?"

"I'm in training." He gave her a wink.

Rachel came up behind Harry and squeezed his shoulders. "He doesn't need training. He knows exactly what he's doing." She walked over to Veronica and leaned on the bar. "No date tonight?"

"Ha!" Veronica scoffed. "Who would want to date me right now?"

"Oh, good point."

"Hey, you don't have to agree with me." Veronica knew Rachel was just teasing her. She'd texted her every day to make sure she was doing okay. "I was bored. That's why I'm here." She'd arrived at her usual time, hoping her friends would be there. And not just Rachel and Charlotte. Harry had become a friend too. Carol and Joe were two of the sweetest people she'd ever met. She hoped she could call them friends as well. "That's not true. I've missed you guys. All of you." She glanced at Rachel but couldn't hold her stare.

"We've missed you too." Harry threw the towel over his shoulder. "How do I look back here?"

"Like a man who knows how to make a..." Carol and Joe perked up. Rachel took a step closer, and Harry rubbed his hands together. "Diet Coke," Veronica said.

There was a collective groan. "You hurt my heart with that order," Harry said. "I've been working on my frilly drink skills."

"Now that Rachel is getting busier with her photography business, Harry is going to work here at the bar," Carol said.

"Speaking of." Rachel sat on the barstool next to her. "I was going to call you later and see if there was any chance you'd want to help me out with a wedding."

Veronica pointed at herself. "Me?"

"My assistant has a nasty cold, and I hate to drag him out of bed."

Veronica looked at her with skepticism.

"Okay, fine. I can't expose all of those people to his cold. From the way he sounds, I'm pretty sure the wedding party wouldn't be thrilled."

"I don't know anything about photography. I can barely take a selfie on my phone."

"I'll worry about the photography," Rachel said. "It's easy. You carry the extra gear, hold a reflector when I need you to, that sort of thing. Basically, you just do whatever I ask."

"Oh. So, I'd be your little bitch?"

Joe snickered. "That's what it sounds like to me."

Rachel nudged her. "That's what friends do, right? They help each other out. They do the bitch work when necessary. They step up."

Veronica stared at Rachel with a blank look. Everyone in her life had been trying to get her out of her apartment. Bea with daily offers for a lunch date. Her mom called every day with some errand she needed to run and would Veronica please accompany her. She had because she loved her mom, but now, with this request from Rachel, she wondered if they were all in cahoots. "Is your assistant really sick?"

"Cross my heart," Rachel said. "And I'll even buy you dinner."

"Fine. But don't expect me to be good company." Everyone grinned at her. Veronica couldn't help but smile back. It felt good to be back in the bar.

❖

Veronica had been surprised when Rachel showed up in a black Audi SUV. There weren't many people with cars in New York. Parking was an issue, of course, but even if you had the cash, most people didn't really need one. Rachel told her that lugging gear to the Hamptons, Westchester, and all over New England made it worth the expense. That's all Rachel told her. The destination was "a surprise," as Rachel put it.

As they merged onto the West Side Highway, Veronica blurted out, "You can't drink tonight."

"What?" Rachel sounded incredulous. "Why the hell would I drink? I'm working!"

"Well, it's a wedding, so I just wanted to make sure," Veronica said. "The thing is, I'm kind of a terrible driver."

Rachel laughed. "I'll try not to drink on the job."

"Does that go for me too? Because this isn't really a job for me if I'm not getting paid."

"Don't most lawyers drink on the job?"

"Only the stupid ones." Veronica paused. "Okay, so maybe I have a flask of bourbon in my desk drawer, but I rarely take a swig."

Rachel giggled under her breath.

"What's so funny?"

"You said swig. For some reason, that struck me as funny."

"It's what you do from a flask," Veronica said. "You don't take a swallow or a sip or a drink. You take a swig." She folded her arms. "You're a bartender. You should know this."

Rachel glanced at her and shook her head. "You're something else."

"Keep your eyes on the road, Monaghan. I don't do personal injury law, but I know Burton Bartholomew personally."

"You do not. The guy on TV?"

"He was Burt the Flirt in high school," Veronica said. "Couldn't keep his hands to himself."

"He's the 'If you've been hurt, call Burt' guy, right?"

"If you like obnoxious flirts, call Burt," Veronica said. "Way more accurate."

"Hmm." Rachel tapped her chin. "If you...get hurt in a yurt, call Burt."

"Or if you slip and hit your head on a grocery curt, call Burt."

Rachel laughed. "A grocery curt?"

"We're riffing. That's my riff."

"It's cheating. I mean, churting."

"Fine." Veronica thought for a moment. "I have one! If you eat bad yogurt and your stomach hurts, call Burt."

"Okay, I'm over it."

"Me too."

Rachel turned up the music. "We don't have to talk. We could just sit here in awkward silence."

Veronica didn't think the moments of silence felt awkward at all. Sharing the same space with Rachel, listening to the same music and breathing the same air, felt like the most natural thing in the world. When they crossed over the state line, Veronica figured they were nearly there. "You left out the part where we're driving all the way to Connecticut," she said.

"Not long now. It's beautiful here, isn't it?"

"Gorgeous."

Rachel turned onto a narrow, tree-lined road. The space between driveways became much longer, and the few Veronica saw had high, wrought iron gates and rock walls lining the properties. This was a whole different level of wealthy.

"Hey, I left something else out too," Rachel said. "I think it'll make you happy."

"The photog and her assistant get to drink champagne and eat caviar on toast points?"

Rachel dug into her leather satchel. She pulled out a protein bar. "Eat this. It'll be nonstop for the first two hours."

Veronica groaned. "Seriously? Do we get to eat anything at all? A chicken wing? A meatball?"

"It's not that kind of wedding. It'll be a sit-down dinner catered by the best chef they can find. And yes, we can always go into the kitchen and grab something, but we don't sit with the other guests. We're working, just like the servers and valets."

Veronica ripped open the wrapper. "How did I get talked into this?"

"My wit and charm."

"You have neither."

"Ouch."

Veronica took a bite and grimaced. "How long has this been in your bag? Seriously, like a year?" She grabbed a bottle of water and tried to push the dry bits down her throat.

"Not sure. I haven't cleaned out my bag in a while."

"You owe me two dinners now. And you better sneak some food for me. I don't want a security guard catching me with a half-eaten taquito."

"He'd be more likely to catch you with a half-eaten sea urchin."

"Seriously?"

"I've seen some crazy menus at these weddings. Everyone tries to outdo each other, but I don't think that's this couple's style." Rachel glanced over at her. "You look great, by the way. You'll blend right in."

Veronica thought it was a strange request when Rachel had texted, asking her to wear beige. Apparently, for outdoor weddings, a lighter color was a better choice than black. The only beige thing Veronica owned was a knee-length lace dress that she'd worn to a wedding a few years back. It was snug on her hips, which made her feel slightly self-conscious, but she didn't have time to find something else. The dress should've been worn with heels, but she chose to go with a toeless suede ankle-boot. It made more sense since she assumed she'd be standing the entire time.

Rachel's outfit was cool, of course. But Rachel always looked great. She was the only person Veronica knew who could make wearing a bar apron look as if it was the latest fad. Today, she had on beige skinny jeans with brown boots and an off-white V-neck sweater. She'd changed her leather belt from black to brown, but the camera buckle was the same. She looked hot, which on some level pissed Veronica off. For the next several hours, she'd be forced to watch Rachel work and try not to get turned on by it. Good God, why did she agree to this?

"V?"

"What?"

"I said, you look great. Love the dress."

"Oh. Right. Thanks."

Rachel gave her a curious look, then focused on the road again. It wasn't long before they pulled into a driveway. The gate had a large *P* on it, surrounded by fancy wrought iron work. There was a small, bare building to the left that didn't seem to fit in with everything else. It was a newer structure, going by the way ivy was growing on everything else. A man dressed in a security uniform stepped out of the building. Rachel unrolled her window, and the man bent down. He scrutinized both of them and then focused on Rachel. "I've seen you before. Do you have your authorization card?"

Rachel handed it to him. "I'm the photographer, and this is my assistant."

He looked at the card, then checked his clipboard. "She doesn't look like a Justin."

"Right," Rachel said. "Justin is sick at the moment, so Veronica will be assisting me today."

"I'll need to see your ID."

Veronica opened her wallet and pulled out her driver's license. Rachel took it and handed it to the man, then turned back to her. "Your middle name is Violet?"

"You caught that, huh?"

"How could I miss it?"

"I'm named after both of my grandmothers. Violet was pissed she got second billing, so that's how I got the nickname V, because Violet refused to call me Veronica."

"Family," the security guy said with a shake of his head. "They're crazy sometimes. I was supposed to be named after my grandfather, the great Robert Howard the Third. A two-star general. Well, at my christening, the priest misunderstood my parents and called me Roger. Instead of correcting him, my parents let it ride, thinking it must be the will of God. So, I walk around this earth with the nickname Roger, and don't think I do it happily." He handed Rachel the authorization card and Veronica's ID. "Have a nice day, ladies." He opened the gate and gave them a wave.

"I think he topped your story, Veevee." Rachel drove at a slow pace through the gate and down the narrow road.

Veronica rolled her eyes. "Don't. No one calls me Veevee. One V. Just one."

"How about V Squared? It kind of fits with the math whiz thing."

Veronica gasped. "Oh my God!" It was a massive estate behind that big gate. Sweeping lawns, huge oak trees, and tall hedges along the perimeter. As they came around a curve in the road, she could see a large white tent set up on the lawn, and behind it was a mansion that looked as if it had been there for hundreds of years.

A handsome guy in a dark suit walked up to the car as Rachel parked. He opened her door. "Hi, Rachel!"

They got out of the SUV and met at the back. "Stephen, this is my friend, Veronica. She'll be assisting me today."

Stephen reached for her hand. "Pleased to meet you, Veronica. If there's anything you need, please find me, and I'll point you in the right direction." He stood a little straighter and buttoned his coat. A slight blush formed on his cheeks. "I found out this morning that I'll be walking a certain someone down the aisle today."

Rachel gave him a fist bump. "Congratulations! Just make sure you walk slow enough so I can get some good shots. And don't look at me, okay? Just keep your eyes straight ahead."

"Straight ahead. Got it."

"And have someone put a flower in your lapel. Everyone in the wedding party should have one."

Stephen looked at his empty lapel. "I knew I was forgetting something." He jogged toward the house.

Rachel turned her attention back to Veronica. "You'd be amazed how much gets forgotten at a wedding. Everyone's nervous, so brides forget their bouquets. Rings go missing. Once, two groomsmen had switched suits. One was drowning in his, and the other was showing off his package like it was everybody's business, and neither of them thought to question it."

"What did you do?"

"I told them to switch suits because here's the thing." Rachel sat on the edge of the car. She had such a serious look on her face, Veronica felt as if she should really listen to what was about to be said. "Even if everything about the photo is perfect—the lighting, the positioning, all of the stuff that's my responsibility—but the people don't look their best, the bride will be unhappy. And an unhappy bride is terrible for business because she won't see that the photo is perfect; she'll see that her brother's tie is crooked, or her mother's slip is showing, and I guarantee you that two things will happen. One, that photo won't end up on a wall or even in a photo album, and two, I won't get a referral from her."

"Wow. So, you adjust slips too?"

"I get consent first." Rachel grinned.

"Well, thank God. I'd hate to think you go around violating people's personal space." Veronica felt a blush rising up her chest as her mind wandered back to the night when "personal space" didn't exist between them. She quickly changed the subject. "So, tell me about the bride and groom."

Rachel's eyes lit up. "That was another thing I didn't tell you. They're brides. Two of them. And it's one of the reasons I wanted you to come with me." She put a camera bag on Veronica's shoulder. "I'll need you to stay behind me with the gear. If I'm moving around a lot, just stay close but on the periphery. You don't want to show up in every shot of their wedding video, so try to keep track of where the videographer is."

"I don't understand. What do you mean it's one of the reasons you wanted me to come with you?"

Rachel stopped what she was doing. "Okay, look. I may be jaded about all of this." She waved her hand around, indicating she was talking about the wedding that was about to happen. "But I don't want you to be. I want you to see a win."

"A win?"

"Yeah. You know, two people who are so in love they almost shine. That's who Madison and Ana are. They shine for each other."

Veronica smirked. "Sounds like Ms. Jaded is shipping a lesbian couple. Madison and Ana, did you say?"

"Madison Prescott. This is her family estate. And Ana Perez. You'll fall a little bit in love with them too. Especially after I tell you their story." Rachel cocked an eyebrow. "And what the hell is *shipping*?"

"It just means you would, or do, like seeing two people together. Like, for me, I totally ship Sandra Bullock and Cate Blanchett."

"Aren't they both straight?"

"If you say so. But I can still ship them," Veronica said.

"This is a side of you I didn't know about. I thought you were strictly business. Thirty dates in thirty days and all that." Rachel grabbed more gear and locked the car.

"Have you forgotten that you had your tongue in my mouth?"

Rachel had taken a few steps, but she stopped and turned around. "No."

Veronica stepped closer. "And other places?"

Rachel's gaze dropped to Veronica's chest. "No, I haven't forgotten."

"Not exactly businesslike behavior."

It was obvious Veronica's words had brought the memories of that night back for Rachel too. Her stare was intense for a few seconds, but she seemed to shake it off. "Thanks for telling me what shipping is. My world feels so much bigger now."

Her tone was sarcastic. That made Veronica smile because she knew Rachel was trying to hide the fact that she'd felt the tension between them in that moment. The attraction was very real on both sides, even if nothing could ever come of it.

They walked past the large tent, and Veronica noticed two smaller tents she assumed were for the caterers. She also saw workers unloading outdoor heaters. That made sense since the weather could be unpredictable in early summer. It was a beautiful day. Veronica hoped it would stay that way.

"We took all of the formal bridal shots last weekend, so that's out of the way." Rachel lowered her voice as they neared the house. "After the ceremony, we'll get some shots of the wedding party together and then straight into the reception, dancing, cake cutting, etcetera."

Veronica felt a sense of excitement as they climbed a few steps to the large wooden door.

"I watched you work at Tiffany's wedding. I know what to expect. It'll be an adventure."

"Ha!" Rachel opened the door. "Tell me that when you're dead on your feet six hours from now."

The house was a beehive of activity. Uniformed staff hustled in every direction. A woman came out of what appeared to be the library and waved. "Rachel, you're here!"

Veronica guessed she must be a mother of one of the brides. She wore a modest but elegant silver-gray dress and had an orchid pinned to her chest.

"Mrs. Perez. Good to see you." Rachel gave her a hug.

"I told you to stop with that. Call me Carmen."

Rachel put her hand on Veronica's back. "Carmen, this is a good friend of mine. Veronica, please meet Carmen Perez. She's Ana's mother."

Carmen took Veronica's hand and held it in both of hers. "Can you please tell your good friend to stop calling me Mrs. Perez? It makes me feel much older than my thirty-five years."

Veronica laughed. "I'll work on that for you."

Carmen gave her a wink, then turned her attention back to Rachel. "Can you believe this day is finally here? Sixteen years ago, Madison gave my Ana her grandmother's wedding ring, and finally, the day has arrived."

"I'm so happy for both of them," Rachel said. "It's been a long time coming."

"You already have the bridal room photos, so Madison said to go on down to the oak tree and set up however you need to." Carmen looked at her watch. "It won't be long now."

They turned to go back outside and Veronica whispered, "A sixteen-year engagement?"

"I'll tell you on the walk down to the oak tree," Rachel whispered back.

"What's at the oak tree?"

"That's where the ceremony will be held. Then a big party under the tent."

❖

By the time they got to the oak tree, Veronica had tears in her eyes. "That's the saddest story I've ever heard. How could a father be so cruel to his own daughter? Keeping them apart like that? It's horrible."

Rachel took a tissue out of her bag and gave it to Veronica. "I couldn't believe it either when they told me."

"It seems like you've gotten close to them. Carmen and Stephen both gave you a warm welcome."

"I have," Rachel said. "I always interview my clients in person. I have a list of questions I ask that helps me get a feel for who they are as a couple and how they want the photos to represent them. One of the questions I ask is, what brought you together, and what will keep you together? Well, Ana put her hand on Madison's knee and said, let me tell it." Rachel looked around. "Can't you see it? Two little girls, running around this place? One, the maid's daughter and the other, the only child of a very wealthy but not-so-nice man?"

Veronica touched the oak tree. "And this is where Madison proposed when they were in college?"

"Right under this tree. And then all hell broke loose, and they were kept apart until the old man's death."

Veronica took a deep breath. "Wow. It makes me so grateful for my parents. They never even flinched when I told them I was gay. Well, I guess my dad flinched slightly because he already had someone in mind for me, but he got over it."

"I bet the guy he'd chosen didn't get over it," Rachel said. "I mean, if he knew he was the chosen one."

"Was that a compliment, Monaghan?"

"Yes, Welch. It was. Remember that I've been in your bedroom and seen photos of the young and vibrant Veronica. She was, and still is, a hottie."

"Well, that guy has a husband and three kids. Pretty sure he got over it. And I'm pretty sure my dad thought he was perfect because he was never anything less than a perfect gentleman with me. Of course, now we know why."

Rachel walked through the rows of chairs and put their gear on the ground behind the last row. "I'll be up and down the aisle, but you'll stay back here."

"I think it's nice," Veronica said.

"What's nice?"

"You getting to know your clients so well." She brushed a piece of lint off Rachel's sweater. "If I didn't know better, I'd say there was a heart beating in that chest of yours."

Veronica went to remove another piece of lint, but Rachel grabbed her hand and held on to it. "I have a heart, V."

"Yeah," Veronica said with a shrug. "You just don't want to use it."

CHAPTER THIRTEEN

Veronica had decided that Rachel was right about two things. The brides did shine for each other, and Veronica was dead on her feet. As the newly married couple were driven out of the gate in a Rolls-Royce with tin cans and streamers tied to the back bumper, she breathed a sigh of relief.

Rachel walked back to her, camera in hand. Did she have to look so damn cute in those skinny jeans and that cool belt buckle? Veronica dropped her gaze. She didn't need to lust after someone she could never really have. Nor did she need Rachel to see the lust in her eyes. God, how embarrassing would that be?

Rachel wrapped her arm around Veronica's shoulder and walked back to the car. "Great job, V. Want a job?"

"You're just being kind, but that doesn't get you out of buying me dinner. I'm starving."

"That canapé I slipped you wasn't enough?"

"I could eat a damn horse." Rachel hadn't let go, so Veronica put her arm around her waist and held on to her belt. "Or breakfast for dinner. I saw a diner not too far down the road."

"How about I cook you breakfast for dinner at my place?"

"Aren't you tired?"

"No," Rachel said. "I'm revved up. It was a gorgeous wedding. Gorgeous brides. I had a great assistant who I didn't have to scold once, and I gave out a few business cards. That's a great day in my book."

It had been a great day. And Rachel was right—it was nice to see a couple who seemed so very right for each other. Veronica tried to imagine herself marrying any of the women she'd had dates with. It almost made her laugh out loud at the thought. But it also brought a sadness to her heart, and after witnessing such a beautiful wedding, she didn't want to feel sad. "They were beautiful, weren't they? Standing under that tree in their white dresses, saying their vows?" A genuine smile popped out again. "Did you notice how they didn't let go of each other the entire night? They greeted everyone together. They held each other close when they danced. Madison kept kissing Ana's hand. And Ana, the way she couldn't hold the tears back. It was…" Veronica took a deep breath. "It was everything."

Rachel leaned in and whispered, "They asked me if I do newborn stuff."

"No, they did not!" Veronica stopped and turned to her. "Is one of them pregnant?" She knew her voice sounded a little too hopeful. "I mean, that would be great, wouldn't it?"

Rachel smiled. "It's what they wanted when they were younger. I'm sure they'd have at least a couple of children if it weren't for Madison's father getting in the way."

Veronica grabbed her by the shoulders. "Tell me what you know. Who's carrying the child? Ana or Madison?"

"Hmm. I think someone else is shipping them too."

"Tell me!"

Rachel laughed. "Okay, okay. It's Ana. They just found out last week."

Veronica squealed and jumped up and down. "They're going to have that family they always wanted!"

"Yes. In this case, love wins." They got to the car, and Rachel stowed her gear in the back.

"They're like the epitome of love overcoming all obstacles," Veronica said. "They're like a fairy tale. One of those stories that gets passed down from generation to generation." She got in the car and turned to Rachel. "Thank you, for bringing me. I got to see a fairy-tale wedding in real life."

"Are you sure you want to go back to being a lawyer? I could really use the help."

Veronica put up a finger. "Number one, I never stopped being a lawyer; I just quit my job. And number two, you're not making me wait until we get into the city to eat. I want breakfast for dinner at that diner."

"And number three?"

Veronica tilted her head. "How did you know there was a number three?"

Rachel tapped her temple with her finger. "My Spidey sense told me you weren't quite done."

Veronica shrugged, even though she kind of liked the fact that they were getting to know each other better. "Number three, I don't share my pancakes."

❖

"Ouch!" Rachel pulled her fork away. "You were serious about not sharing? Everyone shares their pancakes."

"That *ouch* was unwarranted," Veronica said. "I hit your fork, not your fingers."

Rachel's mouth watered as Veronica took a bite of butter- and syrup-laden pancake. She'd ordered eggs benedict, which didn't come with pancakes on the side. That was obviously a mistake. "You're seriously going to eat that whole stack?"

"All of it," Veronica mumbled through a mouthful of food. "Can I see some of the photos you took?"

"No."

"No? I just helped you for a zillion hours, and I don't even get to see the photos?"

"I mean, I'll show you later." Rachel needed to remove the few shots she'd taken of Veronica on the sly before she could show her anything. Okay, maybe there were more than a few. She'd even gotten a shot of her looking as if she was about to cry as the brides said their vows.

"Why not now?"

"I need to organize them first." Rachel also needed to change the subject. "Been on any more dates?"

"Why so interested, Rach? You already asked me that in the bar."

Rachel recognized flirting, and it sure seemed as if Veronica was flirting. "Did I?"

"And furthermore, let's think about what that would look like, because you know what's worse than a successful, arrogant lawyer? An unemployed, bitter one." She stabbed another piece of pancake with her fork. "That doesn't mean I don't have women clamoring at my feet for my attention, though. They just aren't the right women." She slid the fork into her mouth and moaned. "This is so good."

Rachel shook her head as Veronica made a show of licking the syrup from her lips. "You're evil."

"Bitter. I'm bitter."

Rachel wasn't sure if she wanted to know the answer, but she had to ask. Not knowing the current state of things was killing her. "So, these women you mentioned. Is one of them Lemon Drop?"

Veronica's eyes shot up. "I haven't. We haven't talked since I found out."

"It's okay," Rachel said. "I don't begrudge my ex for wanting to date you. Lauren knows a good thing when she sees it."

Veronica blinked a few times. "But she was too stupid to hold on to it."

Rachel smiled. "Thank you for saying that. I'm also of the opinion that it was her loss, not mine. At least, now I am. It hurt for a long time."

Veronica focused on her plate for a moment. "She claims she's grown up since then and is a better person now. Lesson learned, as they say."

"They do say that, but I can't tell you Lauren is a safe bet, if that's what you're looking for."

Veronica let out a huff. "I should've given Piña Colada and her snake named Vicki a chance."

Rachel laughed. "Oh, my number one would be Jägerbomb. She needs in-house counsel for sure."

Veronica shook her head. "God. Who thought it would be so hard to find someone to share my life with?" Her eyes teared up again. She grabbed a napkin. "Sorry. My emotions are all over the place lately."

Rachel moved from her side of the booth to Veronica's. She wanted to wrap her arms around her and tell her everything would work out. But then she'd get wrapped up in her scent and want to stay there, even after she'd stopped crying. She'd want to take her home and kiss away the pain. Make love to her all night. But the morning would come and then what? Sticking to her three-date limit had served Rachel well. Her heart was well healed now, and her preference was to keep it that way.

There was also the fact that sex would surely ruin a friendship she really wanted to keep. She had plenty of friends, both male and female, but there was something different about this one. No, not her ass, although Rachel did spend plenty of time thinking about that. There was something about Veronica that made Rachel believe she would always have her back. That was something she couldn't say of her other friends. And yes, there was also her ass. She opted for resting her hand on Veronica's leg. "You've been through a lot. Don't apologize."

Veronica put her head on Rachel's shoulder. "There has to be a better option for me out there."

"There is. Neither of them deserves you."

Veronica pushed her plate of pancakes over to Rachel and handed her a fork. "That gets you one bite."

Rachel separated a large piece of the stack and stabbed her fork into it. "What would get me two bites?"

"You're a greedy little photographer, aren't you?"

"Oh, come on. No one can eat just one bite of a pancake."

"Well, you currently have the equivalent of four bites on your fork."

Rachel's hand was still on Veronica's leg. She should've moved it, but she didn't want to. It felt nice being this close to her again. "If I can eat this whole bite, can I have another?"

"Bite? That is not a bite. That's half a stack of pancakes on a fork." Veronica sat up and turned her whole body toward Rachel. "Are you seriously going to shove all of that in your mouth?"

Rachel giggled at the look of horror mixed with excitement on Veronica's face. "I have two brothers."

"So?"

"So, we used to have competitions that involved stuffing large amounts of food in our mouths. I couldn't let them beat me just because they were boys."

Veronica put one hand on the table and the other on the back of the booth. "Oh my God, you're serious. If this devolves into hot dog eating contests, I'm out."

Rachel giggled. "Are you ready?"

Veronica's eyes darted between the huge bite of food and Rachel's mouth. "Ready."

Rachel shoved the pancake into her mouth and chewed fast because it wasn't just about how much you could fit in your mouth; it was also about how fast you could swallow it. With her brothers, they would swallow and then open their mouths wide to prove the food was gone. She decided to spare Veronica that last part and just swallowed and said, "Gone."

Veronica stared with her mouth hanging open. "I'm not sure if I should feel turned on or completely horrified."

Rachel laughed. "Turned on? Maybe I should do this with all of my dates."

Veronica furrowed her brow. "This isn't a date." She paused. "Is it?"

"No." Rachel cleared her throat and took a sip of water. That was probably the wrong thing to say. Why did she have to be such a dick when they were having so much fun? "This meal is just a thank-you for helping me today."

"Of course." Veronica sighed. "But that was a pretty firm no when I asked if this was a date." She looked at Rachel. "You've been super clear about what you do and don't want, and I appreciate that. I guess it's just the 'Oh God no, I'd rather gouge my eyes out with a tire iron' tone that felt like a smack in the face. What can I say? It's been a rough month."

"I didn't mean to come off like that," Rachel said. "You're beautiful. And you're brilliant and driven and funny and freaking amazing. Any woman would be lucky to have you."

"Any woman except you."

Rachel's heart sank. "No, V. I would be extremely lucky to have you. I'm just not in that place right now."

"I know. And you're sticking to your guns, I'll give you that much." Veronica motioned for Rachel to let her out of the booth. "Can we please go now? I'm tired."

Rachel slid out of the booth and stood back while Veronica got out. "V."

"I need the restroom. I'll meet you at the car." Veronica's matter-of-fact tone left no room for debate.

Rachel didn't want the night to end on a bad note. Veronica had slept most of the way home or at least pretended to sleep at first so they wouldn't have to talk. Rachel couldn't blame her. Every conversation they had seemed to be filled with highs and lows. Everything would be fine and then, bam, the conversation would go sideways.

"Hey, sleepyhead. We're here."

Veronica stirred awake and yawned. "What time is it?"

"It's almost midnight." Rachel got out of the car and opened Veronica's door. "I'd walk you in, but I'm double-parked."

"It's okay. There's a doorman." Veronica got out of the car and headed for the front door of her building.

"Hey." Rachel shut the car door and stepped onto the sidewalk. "Want to do breakfast again in eight hours?"

"Thanks, but I'm good."

"V, wait." Rachel stepped closer. "You were an amazing assistant. Truly. Thank you for helping me today. And Justin thanks you too."

"Yeah. See you around."

"V!" She didn't turn around this time. Rachel wanted to run after her and somehow make things right, but she couldn't leave her car there. Or maybe she was just too big a wimp. She could have asked the doorman to keep an eye on her car. Besides, everyone double-parked in New York. She threw her hands in the air and went back to her car.

❖

"Double-parked?" Charlotte raised her eyebrows and waited for Rachel to continue.

"I know. I should've followed her in."

"And then what?" Charlotte slid a diet soda across the bar to Rachel.

"What do you mean? We could've talked. She might have invited me in."

"And then what, Rach? Maybe Veronica doesn't need another friend."

"Of course she needs another friend! She lost her job, and she's definitely lost some of her confidence. A good friend is exactly what she needs right now."

"Not from you," Charlotte said. "We've all seen the way she looks at you. Haven't we?"

Joe and Carol nodded from their regular seats. Rachel glanced at Harry behind the bar. He was studying a wine glass as he wiped it dry, but he also nodded.

"So, what are you saying, that I should just leave her alone? Let her contact me if she wants to?"

Carol gave Rachel a disapproving look. "And let a fine woman like that slip through your fingers?"

"Trust me, Rachel. When you find the real deal, you don't let her go," Joe said. He looked at Carol and patted her hand. "I didn't let you slip through my fingers, did I, honey?"

Rachel focused on her drink and let Carol and Joe swoon at each other privately for a moment. It was nice to see the way they were with each other. It didn't restore her faith in the idea of one true love, but she was always happy when someone found it. "How did you know?" she asked. "How did you know you wouldn't break each other's hearts? How did you know you'd last forever?"

Carol and Joe gave each other a quizzical look. "We didn't," Carol said. "We just took the plunge and hoped for the best."

"That's all anyone can do," Harry said.

Did they really think they would convince her with a *throw your arms in the air and hand it over to God* answer? She'd heard more vows said at the altar than the average priest. She'd never once heard someone say that they were hoping for the best. No, everyone was as adamant as they were passionate about their love and commitment. She was sure Carol and Joe had been too. Because everyone was, whether or not they lasted as a happily married couple. Had Lauren made it to the altar and said her vows to Rachel, she was sure they would've been adamant too, even though they would've been a lie said through lips that quivered out of fear, not joy. Fear that she was making the biggest mistake of her life.

Rachel could barely stand the thought that Lauren had felt that way about her. A big mistake? God, how could Rachel not have known? How could she have been so blindsided? How do you become so unsure like Lauren had and not say anything before your wedding day?

Rachel didn't know the answers because she'd never talked to Lauren again. Her heart was too broken. And her rage for how it had happened was too strong. She felt humiliated and broken, and nothing Lauren said would've fixed that.

Thank God they hadn't moved in together before the wedding. Lauren's lease wasn't up on her apartment, and she'd said it was a sign that they should "do things right" and wait until after the wedding to make the big move. It did seem kind of quaint and romantic. Of course, they'd spent plenty of nights together, but they also spent plenty apart. It created a sense of longing, at least for Rachel. Once the wedding-that-wasn't happened, Rachel realized it was a big, giant red flag she'd missed.

Wedding season was just around the corner. Rachel wouldn't be able to help in the bar much for the next few months. She hated that she couldn't be there for Charlotte, but Harry seemed to be enjoying his new part-time job, so that gave her some comfort.

She slipped off the stool and went around to the other side of the bar. She gave Charlotte a hug. "Call me if you need anything. Even if you just need to talk."

Charlotte kissed her cheek. "I will. Love you, Rach."

She gave Harry a fist bump. "Take care of her."

"Will do."

She gave Carol and Joe a wave. "Bye, you lovebirds." Of course, they waved back and then looked at each other longingly. Rachel waved them off with her hand. "Yeah, yeah. Get a room!"

CHAPTER FOURTEEN

Veronica wasn't sure what gave her more pleasure—ignoring Rachel's texts or Lauren's. It was Bea's calls that she hated ignoring, but she really didn't have anything to say. Bea had made it clear that she wanted to go with Veronica to a new firm, but she needed more time before she looked for another job. She needed to build her confidence back up so she could walk into any interview and knock their socks off. In her current state, she couldn't knock an autumn leaf off a tree.

The cold eye mask wasn't helping. Her eyes still burned from all of the crying she'd been doing. She took it off and tossed it on the coffee table, next to the open bag of Cheetos and the empty bowl of ice cream she'd devoured while watching home improvement shows. She was sure she could build an Adirondack chair for her small balcony if she could just get her ass off the sofa.

Her phone rang. It was Rachel. She groaned and then answered it. "Why can't everyone just let me wallow in my dark, dirty pit of despair? If you're calling to cheer me up, fuck you."

Rachel chuckled. "How about if I make an appointment to cheer you up over lunch next Tuesday?"

"Some friend you are. I could be dead by then."

"I'm not going to win this conversation, am I?"

Veronica sighed. "I get to pick the restaurant, but you'll pick the wine."

"Oh, so we'll be day drinking?"

"That's what unemployed, womanless, pathetic people such as myself—"

"Okay, stop," Rachel said. "You are none of those things. I mean, no, you don't have a woman in your life. Okay, also no job, but—"

"I always feel so much better after talking to you, Rachel. It's like talking to a therapist, except without the PhD or the feeling better."

"Let me make it up to you on Tuesday. Good food, good wine, better conversation than this one."

Veronica smiled. "Well, it can't get much worse."

"Is that a yes?"

"Fine. Yes."

"Good. Make the reservation, and let me know where we'll be having this fancy, drunken lunch."

"Will do. Bye, Rach."

"Bye, V."

"San Francisco?" Veronica's mom passed the mashed potatoes to her dad.

"It's the most expensive city in the country," her dad said. "CEOs are homeless."

"Are you seriously going to spout that nonsense from your Upper West Side co-op?" Veronica took the potatoes from her dad and slapped a spoonful on her plate. "Besides, I think it's their assistants who are homeless."

"That's shameful." Her mom spooned some roast beef and carrots onto Veronica's plate. "Imagine if that was poor Bea. Oh, honey, promise me your assistant won't be homeless."

"That's too much, Mom."

"You're getting thin, and you were already thin."

"Eat your supper," her dad said. He took a bite and pointed his fork at Veronica. "Those bastards didn't do right by you."

"Which is why I need to move on." Veronica took a bite and waited. She knew this conversation would be a difficult one, but how could she turn down an in-house counsel position at one of the largest tech firms in the country? They'd been after her forever and had made clear in the email she'd received a few hours ago that the interview was a formality. "The pay is outstanding. You could come and visit me whenever you want. I'll get a big enough apartment for all of us. Wouldn't you love to get out of the city in the winter?"

"How do they even know about you?" Her mom put a big spoonful of peas on Veronica's plate.

"Mom, I can't eat all of this."

"Eat your supper." Her dad kept his head down while he ate. "And answer your mother's question."

Veronica rolled her eyes and pushed the peas around her plate. With the way her dad was talking to her, she felt as if she was back in junior high trying to defend the D she got in art class, never mind that she had straight As in every other subject. "I worked on a case with them last year. They must've heard through the grapevine that I left the firm and reached out to me."

Her mom put her elbows on the table and clasped her hands together. "What about Rachel?"

Her dad looked up from his plate. He didn't say anything, but Veronica knew what that hopeful look in his eyes meant. "What about her?"

"Well, you said you connected with her, and she certainly came running when you needed her."

"She's a friend. That's all." Veronica ate a spoonful of peas. "Dad, stop looking at me that way."

Her mom frowned. "Don't talk with your mouth full, dear."

Veronica dropped her fork on her plate. "Okay, look. I'm an adult, and I'd like to have an adult conversation with the two of you, so stop acting like I'm fifteen with braces and acne!"

"It cleared up." Her mom gave her a nod. "The acne. It cleared up."

Veronica threw her hands in the air. "Agh! I'm not dating Rachel, okay? I know you both like her, but she doesn't like me that way, so don't mention her again."

"Impossible," her dad said. "How could she not be completely enamored by you? And why would you leave town if you've become friends? It could turn into something more."

"No." Veronica lowered her head. "It won't. She's made that pretty clear."

Her mom reached for her hand. "You really like her, don't you, dear?"

Should she be honest? She always had been with her parents,

except when it came to Avery. They didn't know she'd slept with the woman who stole her partnership, and what good would it do to bring it up now?

But Rachel was a different story. She looked at them and said, "She has that thing that makes me want to rush into her arms every time I see her and never let go, you know?" They both nodded their understanding. "It's hard when that feeling isn't mutual." She took a deep breath. "I think a new start would do me good. New people. Different surroundings. And I wouldn't have to work night and day just to prove myself." She reached for their hands. "This could be good for me. Maybe this job will be amazing for my career *and* my love life. Maybe that special someone lives in California, and this is God's way of putting us together."

Her parents looked at each other and did that silent communication thing they were so good at. It used to infuriate her that she couldn't tell what they were thinking, but watching them now, it seemed like a beautiful thing that only two people who had been together as long as they had could accomplish.

Her dad turned to her and said, "Buy a good mattress for that spare bedroom."

Veronica stood and wrapped her arms around her dad's neck. "I promise I'll call every week."

❖

"Thank God." Rachel closed the weather app on her phone and breathed a sigh of relief. The last time she'd shot a wedding at a ski resort, she ended up getting second-degree frostbite on four of her toes. Charlotte, who was like a sister in good and bad ways, loved to remind her that it was not "the really bad kind of frostbite." Well, it still sucked, if you asked Rachel.

Of course, that time, it had been in the dead of winter, and the couple insisted on saying their vows in the exact spot where they'd met—on a black diamond ski run.

The story was sweet. The bride, who was new to the sport, had taken a wrong turn and ended up on one of the most difficult runs. The groom, who'd been skiing since he was a child, skied up to her and said, "You look like you need some help."

The bride did indeed need help. She'd broken her wrist when she fell and couldn't push herself back up onto her skis so she could get down the mountain. The groom stayed with her while the rescue team took her to the bottom and then to the hospital. He didn't leave her side that day, and they'd been together ever since.

Rachel, along with a videographer and a local pastor, were taken to that spot on snowmobiles, which was handy since Rachel didn't know how to ski. The plan was for the bride and groom, along with their parents, siblings, and friends, to ski from the top down to that spot. It sounded simple enough if everything went as planned.

As it turned out, the bride was late, the temperature had plummeted, a storm was rolling in, and Rachel hadn't worn the right boots.

It was only when she got back to her hotel room and her feet started to thaw out that she realized something was wrong. She now regularly referred to the experience as *that time I almost lost my toes.*

She looked at her phone to see where the Uber was. Still five blocks away. Because of course, the driver who picked her was "completing another trip nearby." Apparently, the driver was also having trouble saying good-bye because his little car avatar hadn't moved for several minutes. Good thing she'd allowed for an extra hour in case traffic was heavy. Her phone rang. It was Justin. "Dude, please tell me you're on your way to the airport."

"I'm at the Urgent Care."

"What?"

"That stupid cold, it's turned into bronchitis with a bonus ear infection. Rach, I can't fly."

Rachel was speechless. She couldn't do the wedding alone. Not on the top of a freaking mountain. Sure, the snow was gone, and it would be semi-warm, but there could be wind up that high. She needed an assistant, damnit!

Justin sounded horrible. If she was going to get mad at him for not telling her it had gotten that bad, she'd have to do it after the trip. Besides, she knew how excited he'd been to go with her. It had to be bad for him to back out. Another call came through. "Hold on, Justin. Hey, V. I'm kind of in the middle of a crisis here."

"Okay. I just need to cancel lunch on Tuesday."

"What? Why?" Rachel waved the Uber driver down.

"I'm going to San Francisco for a job interview. What's the crisis?"

Rachel and the driver loaded her suitcases into the trunk. "Justin is still sick, and I have this wedding to shoot in Tahoe."

"Oh."

Rachel got in the back seat. "Anyway, don't worry about Tuesday. I've got Justin on the other line. I need to go." Veronica didn't reply. "V?"

"Yeah, um, I could go with you."

"Wait. Did you say San Francisco?"

"Yes, and I also said I could go with you."

"It's too late. The wedding is tomorrow, and this is the only flight I could find to make the timing work. I'm on my way to the airport right now."

"Never say never, Rach. What time is the flight?"

Rachel looked at her watch. "Eleven thirty."

"I'll be there," Veronica said.

"You don't have time. Veronica…"

"I'll be there. Getting in a cab now. Hey, Rach?"

"Yeah?"

"Which airport?"

"JFK."

Rachel heard Veronica direct the driver to get to the airport as fast as they could go. "Okay. Hold on. Let me hang up with Justin." She switched over to Justin's call. "Dude, I hope you feel better soon. Take care, okay? Don't worry about the job. I have a friend going with me."

"A friend named Veronica? That friend?"

Rachel rolled her eyes at Justin's teasing tone of voice. "She's saving your sorry ass, so just be grateful, okay?"

"I'll kiss her next time I see her."

"You'll do no such thing. Get better, okay?"

"Okay, boss."

When Rachel switched the phone back over to Veronica's call, she half expected her newfound assistant to have come to her senses. "V, you really don't have to do this."

"Too late, I'm already headed crosstown on Ninety-sixth. Besides, this is what friends do."

Rachel settled back into the Toyota Camry belonging to a man named Bill. She rested her head on the back of the seat. She couldn't help herself. She was excited about this unexpected turn of events. She pictured herself showing Veronica around town, riding the gondola together, maybe going out on the lake. She pictured other things too, none of which involved working. "Well, you're an amazing friend. Now, what's this I hear about San Francisco?"

As Veronica shared the details, Rachel did her best to feign enthusiasm. "Wow, what great timing for you" and "San Fran is such a wonderful city" and whatever other bullshit she could conjure up.

"It's an amazing opportunity, and it's mine if I want it. I figure I'll just rent a car when we're done and head over from there."

"Wait! You don't have any clothes!"

Veronica laughed. "Believe it or not, I'm pretty self-sufficient. I think I'll manage."

For a split second, Rachel found herself hoping that Veronica wouldn't "manage" and that all of the clothing stores in Nevada would be on strike. "I'm sure you will. And seriously, I can't tell you how much I appreciate this. You're saving Justin's ass."

"And yours."

Rachel smiled. "And mine. See you soon."

Rachel ended the call. She thought back to her little lecture about how friends step up. Veronica was definitely stepping up.

❖

Was she into self-torture and humiliation? At this point, Veronica wondered if therapy would help. She'd felt such a sense of relief when she had a good reason to cancel the lunch date. She knew Rachel was trying to be a good friend by inviting her out, but Veronica was done feeling sorry for herself. She didn't need her mother or Bea or Rachel or anyone else calling up with random invitations that would get her out of her apartment. She was a damn good lawyer, and on top of that, she was a good person. Any firm would be lucky to have her. And any woman would be lucky to date her. She would take that job in California and move on with her life. That was the plan, anyway. But here she was, ready to lug Rachel's gear around at another wedding.

Why had she jumped at the opportunity? Why hadn't she just told Rachel that she hoped she'd find someone to help her out and ended the conversation? Why did she have to be a hero? The BFF? And she doubted that was how Rachel saw it. No, Rachel probably thought Veronica had jumped at the chance because she wanted to be near her again, hence the humiliation.

The self-torture part? That was the way she felt when she was around Rachel. It was a weird mix of excitement and sadness. The part that made her sad was knowing Rachel would never give them a chance to see if they could mean something to each other. She wasn't willing to open up her heart to anyone, and Veronica could understand that on some level. But wasn't it time for Rachel to get on with her life too?

Luckily, they hadn't sat together on the plane, and the hour drive to the hotel was spent in the back of an SUV with plenty of room between them. Veronica had shopped for clothes on her own while Rachel got them checked into the hotel. She'd have to get a suit for the interview in San Francisco since the little shops in Lake Tahoe only carried casual clothing and ski wear.

Veronica looked at her watch again. Rachel was supposed to meet her for a late dinner after she'd had a brief meeting with the bride and groom to finalize the plans.

"Well, don't you look adorable."

Veronica turned and found Rachel standing right behind her. She looked like her usual cool self in jeans and a brown leather jacket that had a fleece lining. "Hey."

Rachel looked her up and down. "Puffer jacket, leggings, and hiking boots. You fit right in."

"You said it gets chilly at night, and I didn't know what kind of conditions we'd be working in on top of the mountain, so I got boots."

Rachel narrowed her eyes. "Didn't one of your dates offer to take you hiking? Dirty Martini, wasn't it?"

"Keeping track of my dates, Monaghan?"

Rachel smirked. "Someone needs to make sure you don't date a serial killer. Now, let's eat. I'm starving."

Veronica dropped onto a chair in the hotel ballroom. The guests had just sent the couple off on their honeymoon and were trickling back in. The DJ was still playing, and drinks were still being served.

The mother of the bride put her hands in the air and danced her way to the middle of the dance floor. The mother of the groom joined her. It seemed that this party wasn't over.

Veronica had learned that the groom was one of six sons. So far, Rachel had shot the three oldest sons' weddings, and number four had a serious girlfriend. Important client indeed.

She spotted Rachel in the crowd, taking two glasses of champagne from a waiter's tray. God, Veronica hoped one of those glasses was for her. She smiled when Rachel headed right toward her.

"Here's to the best assistant I've ever had. Are you sure you want to go back to that lawyering business?"

Veronica took the glass and clinked it against Rachel's. "Remind me to never get married on top of a mountain."

"Or in a hot air balloon. And definitely not on a camel in Morocco, or your photographer will curse your name for years to come." Rachel turned a chair so it was facing the dance floor and sat. She stretched her legs out in front of her and crossed her ankles. "They plan to party until the wee hours, but we're officially off duty."

"Thank God." Veronica leaned back in her chair and sipped on the champagne. "I'm not saying it wasn't beautiful up there, with a view of the lake."

"Gorgeous. I can't wait to see how the photos turned out. How's your ankle?"

"It's fine." Veronica wished she could say she'd twisted her ankle on a rock or even jumping out of the way when she saw a snake on the trail. And she had in fact jumped a bit when she heard what she thought was a rattlesnake only to realize it was just some pills in her purse. The truth about her ankle was much less exciting, not to mention embarrassing. "Can we make up a story so I don't have to admit I tripped getting out of the gondola because I'm not used to wearing boots like this? And also because I'm not used to getting off gondolas?"

Rachel laughed under her breath. "Sure! How about we tell everyone that you swooped in and scooped up the bride so her dress wouldn't get wet crossing that little stream?"

"Too much. I don't swoop, and I definitely don't scoop."

"Do you shoop?"

Veronica glared at her disapprovingly.

"Okay, okay. How about this. Do you dance?" Rachel motioned toward the dance floor with her thumb. "Bust a move? Shake your booty?"

Veronica looked at her feet. She'd changed into her sneakers for the reception. They were what she was wearing when she'd grabbed a cab for the airport. Luckily, they were a newer pair and still bright white. They didn't look too bad with the black cropped jeans she'd found in a cute little boutique on the main drag.

Rachel stood and held out her hand. "No one cares what you're wearing. Besides, I think you look adorable."

They were playing one of Veronica's favorite 80s songs, and her ankle felt fine now. She took Rachel's hand and stood. "It felt too big."

"What did?"

"The mountain," Veronica said. "Too big and too open. It was all sky and not at all intimate. It felt like we could all get swept up in a gust of wind and blow away. That's not how I want to feel on my wedding day."

The song stopped, and the DJ spoke into the microphone. "Okay, folks, I have a special request from the grandparents of the bride. They'd like to dance to a song that played at their wedding sixty-one years ago. Here's Elvis Presley singing 'Can't Help Falling in Love.'"

People started pairing up around an elderly couple. Rachel turned to Veronica. "We don't have to."

"Is this a thing with you? Ask women to dance and then ditch them?"

Rachel took Veronica's right hand and pulled her into an embrace. "I owed you one, but the truth is, I never dance at weddings. Consider this a one-time deal."

"Just like sex." Veronica looked around. Most of the guests had moved to the dance floor and were watching the elderly couple. Their movements were careful, but she imagined that in their prime, they were a sight to behold on the dance floor, moving as one and totally in tune with each other.

"What do you mean, just like sex? And don't step on my toes; these are my favorite boots."

Veronica couldn't take her eyes off the couple. "Look at them, Rach. Aren't they adorable?"

"Yeah, they are. Did you hear the groom earlier when he thanked his grandfather for teaching him how to treat a woman? I wonder why he didn't thank his own dad."

Veronica leaned in close and whispered, "His dad is having an affair with the wedding planner."

Rachel gasped. "Meghan? No."

"You're not the only one who can read people. In fact, I'd put money on it."

"That son of a bitch." Rachel shook her head. "I can't think about that. I have to work with her."

Veronica let go of Rachel's hand and wrapped her arms around her neck. "Forget I said anything. Just focus on these awesome dance moves we've got going on."

Rachel chuckled. "We're barely moving."

"I might step on your toes if I try too hard. And those are your favorite boots."

"So, you did hear that."

Every word that comes out of your gorgeous, stubborn mouth. Veronica rested her head on Rachel's shoulder. It was too hard to be this close and hide everything she felt. Rachel's hands on her hips gave her a sense of safety she'd been missing all day up on that mountain. Her voice and the warmth of her body were things she could bask in for hours, given the chance.

The song ended too soon, but Veronica made sure she let go first. "Consider that debt paid, but you still have another one." She pointed at her belly.

"Oh, right!" Rachel looked at her watch. "Go order some room service, and I'll be up after I say good-bye to the parents."

Veronica backed away. "Those are dangerous words. I might order the most expensive thing on the menu."

"I think I can handle whatever's on the room service menu."

"I really need to make bigger demands," Veronica said. "You're getting off too easy with these cheap dinners."

"Hey, you got a dance, didn't you?"

"Yeah. Your moves are fantastic. That back-and-forth thing? The swaying? You nailed it."

Rachel waved her away. "Get outta here, smart-ass."

❖

Veronica opened her hotel room door. Rachel held up a bottle of champagne and two flute glasses. "A gift from the parents. It's the good stuff."

"So, it's a pajama-slash-champagne party?" Veronica wagged her finger up and down Rachel's body. "I never would've taken you for the flannel pajama bottom type." She bent down to get a closer look. "Are those beavers?"

"Ha! That would be awesome, but no. They're sloths. Can I come in, or are you just going to stare at my crotch while I freeze in this hallway?"

Veronica shot up and moved out of the way. "Sorry. Come in."

"Are we feeding an army?" Rachel set the bottle on the room service table.

"No. Just two very hungry women."

Rachel turned back around. "You forgot to buy pajamas, didn't you?"

Veronica had put on the black leggings she'd bought, along with a T-shirt that had the words *Chillin' in Tahoe* printed on it. "Maybe I sleep naked."

"Do you?"

"No. I would freeze to death." Veronica lifted the cover on a plate. "Chicken fingers and fries. It's the late-night menu, so don't judge."

Rachel put up her hands. "Hey, I'll eat anything you put in front of me at this point."

"Good." She lifted another cover. "Burger and fries, but this is mine." She stole a fry and lifted another cover. "Another burger with cheese and fries. And last but not least, spaghetti and meatballs."

"Would you be totally disgusted if I ate the burger *and* the spaghetti?"

Veronica took her burger and the chicken fingers over to the bed. "I'll join you in your gluttony." She sat with her legs crossed under her and grabbed the remote. "What should we watch?"

"I haven't seen *Bohemian Rhapsody* yet." Rachel uncorked the champagne and poured two glasses. She set them on the nightstand and grabbed the burger and fries. She propped a pillow behind her head and lay down, then set the plate on her stomach.

Veronica gave her a quizzical look. "You can't eat like that."

"Why?" Rachel took a bite of a French fry.

"Because you'll choke if you eat lying down."

"Did your mom tell you that? Seems like an old wives' tale to me." Rachel picked up the burger and took a bite. A dollop of mustard landed on her T-shirt. "Shit."

"And that will happen!" Veronica handed her a napkin. "Speaking of mothers, I know nothing about your family except that Charlotte is your cousin."

"My parents live upstate, along with my two brothers. They're good people."

"And what would your mother think about the way you're eating that hamburger right now?"

Rachel took another bite. Her mouth was so full, she just shrugged. Veronica covered her eyes. "I can't watch. I don't know the Heimlich maneuver. I mean, I know the general idea. Just get behind the person and squeeze them, but I don't want to be responsible for breaking a rib or something." Veronica felt a tap on her arm. She uncovered her eyes. Rachel was sitting up. "Oh, thank God."

"Do you always do the worst-case scenario thing?" Rachel popped a French fry in her mouth.

"About practical things like riding a motorcycle or running with scissors or eating in bed like that? Yes. Oh, and God help me if you ever go jogging while chewing gum. Chicken finger?"

Rachel grabbed it and took a bite. "They're delicious, but they have a gross name." She leaned over and dipped it into the honey mustard on Veronica's plate. "Food should not be anything fingers or toes related."

"What about ladyfingers?"

Rachel snickered. "Yeah, I love a good ladyfinger."

Veronica shrugged. "Or three."

Rachel went still.

"What, you didn't think I'd get your little joke?"

"I thought you'd ignore it," Rachel said.

"Where's the fun in that?"

Rachel stared at her for a few seconds, then said, "Champagne?"

"Absolutely." Veronica took the glass and downed half of it. Rachel gave her a strange look. "What?"

"I just wondered about what you said on the dance floor. About me and sex?"

Veronica looked surprised for a second before realization dawned on her. "Oh, when you said the dance was a one-time thing? Yeah, that's what you told me about sex too."

"I believe I told you I couldn't promise anything beyond that night or possibly the next day."

Veronica's eyes widened. "Ooh, so maybe sex in the morning too? How generous of you."

"Hey, I could've not said anything and just fucked you."

"Yeah, that's how people usually do it. They don't announce their commitment issues up front. And who knows, I might have hated it, and then you'd have no problem, right?"

Rachel laughed. "Not likely." She finished off her glass and got up to grab the bottle. "More champagne?"

Veronica held out her glass. "Hit me."

"Tell me about this job in California."

"It's a tech company. I'd be on their legal team."

"Want a meatball? I'm getting a meatball." Rachel put the bowl of spaghetti on the bed and cut a meatball into four pieces, then stabbed a piece with her fork and offered it to Veronica. "What's the upside? Because I imagine leaving your home town and your parents wouldn't be your first choice."

"My first choice would be to make partner this year like I was supposed to do, but since that's not happening, I think a fresh start in a new place might do me good."

Rachel tilted her head. "You don't sound so sure about that."

Veronica pulled her knees up to her chest and wrapped her arms around them. "I'm not. But the money is great and so are the hours. It's worth a trip to see what they have to offer."

"I'll be shooting a wedding in San Francisco in August."

"Let me guess. They're a young couple. He's a tech billionaire, and she's got a PhD in molecular biophysics and the looks of a supermodel. Also, they're adventure seekers who want to get married while parachuting out of a plane."

"Not even close, thank God." Rachel put up two fingers. "Second marriage. Old money. Guess what the age gap is."

"Prime childbearing years meets enlarged prostate?"

Rachel put out her fist. "Exactly."

Veronica gave her a bump and blew it up. "I should be going for someone way younger than me. Why did I tell Bea to find me someone near my age?"

"You're only thirty-five. How much younger could you go?"

"Legal drinking age?"

"You're kidding, right?"

Veronica sighed. "Totally. I could never date someone who's in such a different place." She contemplated it for a moment and said, "Hey, what about someone older though? Like, fifty-ish."

"Older women are hot," Rachel said. "They know what they want."

Veronica grinned. "There's this hot judge. I always felt nervous in her courtroom, afraid that she'd read my mind and know that in my head, we were fucking in her chambers."

"That's naughty, Veronica Welch. Here's the thing about an older woman. You want kids, right?"

"Oh, yeah. I guess that would be a tough sell."

When they couldn't eat another bite, Rachel moved all of the food back to the table and filled their champagne glasses again. She held hers up for a toast. "Here's to the woman who saved my ass today. I kept an important client thanks to you."

Veronica held her glass up too. "I make a damn good lackey. Who knew?"

Rachel shook her head. "No. You make a damn good friend." She clinked their glasses together. "Thanks, V."

Veronica patted the spot next to her. "Let's watch a movie."

Rachel resisted the urge to reach over and move Veronica's hair from her eyes. She'd been watching her sleep for several minutes, and now that the movie was over, she had no reason to stay. But she wanted to stay. She wanted to curl up next to Veronica and fall asleep too.

They were obviously attracted to each other, but the desire for intimacy outside of sex unnerved Rachel. She could barely admit it to herself, but the truth was, she'd loved dancing with Veronica. She hadn't wanted that dance to end. And she didn't want to leave her bed, either.

She could stay and claim that she'd fallen asleep too. Hell, if she closed her eyes for five seconds, she'd probably be dead to the world until morning, she was so exhausted. She rolled onto her back and threw her arm over her eyes. She couldn't feel this way. She wouldn't allow herself to need someone like this. Not ever again. Especially someone who might or might not continue to date Lauren. *Please don't let that be true.*

When Veronica volunteered to be her assistant again, she'd felt relieved and excited. When they couldn't sit together on the plane, she'd felt disappointed. Veronica asked if her new jeans looked okay, and it was all Rachel could do to keep her tongue in her mouth. When Veronica tripped and fell while getting out of the gondola, Rachel felt glad she had a reason to touch her, if only to help her up and hold on until she'd steadied herself.

She was drawn to Veronica like a moth to a flame, and all of her efforts to hide that fact, from herself mostly, had failed. She rolled onto her side again and was startled to find Veronica staring at her. "Hi. I fell asleep."

"Yeah," Rachel said. "That's the second time you've fallen asleep in my presence."

Veronica rolled onto her back and stretched. "Stop working me so hard." She rubbed her belly. "I can't believe I ate all that food."

"And drank all that champagne. We killed the whole bottle."

"It was like a food orgy."

"Wanna do it again in the morning? There's a little place here that's famous for their pancakes."

Veronica turned and looked at her. "You know the way to my heart."

Rachel smiled. "I still don't know what your favorite alcoholic beverage is."

"Tequila body shots."

Rachel's eyes widened. "Don't tease me like that."

Veronica laughed. "I've never done that before. Does that make me a bad lesbian?"

"It makes you a respectable, upstanding lesbian. And in my experience, those are the most fun in bed."

Veronica glanced at Rachel, then looked away.

"Did I say something wrong?"

"No," Veronica said. "I just can't tell if you're flirting with me."

Rachel was totally flirting. "I'm just stating the facts, V."

"Oh." Veronica got up. "I'm going to shower and then sleep like a log. Don't wake me up before nine."

Rachel had ruined the mood with her useless flirting. She blew air through her lips and got up. She heard the shower turn on and went still for a moment as she pictured Veronica soaping herself down. Water dripping from her nipples. Hair wet and slicked back. She took a few steps closer to the bathroom door and listened.

"Hey, Rach? Are you still there?"

Rachel swallowed hard. "Yeah!" Her voice squeaked. She cleared her throat and stepped right up to the door. "Yeah, I'm here."

"Thanks for dinner! I had fun!"

Rachel put her forehead against the door. "Yeah," she said under her breath. "It was fun." She grabbed a notepad and pen and wrote a quick note.

Don't forget to double lock your door.
I'll pick you up at 9:30 for pancakes.
R.

CHAPTER FIFTEEN

"Y ou seem so relaxed today." Rachel could see the hotel coming into view. Since it was a sunny morning, they'd decided to walk back instead of getting an Uber.

"Well, for one, I slept great after that hot shower. And number two, I didn't have to fight you for my pancakes."

"Is this an only child thing, you not wanting to share?"

"It's more of a dad thing," Veronica said. "When I was young, he always tried to steal a pancake off my stack. I got good at protecting my plate because if I let him get it, he wasn't just playing around. He would eat it."

"He scarred you for life."

Veronica shrugged. "He also gave me a great life with lots of love and support, so if that's the only scar I have, I guess I'll take it."

"My dad's a good guy too. In fact, when I came out to my parents, he broke down crying and asked if it was something he had done to turn me off men. When I told him it wasn't that men turned me off, it was that women *really* turned me on, he seemed relieved."

"Parenting is hard," Veronica said. "Sometimes I wonder if I'm up for it."

"Oh, you'd be a great parent, and I don't say that lightly. I've known plenty of people who clearly don't have the patience or temperament to raise a child. You're not one of them."

Veronica looked at her. "What about Lauren?" Rachel didn't answer. "Sorry. I shouldn't have mentioned her."

"I guess it depends on why you're asking."

"Oh!" Veronica exclaimed. "I wasn't asking for me. I just wondered if you two wanted children."

Rachel saw no reason to answer the question. What she and Lauren did or didn't want in the way of a family was of no consequence now. "Lauren will be a great mom one day. She's very playful. Not afraid to get down on the floor and romp around with her nieces and nephews." Rachel stopped abruptly. "Please be honest with me. Are you still interested in her?"

Veronica shook her head. "I don't know. I mean, I see why you wanted to marry her."

"Don't try to soften the blow. Just tell me."

"I honestly haven't figured that out yet. And now I might be moving across the country, so it won't even matter."

Rachel considered that for a moment. "When you think about moving to San Francisco and what that might mean, where is Lauren on the list of things you think about?"

"Um." Veronica gave the question a good long think. "Maybe forty-fifth?"

"Right." Rachel had no right to tell Veronica not to date Lauren. If it happened, she'd either have to deal with it or end their friendship. Neither option sounded appealing. But she knew Lauren, and moving to California for a special woman like Veronica was something she'd fully embrace. She had an adventurous spirit. It was something she'd always loved about her.

Rachel needed to change the subject before she got worked up about Lauren. She took her phone out of her back pocket. "Let's get a shot of you with the mountains in the background. Your parents will love it."

Veronica touched her head. "I slept on wet hair. You can't take a pic of me right now."

"You look like you've been camping for days without a shower. They'll think you're getting some rest and relaxation in the great outdoors. Think about how happy that will make your mother."

Veronica grabbed her head with both hands. "That's what I look like, and you didn't tell me?" She licked her fingers and tried to smooth it down.

Rachel pointed her finger. "Did you just..."

"Shut up. You should've told me about this before we left my room."

"And miss out on that naturally formed Bumpit on the back of your head? I mean, you almost look like a blond Jackie Kennedy." Rachel put a hand on her chest. "Be still, my beating heart."

Veronica put her hands on her hips. "I'm so glad my hair could entertain you over breakfast. Now, take the damn shot, and let's move on."

Rachel looked at their surroundings. "Lean against that log fence, but don't do it like you're posing for your senior portrait."

"Should I lie on it like a stripper would? Or maybe straddle it like a horse?"

"I'm not against that, but remember, I own the rights to all of my photographs."

"Oh, bless your cold, dark heart. I think you forgot I only moonlight as an assistant. In real life, I'm an attorney. And I never signed a model release." Veronica leaned against the fence with one hip, folded her arms, and flipped her head around. She grinned stiffly and said, "How's this?"

Rachel chuckled. "I said *don't* pose for a senior portrait." Her jaw dropped. "My God. Is that really how you posed for yours?"

"Take the damn photo," she mumbled through her wide smile.

Rachel took a few shots. "Okay, now the stripper pose."

"I was kidding. There's no way I'm going to let you make a *Veronica in Tahoe* calendar."

"Oh my God. I could hang it up in the bar right next to the cash register. Come on, V. Eleven more shots, and you'll be world famous." Rachel counted on her fingers. "You could do the stripper pose, the straddle pose, the boob pose…"

Veronica folded her arms. "The boob pose?"

"Yeah." Rachel pulled her T-shirt down with both hands, revealing her cleavage. "Just lean over and do this."

Veronica pulled her phone out of her pocket. "Nice tits, Monaghan. Don't move."

Rachel straightened back up. "I take the photos. I don't pose for them."

Veronica pushed her toward the fence. "But you pose so well."

"I'm not doing that pose."

"No. You'll do exactly what I tell you to do."

Rachel huffed out a sigh and stood by the fence with her hands stuffed in her jeans pockets. "Hurry."

Veronica pointed at the middle log on the fence. "Put your left foot on that."

Rachel looked at the fence. "Isn't that a little high? How about the bottom log?"

"Middle log, and then rest your left forearm on your thigh and look at me."

Rachel followed the instructions. "I look ridiculous."

"Now, put your right hand on your hip and smile. Perfect!" Veronica took the photo and bent over in a fit of giggles.

"Give me that phone." Rachel held out her hand, but Veronica ran from her. "V!"

Veronica screamed through her laughter as she ran. She slowed down to a fast walk when she got to the hotel lobby. Rachel wasn't far behind, so she jogged to the elevators and caught the door just as it was closing.

She heard Rachel yell, "Hold the elevator!"

An older gentleman was in the elevator with Veronica. She looked at him and shook her head. "Don't wait. Just push the button."

"Why is everyone in such a hurry this morning?" he grumbled under his breath.

Rachel's arm flew through the opening just as the doors were about to close. She stepped in and leaned against the wall while she caught her breath. "I didn't know you could run that fast."

"Treadmill." Veronica wiped the sweat from her brow. She unzipped her jacket and tucked her phone into her bra, then zipped it back up to her chin.

Rachel raised an eyebrow. "Is that supposed to stop me?"

"I had no idea you'd be so compliant with that pose. Seriously, I wish my clients listened to me that well." Veronica covered her mouth to hide her laughter.

"I was humoring you, but now I don't trust you with that photo."

"Rachel, this is like attorney-client privilege. How can you not trust me?"

The older gentleman glanced over his shoulder. "Don't ever trust a lawyer. No matter what they tell you, they're in it for themselves."

"See?" Rachel held out her hand. "Give it to me."

The door opened on Veronica's floor. She stepped off the elevator and then sprinted to her door. "I'll probably post it on Twitter!" She took the key card out of her pocket and shoved it into the door. Just as she opened it, Rachel pushed her into the room and closed the door behind them.

Veronica turned around and backed her way into the room. "You wouldn't really go down my shirt for it."

"The hell I wouldn't," Rachel said. "So, you have two choices. Give it up willingly or wrestle me for it."

"I may be fast, but you have a longer wingspan. That doesn't seem fair."

Rachel followed her, keeping a few steps away. "We're not going to box, V."

Veronica's back hit the window. "Right. Wrestling is about strength and agility."

"If you say so." Rachel left only a few inches between them. "But I think it's more about who can stay on top."

Rachel's close proximity made it hard for Veronica to breathe. Should she flirt back? Because this time, there was no question that Rachel was in full flirt mode. Veronica's coat was still zipped up to her chin, so she held Rachel's stare and slowly unzipped it to just below her breasts. "One doesn't have to be on top to hold all the power."

Rachel didn't move, but her eyes lingered on Veronica's chest.

"It's your move, Monaghan."

Rachel met her gaze. "You're much more confident this time around."

"Am I? Or am I leaning against this window because I can barely breathe, I'm so attracted to you."

"You're moving to San Francisco."

"Which means we both get to walk away. Isn't that kind of perfect?" Veronica wanted this. She didn't care about tomorrow or the next day. She took off her coat and pulled her V-neck shirt down like Rachel had done a few minutes ago. "The phone is yours if you want it." Her chest was heaving, and her cleavage was exposed.

Rachel's gaze fell to the phone sticking out of her bra, then back up again. "I want it." She lunged forward, and their lips crashed together.

Veronica grabbed Rachel's face and deepened the kiss. A burst of electricity shot through her and landed in her core, just like it had the first time they'd kissed. It felt like magic and mayhem, and nothing would stop them this time. Nothing would keep Veronica from having what she'd craved for so long. Even if it only happened once, she'd come to terms with it. She'd live to see another day and carry with her the memory of becoming one with Rachel Monaghan.

Veronica pushed Rachel's jacket off her shoulders. Rachel freed her hands and pulled Veronica's shirt over her head. She took the phone out of her bra and tossed it on a chair, then stopped and stared. "My God, you're beautiful." Her eyes met Veronica's again. "Stunning."

"I'm yours, Rach." Veronica pulled her into a kiss. Rachel's grip on Veronica's hips was firm, then it loosened, and Rachel's hands slid down to Veronica's ass. Rachel squeezed her ass and pulled her closer. Veronica broke away from the kiss and whispered against Rachel's ear, "Oh my God, I want you."

Rachel's grip on Veronica's ass eased. She wrapped her arms around her waist and stopped all movement. Veronica tried to pull back enough to look her in the eye, but Rachel held on tight. "Rach?" Rachel didn't respond. She kept her face buried in Veronica's hair. "Rach, what's wrong?" Rachel's grip on her loosened. She pulled back but wouldn't look Veronica in the eye. "Oh God. You're tapping out again, aren't you?"

Rachel took a step back. "I can't."

Veronica grabbed her hand. "I know what I'm getting into, and I'm okay with it."

Rachel shook her head. "No. You don't mean that."

Veronica did mean it. She meant it with all of her heart. She took both of Rachel's hands and held them to her chest. "I don't need you to be the bigger person right now. I need you to be who you are. Who you *really* are. Let me see you, even if it's just for one night." Veronica could tell Rachel was holding back tears. She reached up and cupped her face. "Talk to me."

Rachel broke free of Veronica's grip and backed away. "It's best if I just leave." She grabbed her coat off the floor and rushed out of the room.

❖

Rachel closed the door to her room and leaned against it. She was out of breath, and her heart pounded against her ribs. The thought of letting Veronica see past the walls she'd so carefully built around herself terrified her. She bent over and tried to catch her breath. If only she had a paper bag she could breathe into.

Was she really going to do this again? Rebuff an intelligent, kind, funny, sexy-as-hell woman? And why were tears surfacing? She straightened up and wiped her eyes. She walked into the room and caught a glimpse of herself in the mirror. She stopped and whispered, "Coward."

She couldn't leave it like this. Whatever Veronica was thinking right now, it was wrong. Rachel wanted this. She wanted to feel Veronica's skin against hers. She wanted to taste every inch of her. She wanted her to know how much she loved her laugh and the way she talked with her hands. She wanted to tell her every thought she'd ever had about her, like that time when Veronica had gotten drunk on Jägerbombs and how even her hiccups were adorable. Or how every time she smirked or rolled her eyes at something Rachel said, it made her want to kiss that smirk away.

But Rachel couldn't do any of that without exposing her heart. The other thing she knew she couldn't do was sleep with Veronica. Not even just once. The pull had become too strong. The desire too deep. The ability to follow her head instead of her heart too difficult.

So where did that leave her? She fell back on the bed and stared at the ceiling while she contemplated what to do. Should she apologize via text? Show up at Veronica's door with pizza and beer and act as if nothing had happened? Over breakfast, they'd talked about maybe going on a tour around the lake. She could book that for this afternoon and hope for the best. And maybe a nice dinner afterward. She needed to do something. And fast. A quick text, and then she'd get on the other stuff. She pulled her phone out of her pocket.

I'm so sorry. Please, let's talk.

She backspaced because talking about it wasn't really in the cards. What would she say? That it was her own heart she was protecting, not Veronica's? That it was she who would fall in love first? No way.

I'm so sorry. Making plans for us tonight. Ttys.

It took some time on the phone, but Rachel finally found a yacht tour that left in two hours. She also made a reservation at a restaurant with a view of the lake. She texted the information to Veronica and hopped in the shower.

❖

After everything Veronica had done for her, Rachel wondered if flowers would be a nice touch. Just a small bouquet that expressed appreciation and possibly some remorse. She opened the cooler in the hotel gift shop. Everything looked too much like romance, except for a small bunch of pink tulips. She was just about to reach in and grab them when someone tapped her on the shoulder and said, "I'm so glad I caught you."

It was the father of the bride. Rachel had only met him the night before the wedding. He seemed to be a man of few words. Not exactly stern but not very friendly either. The one positive thing Rachel had noticed was how much he doted on his wife and daughter. They seemed to be his whole world. "Mr. Jensen." Rachel shook his hand. "Good to see you again." She glanced at his bright blue trousers. "Golfing today?"

Mr. Jensen sighed. "I've been waiting in the lobby for over an hour. I have a feeling that my daughter's new in-laws aren't sticklers for being on time." He stuck out his neck to see what she'd been looking at. "Buying flowers for someone?"

"Yeah, um…" She had to tell the truth. Who else would she be buying flowers for in Lake Tahoe? "I thought I'd get a small bouquet for my friend. She really stepped up and helped me out when my regular assistant couldn't make it."

"I told that girl she did a spectacular job. You both worked very hard to make sure we'd have cherished photos of a very special day." He glanced at the lobby. "I hope I didn't offend her by trying to give her a generous tip before she left." He pulled out his wallet. "I wanted to do the same for you, Rachel. I would've left it at the front desk, but since you're here…"

Rachel's heart sank. "Did you say Veronica left?"

"Yes. Unfortunately, you're a little late on the flowers. I think they would've really brightened her day, considering."

"Considering?" Rachel went to the door and scanned the lobby. "Considering what, Mr. Jensen?"

"Well, her blue mood, to be honest. I know when a woman is struggling to keep her emotions at bay." He held out several Benjamins. "She said I could only give the tip to you."

Rachel was in no mood to be gracious. She wanted to run out of there and find Veronica, but she couldn't offend Mr. Jensen. She took the money and shook his hand again. "Thank you, Mr. Jensen. That's very kind of you. Did Veronica happen to say where she was going?"

"I'm not sure. One of those rental car places picked her up."

Rachel forced a smile. "Of course. I forgot that was her plan."

"We're on the red-eye tonight. You're welcome to catch a ride with us in the limo. Just be in the lobby at seven thirty."

Rachel's flight wasn't until the next morning, but the thought of staying in Lake Tahoe when Veronica was already off to San Francisco felt like torture. God, how could she have been so stupid? She should've gone back to her room immediately and apologized. "Seven thirty. Thank you, Mr. Jensen. I really appreciate it." She went to the elevators and took her phone out. She needed to call the airline and see if she could get on that red-eye back to New York.

"You okay in there?"

Veronica put her hand against the dressing room door that for some strange reason didn't have a lock. "Yeah. Just answering an important email." She appreciated the service, but this woman was taking it too far.

"Let me know if you need a different size. You look more like an eight to me than a six."

Perfect! What she really needed was another blow to her ego. "Thanks! I'll keep that in mind."

"Just an observation," the woman said.

"You can shove your observation up your ass," Veronica whispered. She looked at the text message on her phone again. Rachel had thanked her profusely for her help and apologized if she had somehow offended Veronica. That wasn't her intention, it said.

Rachel's intentions were never clear. She was a volcano one minute and glacial the next. Flirty and all business. Snarky and effusive. Coming and going at the same time. *Speaking of coming.* Would it be terrible to give herself a bit of relief in a dressing room? If only she hadn't said those words out loud yesterday, maybe they would've stripped each other's clothes off on the way to the bed. If only she hadn't said, *I want you.*

Was that what freaked Rachel out? Too much communication in the heat of passion? Did she need to fuck in silence and then quietly sneak out of the room afterward? Veronica had convinced herself she'd be okay with that. Whatever she could get of Rachel, she'd gladly take. But was that the truth?

The truth didn't matter. The last two days didn't matter. All that mattered was making sure she looked her best for this meeting so she'd never have to lay eyes on Rachel Monaghan again.

Veronica tossed her phone in her purse and tried on another skirt. It was way too tight. She definitely didn't want to get the job because they liked the way her ass looked in a skirt. She heard the nasty woman's footsteps. "Hey, um. I think I need a size eight." Three skirts appeared over the top of the door. Veronica rolled her eyes and grabbed the hangers. "Thanks."

"She hates me." Rachel set her phone on the bar and covered her face with her hands. Maybe she'd gone overboard with all of the apologetic texts. The reply she'd just received from Veronica seemed final.

I don't think we have anything else to say to each other.

"Of course she hates you," Charlotte said. "You're an ass."

Rachel took her hands away. "Hey! A little support here?"

"No." Charlotte put the bottle of whiskey back on the shelf. "And you're cut off."

"Great! I guess I'll just have to *feel* all of the horrible things I'm feeling right now."

Harry threw a bar towel over his shoulder and stood in front of her. "Or maybe you could deal with all of those things you're feeling."

"What are you talking about? I've tried to apologize, but she obviously wants nothing to do with me."

"I'm not talking about Veronica," Harry said. "I'm talking about Lauren."

Rachel shot him a glare. "Don't say her name."

"I think that says it all." Harry turned to Charlotte. "You okay if I take our friend on a little outing?"

Charlotte handed him a bottle of water. "Make sure she drinks this."

Rachel slid off the stool and backed away. "What are you talking about? I'm not going anywhere."

Harry took off his apron and rounded the bar. "Sweetie, it's the only way." He put his arm around her and urged her toward the door.

Rachel wasn't sure where they were going, but having Harry's strong arm wrapped around her shoulders provided some unexpected comfort. "Where are you taking me?"

"Where you should've gone a long time ago."

Rachel stood in front of Lauren's door, unable to make herself actually knock. Harry was waiting for her downstairs. He said he'd get her back home if she couldn't do it herself. She knew he wasn't referring to the two shots of whiskey she'd had over an hour ago.

She took a deep breath and plucked up the courage to knock on the door. A female voice yelled, "Just a second!" She took a step back and waited for the door to open.

"I didn't expect you so soon." Lauren stopped short. "Rachel." She looked down the hall. "I thought you were dinner."

Rachel lifted a brown bag she'd accepted from the delivery guy. "Still getting it from Woo's." She handed the bag to Lauren. "Can we talk? It won't take long."

"Sure." Lauren adjusted the towel on her head. "I just got out of the shower. Give me a minute."

It was an odd sensation, standing in Lauren's personal space again. It felt familiar yet completely foreign. She wore the same perfume. Rachel recognized the scent when Lauren opened the door. Everything else was different except for a few family photos that sat on a sofa table. Rachel knew those people well. Or she used to.

Lauren came out of the bedroom dressed in a gray sweatshirt and black leggings. "How's the wedding business?"

Lauren was never great at small talk. She might as well have asked how the weather was outside. "Good," Rachel said. "My summer is packed solid."

"Anything in Italy?" Lauren opened the take-out bag.

"Wealthy people do love to get married in Italy," Rachel said. "Two this year."

"I loved Italy when you took me there. There's plenty here, if you're hungry." Lauren stopped, the realization of what she'd just said written all over her face.

Rachel shook her head. "Not hungry."

"Rach. God. I'm sorry. I didn't mean to—"

"Bring up where I proposed to you? I'm sure you didn't mean to do a lot of things, did you, Lauren?"

"Rach, I never meant to hurt you. I loved you. I really did."

Rachel was surprised to realize there wasn't even an ounce of attraction anymore. She didn't care that Lauren had answered the door in nothing but a short silk robe. Her eyes hadn't wandered over her body the way they used to. She didn't find herself wondering if there was a sexy black bra under that sweatshirt or maybe no bra at all. It was a relief in a way. It made it easier to say what she needed to say.

What *did* she need to say? This little outing, as Harry had called it, wasn't something she ever planned on doing. She'd banished Lauren from her life, never to be seen or spoken to again. And yet the ghost of Lauren remained. She was always there, haunting Rachel's dreams. Making decisions for her. Controlling her life in a way.

She'd fallen hard, and she'd never really gotten back up. It was a sobering thought. One she had no desire to address, no matter what Harry had to say about it. She turned to leave.

"Rachel? Can't we at least be friends?"

Friends? Was she insane? Rachel turned back around. "You really don't know just how badly you hurt me, do you?" Lauren started to reply, but Rachel stopped her. "No! You obviously have no idea how hard it's been to trust anyone in my life. You did that, Lauren. You took away a part of me with your irresponsible behavior. And if you really loved me, you never would have left me standing there in front of everyone who mattered to me."

Lauren folded her arms and dropped her gaze to the floor. "I'm sure that was a difficult moment."

"A difficult…" Feeling completely exasperated, Rachel put her hands on her hips. "A difficult moment? Is that what we're calling it when I lose the love of my life seconds before I'm supposed to marry her? My God, Lauren."

"I panicked, okay? It was too much."

"You had six months to panic. Six months to tell me you didn't want to be married to me, or you weren't quite ready or whatever it was that made you run."

"You could've run after me. You could've tried to convince me. Maybe I would've calmed down and taken a deep breath and walked down the aisle again."

"Yeah," Rachel said with a nod. "That sounds like a great way to start a marriage. Because I wasn't humiliated enough. God, Lauren, is that what you wanted? You wanted me to beg you to marry me? Drag you back down the aisle? Don't you think I deserved better than that?"

Lauren straightened her shoulders. "Why are you here?"

Rachel wondered the same thing. Lauren had her defenses up and was unlikely to give her a straight answer, but she needed to try, or this whole conversation was for nothing. "Somewhere between me getting down on one knee in Italy and our wedding day, you started having second thoughts. I want to know when that happened. I need to make some sense of this so I can move on with my life. I need to understand."

"I don't know exactly when."

"Was it days? Months? I mean, for how long were you faking your excitement?"

"I never faked anything with you, Rach. I just panicked. I woke up that morning with a feeling of panic, and it didn't go away."

"So, you knew *hours* before the ceremony, and you didn't say anything? You know what that tells me, Lauren? It tells me you didn't want that feeling to go away. You didn't want to talk to me about it. You didn't want any reassurance from me or anyone else that it was just nerves and everything would be okay."

Lauren responded with a big sigh, but she wouldn't look at Rachel. She kept her eyes on the floor. "You're right," she said softly. "I wasn't ready, and deep down inside, I knew it. But I loved you so much, and you were so perfect in every way. My friends loved you. My parents loved you. The whole world spent six months telling me how lucky I was. I just kept thinking that if I got to the moment and saw you in that beautiful dress, everything would fall into place. The only problem is, it didn't."

"Wow. So much time. So many tears. Only to hear 'It's me and not you.'" Rachel had heard enough. She knew the truth now. She went to the door.

"That's not what I said at all, Rach. I said I was young and immature and stupid. So very, very stupid. Those aren't good excuses, but they're the only ones I've got. And you can be damn sure if that wedding were today, the outcome would be very different."

Rachel took one final look at her ex before walking out the door. She found a little bit of relief in the realization that if the wedding were today, she would be the one calling it off, not Lauren.

Harry was at the bottom of the stairs, just like he said he'd be. Her emotions were bubbling to the surface. "Let's go home," she whispered.

❖

Veronica's black heels slipped with every step she took. Maybe buying shoes after doing a walking tour of the city she'd soon be living in was a bad idea. She definitely needed a half size smaller now that her feet weren't swollen. At least she was going down a size instead of up, like she'd had to do with the skirt. Damned store clerks and their sassy attitudes.

She needed a coffee but not from the hotel lobby. Hopefully, there would be a place on the way where she could sit and gather her thoughts. There would be some fibbing involved with this meeting. Or interview. Or whatever it was. Did the thought of moving to the West Coast excite her? Not really. Did she think the corporate environment would suit her? How could it? Did she always wear shoes that were too big for her? Only when it was of the utmost importance that she look her professional best.

She spotted a Peet's and caught the crosswalk sign just in time. Her phone alerted her that Bea was calling. "I don't have time, Bea." It went to voice mail and rang again. This time, she answered it. "I don't have time, Bea. Big interview in San Francisco. Hey, do you want to move to San Francisco?"

"Sit down."

"I can't. I'm headed for coffee, and nothing can stop me, except maybe these damn heels."

"Find a bench and sit down," Bea said.

"Oh, for God's sake, this better be earth-shattering." Veronica inspected the bus bench for chewing gum before she sat. Some mistakes you only had to make once. "Okay, my ass is seated. Speak."

"The partnership fell through."

"Partnership? What partnership?" Veronica paused. "Wait. Do you mean Avery?"

"Her big client bailed, V. Word in the lunchroom: She was fucking the wife of this bigwig CEO, and the relationship went south."

"It's not like you to use that kind of language, Bea. I'm shocked."

"Sorry. I'm excited. Like, jumping out of my vintage Christian Dior excited!"

Veronica shouldn't have been surprised by this news. Avery was a walking sex toy. Of course she'd used it to her advantage. But the timing couldn't have been worse. "You're telling me this right before I walk into an interview for a job I will most likely take. How is that even remotely helpful?"

"I swear, V, this isn't a rumor. I got it straight from Mr. Snow. He said he never wanted to offer Avery the partnership, but he was outvoted by the younger partners. He said their greed usurped their loyalty to you and the firm. He said it was wrong, and he hoped he could make it right."

"Why did he tell you this?"

"I think he wants me to soften you up. I mean, I think that because he basically told me to see if there's a chance to smooth things over. He knows how angry you were."

Veronica didn't know what to think. She couldn't just blow this job opportunity on Bea's word. "Tell Mr. Snow he needs to call me with an offer now. Not tomorrow. Not an hour from now. Right now. Or I'm taking this job."

Bea squealed into the phone. "I'm on it."

Chapter Sixteen

I should've stuck with the black. That's the third person who thought they were getting a wedding invitation from you because of the gold foil."

Veronica put her arm around her mom. "Who cares? It's a great party." She kissed her cheek. "Thanks for doing this."

Of course, Veronica didn't need a party to celebrate. Making partner was celebration enough. The last month had been good. She was back in her comfort zone. Back on her feet, ready to take on the world again. The map of her life had a few twists and turns on it, but she'd righted the course, and all of her hard work wouldn't be for nothing.

"Oh, there's Tiffany," her mom said. "I'll let you two catch up." She cupped her hand around her mouth and said in a not so quiet whisper, "Try to find out if she's pregnant yet."

"Pregnant? She just got...hey, Tiff!"

Tiffany hugged Veronica. "Hey, V. And no, I'm not pregnant yet, much to my mother's chagrin."

"And mine, apparently."

Tiffany took a step back but kept hold of Veronica's hands. "Look at you, all grown-up and playing with the big girls and boys. It took them long enough to realize what they had."

"Oh, you mean a workhorse in a fancy suit who doesn't screw the client?"

Tiffany wrapped her arm around Veronica. "Speaking of screwing, why don't you direct me to the nearest glass of champagne, and on the way, you can entertain me with lesbian sex tales that involve a certain wedding photographer."

"Rachel? There's nothing to tell."

"I heard you were searching for her at my wedding. Something about the last dance?"

"God. Does nothing get by our mothers?"

"Not since we exited the womb. Now, tell me, is she good in bed? Back in college, I was very tempted to find out for myself, but I just couldn't go there. Not that there's anything wrong with going there."

Veronica gave her a sideways glance. "I'm finding it hard to believe that boy-crazy Tiffany was ever curious about girls."

"Not girls in general. Just my hot, gay roommate." Tiffany picked up two glasses of champagne. "Cheers. Now, answer the question."

"What was the question again?" Veronica took a long sip of champagne. Getting drunk sounded good right about now.

"Is my hot, gay ex-roommate good in bed?"

"Right." Yes, definitely time to get drunk. "I would imagine Rachel is great in bed, but I wouldn't know. And before you gasp out your shock or disappointment or whatever, it's not that I didn't try."

"Well, that's disappointing," Tiffany said with a sigh. "I was hoping for a love connection between my old friend and my favorite cousin."

"You should've set us up fifteen years ago when we were young, idealistic, and unafraid."

Tiffany set her empty champagne glass down and picked up another. "I have news for you, Double V. You were never idealistic. Even now, you're interviewing women instead of dating them, as if love is something you can schedule in your Outlook calendar."

Veronica covered her eyes with her hand. "Oh my God, my mother needs to shut her big mouth."

"Our mothers share every detail of their lives with each other. I'm sure my mom knows exactly how girthy your dad's dick is and vice versa. Why do you think I'm so private? Hell, I don't even have Instagram. Eric's family thinks I must have something to hide, but really, I'm just hiding from my mother."

Veronica blinked several times. "I can't believe you just casually mentioned my father's…"

"Dick, V. I know you prefer a nicely landscaped pussy, but half of the population has this magical thing that—"

Veronica put her hand over Tiffany's mouth. "Stop talking. You're being gross right now."

Tiffany shrugged. "I'm in a mood, that's all. I should probably pick a fight with my mother and get some of this tension out. All I'd have to do is tell her I've been too tired to cook for Eric all week. That'd get her going."

The mention of Tiffany's husband got Veronica thinking about Rachel's Spidey sense. "How's it going with Eric?"

"Eric is great," Tiffany said.

Veronica waited for more, but Tiffany didn't seem to have anything else to say on the subject. "Great! I'm glad you're happy."

Tiffany set her second empty glass down. "You really couldn't get in Rachel's pants? What the hell is wrong with her?"

"She's…" *Perfect, except for one minor detail?* "We're in different places, that's all."

"Since when did that stop Rachel? Ever since Lauren, she's been going through women like I just went through that champagne—all she wants to do is keep the party going." She put her arm on Veronica's shoulder. "I wouldn't take it personally, V. This is about Rachel, not you."

"Were you there when it happened? The thing with Lauren?"

"Oh my God." Tiffany shook her head. "You can't imagine how bad it was. The music stopped when she ran. Everyone's head went from the door to Rachel to the door to Rachel. No one knew what to do. I mean, what should you do?"

Veronica wondered what she would do in Rachel's shoes. She'd be paralyzed, most likely. Stuck there, witnessing the horrified looks on everyone's faces while her heart shattered into a million little pieces. "I know what I'd do," she said. "I'd never let it happen again. Even if it meant spending the rest of my life alone."

"That's depressing," Tiffany said. "I'm going to need three glasses of champagne if you keep this up."

"Yeah, but we can't really blame Rachel, can we?"

"Honestly, I would've killed Eric. He would not still have his balls, and he loves his balls."

"Okay. I don't need to know that about your husband. You've really started oversharing since you got married."

Tiffany laughed. "Thank God we're not like our mothers." She pointed across the room. "Here comes your dad. I bet my mom twenty bucks it would be a tennis bracelet. She said no way; it's a diamond pendant to match your earrings. What I wouldn't give to be an only child."

Veronica's father's gifts were always an exciting surprise when she was young, but now she felt a little embarrassed that the tradition hadn't run its course. Here she was, a grown woman with a successful career, accepting a gift in front of family and friends to mark another milestone in her life. It seemed there was no getting around the fact that she would always be his little girl.

Her dad walked up to her and put out his hands. "I couldn't be any prouder than I am right now."

Veronica took his hands and leaned in for a kiss on her cheek. "Thank you, Dad."

He turned to the crowd and cleared his throat. "Everyone, can I have your attention? Thank you. Karen and I...where is she? Where's my bride? There she is." He blew her a kiss. "Karen and I are so happy to be here with all of you, the people we love, who enrich our lives every day. Moments like these make us so grateful for strong family ties and friends who are always there through the good and the bad. Today, we're gathered for something very good. And Karen would like to apologize to those of you who thought you'd received a wedding invitation. I told her if it got your heart beating faster for a moment, that's not a bad thing. Especially Uncle Gene's heart. Where is he? Is he awake?"

Uncle Gene gave him a wave from his Jazzy scooter. "I'm awake but barely. You're boring the hell out of me!"

While everyone laughed, Veronica nudged her dad, letting him know he should wrap it up.

"Okay," he said. "I'll get to the point." He turned to Veronica and pulled a long velvet box out of his jacket pocket. "You are our greatest blessing, our pride and joy, our legacy in this world. We love you with our whole hearts, Veronica Violet Welch. Be everything you were meant to be."

Veronica couldn't hold back the tears. She hugged her dad and held him tight, then crossed the room to her mother. "I love you, Mom."

"Love you too, honey. Now, open it. I hear there's money on the line." She winked at her sister.

Veronica looked around the room. Her heart was full of emotion. People she'd known her whole life were there, happy to celebrate her success. "Thank you for coming, everyone. I worked my butt off to get to this place in my career, and in doing so, I'm sure I've neglected to be there for you the way you've always been there for me. That's going to change, starting today. Because family is everything. Good friends are everything. The rest is just noise. So, thank you, for being here. I love all of you."

Tiffany cupped her hands around her mouth. "We love you too, Double V! Now, open the damn box!" Veronica opened the box and held the tennis bracelet up for everyone to see. Tiffany let out a loud whoop and said, "You owe me twenty bucks, Mom!"

Veronica let her mom help her put the bracelet on her wrist. "It's gorgeous, Mom. Thank you so much."

Her mom turned them away from the crowd. "I hope you don't mind, honey. I invited Rachel tonight. Have you seen her yet? She came in while your dad was speaking."

Veronica's mouth went dry. She hadn't told her parents about what had happened in Lake Tahoe. Obviously. She spotted Rachel chatting with Tiffany. She decided to mingle with the other guests. Uncle Gene was trying to get her attention, so she went and sat next to his scooter. "Hi, Uncle Gene. How's the hip replacement doing?"

"Well, it's not getting me any more action with the ladies than I had before."

"That's because you're married, remember?"

Uncle Gene scratched his whiskers. "Am I?" He leaned in close. "Is she a knockout?"

Veronica knew the answer to that question. Gene had been playing this little game with her since she was a young girl. "Prettiest woman this side of the Mississippi," she said.

Uncle Gene slapped his leg. "Hot damn! I better go find her."

They both laughed, and Gene took her hand. "You've done well, kiddo. Now, go find yourself a good woman like I did when I was your age. It'll be the best thing you ever did." He looked over Veronica's shoulder, and his eyes lit up. "Who do we have here?"

Rachel stood there. God. Did this woman ever not look cool? She wasn't wearing her usual jeans and T-shirt. She had on skintight black leather pants and a sleeveless silk blouse. Veronica could've sat in that chair and stared at her all night. "Uncle Gene, this is Rachel Monaghan. She's a wedding photographer. In fact, she shot Tiffany's wedding."

Rachel leaned down and shook his hand. "It's a pleasure, Uncle Gene. As I recall, you have a very beautiful wife."

"She only married me because she felt sorry for me," Uncle Gene said. "But I wasn't above taking a little charity. Not when it looked like that."

"Charity is my aunt's name," Veronica clarified for Rachel. She kissed Uncle Gene's cheek. "Behave yourself."

He waved her back with his finger. "Do you know how to flirt with a pretty woman? It can be intimidating."

"What did I just say?"

He leaned in and said, "Let me give you the secret to success. Say her name a lot. I said Charity so much it started to sound like a foreign word to me, but to Charity, it sounded like a siren song."

Veronica pulled back so they were eye to eye. She wasn't sure if this was another one of Uncle Gene's jokes or genuine advice. "Seriously?"

He winked at her. "Rachel needs a glass of champagne."

"She does," Rachel said.

"Then I should get *Rachel* a glass of champagne." She gave Uncle Gene's shoulder a pat and led Rachel to the drinks table.

"I hope you don't mind that I came," Rachel said. "I wasn't sure if you'd sent the invitation or if it was your mom."

"Do you think I would've chosen those invitations?"

"For a split second, I wondered if it was a wedding announcement, but then I thought, it's only been three weeks since Tahoe."

Veronica shuddered. "Can we not talk about Tahoe?"

"I shouldn't have come."

"No, it's fine. I shouldn't keep hitting on you." Veronica stopped and turned to her. "Look, I get it, okay? I understand your desire to be free from drama and relationships and emotional agony. It's cool. We're cool. I would just rather not talk about what an ass I've made of myself around you." She picked up two flute glasses. "Now, congratulate me on making partner. And smile. Along with Uncle Gene, every woman in this room is watching us."

Rachel clinked their glasses together and glanced around. "Oh my God, you're right." She took a sip and smiled. "Congratulations, Veronica. Until I got the invitation, I thought for sure you'd taken that job in San Francisco."

"Turns out Avery used more than her legal wits to land that big client." Veronica shrugged. "And apparently, her vagina only has so much pull."

"I've met her, remember? I can't say I'm surprised."

"Anyway," Veronica said. "It went south on her, and they rescinded the offer, then offered it to me. Not easy to be the runner-up, but it should have been mine in the first place, so I put my ego aside and accepted their offer. How's wedding season going?"

"I'm in the thick of it now. It's why I was late. In fact, I leave for Europe tomorrow for two weeks. Justin is so excited to go, I swear he's going to pee his pants on the plane."

"Europe? Wow. I only got Lake Tahoe."

"I thought we weren't talking about Tahoe," Rachel said.

"You brought up Europe, and I needed to express my jealousy."

"You're welcome to." Rachel stepped closer. "As long as I can be allowed to express my regret."

"I'd rather we just—"

"V. I want to touch you, but everyone is watching. Please, just know how sorry I am."

Veronica couldn't do this here. Sure as Tiffany was getting drunk tonight, she'd cry in front of everyone if she talked about Tahoe. "Say something funny so I can fake laugh."

"Okay. Vaginas are pretty awesome. You said the word first, so now I feel comfortable saying it. It's even more fun if you sing the word. Vagina, vagina, vagina." Rachel waved her hands in the air. "Vagina." Veronica didn't react. "Nothing? Wow, you're a tough audience."

Veronica tried to hide her smile. "I'm just wondering what my family is thinking right now. Could they read your lips? And that little dance move was just, wow." She giggled under her breath.

"Which one?" Rachel turned around and shook her booty. "This one? It's kind of my signature move."

"Now everyone is *really* confused." Veronica was dying inside, but she managed to keep her cool and not give Rachel the satisfaction of seeing her laugh her ass off.

"Are you telling me they've never seen a lesbian mating call before?" Rachel cupped her hands over her mouth and tilted her head back.

Veronica grabbed Rachel's hand. "Don't you dare howl, Rachel Monaghan, unless you want a chapter in the *family stories that never die* book. Your dancing is already getting you a reputation."

"Would I be right next to the chapter about Veronica's bridesmaid's dress that was cut so low you could see her belly button? Because that's where I'd like to be."

Veronica put up a finger. "Number one, it wasn't cut that low."

"But that's how these stories go, right? Years from now, I'll be the creepy lesbian who thought she was a werewolf."

"And number two," Veronica dropped her hand. "Damnit, I forgot number two. All this talk about vaginas and dicks and werewolves has me in a dither."

"Dicks? That definitely wasn't me. You must've been talking to Tiffany. That's always an adventure."

"She thought about fucking you in college. Don't ever tell her I said that."

Rachel laughed. "And she's just arrogant enough to believe I would've jumped at the chance."

"Wouldn't you?" Veronica glanced at Tiffany, who it seemed had indeed picked a fight with her mom. "I mean, look at her."

"I'd prefer to look at you," Rachel said.

Veronica threw two fingers in the air. "I just remembered number two. Don't flirt with me, Monaghan."

Rachel put her hands up. "Okay. Can I at least show you something?" She pulled her phone out of her back pocket. "Remember in Tahoe when I asked you to take some long-distance shots with the wide-angle lens?" She handed the phone to Veronica. "They wanted this one blown up so they could hang it over their fireplace."

It was a shot from the top of the mountain. The light blue sky was offset by the deep blue lake and the pine-covered hills. She'd taken the shot as the couple kissed for the first time as husband and wife. Veronica had to admit it was beautiful. "Who knew I had it in me?"

"You captured their vision perfectly. This is what their wedding was all about. A shared future full of blue skies and adventure."

Veronica handed the phone back. "Careful, someone might think you believe in true love with all that mushy talk."

"Or they might think I can fully appreciate a good shot. And this is a good shot." She gave Veronica a fist bump. "Also, I liked what you said about family earlier. It made me realize I could do better at the daughter thing. Like, maybe call my parents and check in on them before I leave for Europe tomorrow." She took Veronica's arm. "Gorgeous bracelet. Your parents have good taste. Speaking of taste, I'm starving."

"And you're talking a mile a minute." Veronica led Rachel to the other side of the room where a buffet was laid out on a long table. She handed her a plate. "What's this about, Monaghan?"

"You keep using my last name." Rachel leaned in and lowered her voice. "I think when Uncle Gene told you to use my name a lot, he meant my first name."

"Oh my God! Are your ears bionic?"

"No, he just whispers loudly. Also, I'm nervous. That's why I'm talking fast." Rachel slapped a large spoonful of mashed potatoes on her plate. "And I'll probably stress eat in front of you, so be prepared."

"Just don't hold your spoon with your fist, or my mother will politely correct you. Also, I've seen you eat pancakes, so nothing will shock me."

Rachel took two pieces of roast beef from the carving board. "I know how to eat in front of mothers."

"Wow. You really are hungry."

"I've been nervous all day, so I haven't eaten much."

Tiffany put her arms around both of them. "Who wants to make a plate for me? I'm too tipsy to carry anything at the moment."

Veronica grabbed another plate. "How hungry are you?"

"Not as hungry as Rachel here. What's up, Rach? You only stress eat when you're really worried about something."

"She's nervous," Veronica said. "Look how her hands are shaking."

Rachel put a spoonful of horseradish sauce on the roast beef. "They're not shaking."

"Don't make us guess," Tiffany said. "We're all family here."

"Fine. I'm nervous because there's this woman I like."

Veronica froze with a spoonful of green beans hanging in the air. She cleared her throat and said, "Green beans, Tiff?"

"We used to feed anything green to my dog, remember?" Veronica glanced at Rachel. "And then we grew up."

"Fine. A small spoonful." Tiffany looked at Rachel. "So, not just a quick fuck with this one, huh?"

Rachel grimaced. "Don't be so crass, Tiff."

"Look, I'm excited for you! If you're nervous, that means you really like her, right?"

"Yeah, I really do. But I'm leaving town for a while, and I don't know if I should ask her out before I leave or wait until I get back."

Veronica kept her focus on Tiffany's plate. "I think you should wait."

"Pardon me?"

"I think you should wait until you get back," Veronica repeated. "You might meet someone else in Europe, and then what? You'd have to cancel on the poor woman you left here. It has the potential to put you in a bad light if you ask her out now."

"Ha! Since when does Rachel care about her reputation? She's a regular customer at the In and Out, and everyone knows it."

"Shut up, Tiffany." Rachel stormed off, leaving Veronica and Tiffany standing there.

Veronica watched Rachel sit at an empty table, then turned to Tiffany. "That was rude."

"Maybe, but it's true." Tiffany took the plate from Veronica. "Fine. I'll go apologize, but if you want to talk about rude, I think it was super rude of Rachel to show up here talking about some flavor of the month when she knows you like her."

Flavor of the month. Huh. Veronica had assumed Rachel was talking about her. Was that just arrogance? Was Rachel that insensitive? She had been in the past. But still, she knew Rachel a little bit, and this reeked of yet another flirty move the photographer wouldn't follow through on. Veronica shook her head and decided to mingle among her guests again.

Tiffany was getting an earful in between big bites of food. Veronica was glad she'd stayed on the other side of the room. She wanted no part of whatever they were arguing about. She hugged a few relatives and thanked them for coming, then grabbed another glass of champagne.

When she turned back around, Tiffany was alone at the table. She scanned the room for Rachel, but she was nowhere to be found.

Tiffany stood and walked toward Veronica. She looked so downtrodden, Veronica rushed over and met her halfway. "What happened?"

"I blew it. I'm drunk, and I blew it."

"What does that mean? Where's Rachel?"

Tiffany's eyes teared up. "It's you, V. Rachel wanted to ask you out, but now she's too embarrassed because of what I said."

Veronica shook her head. "Tiff, I assumed it was me, and I'm not interested. You didn't blow anything."

Tiffany wiped her eyes and giggled. "You said I didn't blow anyone." Then came a giggle-hiccup. "But that's not true."

"Okay, I walked into that one."

"Rachel likes you," Tiffany slurred. "But she has issues, which is too bad because she belongs with someone."

"She doesn't have issues. She was hurt by someone. You were there, remember?"

"Oh! It's you. You're the someone she belongs with." Tiffany wasn't quite keeping up with the conversation.

Veronica stood and waved to the waiter. "Can you bring a water for my cousin, please?" She turned to Tiffany and said, "Drink the water. And thanks, Tiff."

Veronica found Rachel out in the hall waiting for the elevator. "Hey," Veronica said. "Are you just going to eat and run?"

"I have an early flight."

Rachel's face was flushed. Veronica stepped closer. "You okay?"

"I'm good."

"Why don't you come back in and have cake with me? We could smear it all over each other's faces and then people might feel like the invitation actually matched the party."

Rachel kept her eyes on the elevator. "I've never understood that tradition."

"Well, like a lot of traditions, I think it started with a real cake fight."

"How do you figure?"

"Can't you see it? A clumsy groom tries to feed his new bride some cake, but he gets it on her face. She's embarrassed and angry, so she takes a piece and smears it on him like, take that, bitch! But he doesn't just take it. He digs into the cake with his fingers and wipes them clean on her face. And then, they laughed and lived happily ever after for sixty-five years."

Rachel turned to her. "You're such a hopeless romantic, Veronica Welch."

Veronica took in Rachel's features. She had a sad expression on her face, but it didn't take away from her beauty. In fact, it made her look vulnerable. "So, about that cake, Rachel."

That got a smile. "You said my name. Uncle Gene would be so proud." The elevator doors opened. "I really do have an early flight. I just wanted to congratulate you on making partner. And apparently, snarf down some food. Please, thank your parents for me."

Veronica didn't know what to think or what to say next. Had Tiffany misunderstood? One thing was sure, she wasn't about to make a fool of herself again. "I will." Rachel got in the elevator. "Rach." Veronica held the door open. "Come back safe. From what I hear, you have a girl to ask out."

Rachel smiled. "Maybe I do."

Chapter Seventeen

"Nice office."

Veronica waved Tiffany in. "What are you doing on this side of town?"

"Just thought I'd come and check out your new digs."

"No, you didn't." Veronica pointed at the sofa that came with her new office. "That should be illegal. I never sit there because I'd fall dead asleep, that's how comfortable it is."

"You had me at illegal." Tiffany sat and put her head back. "Can I sleep here tonight?"

Veronica sat next to her. "Wouldn't Eric miss you?"

Tiffany closed her eyes. "The question is, would I miss him?"

"Uh-oh. Trouble in paradise?"

"Nah. I think we're just getting used to being in each other's way all the time. We'll figure it out."

Veronica gave Tiffany's leg a pat. "Of course you will. You're so perfect for each other."

Tiffany lifted her head. "You're right. I'm not here to check out your new digs. Although for someone who was a terrible cheerleader, you've come a long way, V."

"Hey, I have trophies that say otherwise."

"And you still admire them from time to time. It's quite sad, actually." Veronica slugged Tiffany's shoulder. "Okay," Tiffany said. "I'll stop harassing the fancy lawyer and get to the goddamned point."

"Thank you."

"I have someone who's so perfect for you, it's astounding."

Veronica shook her head. "Oh, no. No, no, no, my dear cousin.

I'm done with the whole blind date thing. My focus is here. If one day, it happens, then it happens. But I'm not going to force it anymore."

"She's hot. I mean, smokin' hot."

"So? You say that like it's number one on my list. It's not. And PS, I've been on dates with fourteen hot women this year alone. It's not all it's cracked up to be."

"You're so full of shit." Tiffany leaned back again and stared at the ceiling. "Seriously, I want to live on this sofa. Can you order us a pizza?"

Veronica looked at her watch. "It's three thirty."

Tiffany punched the air in apparent victory. "Pizza time!"

Veronica leaned back and also stared at the ceiling. "How hot?"

Tiffany giggled. "I knew you were full of shit." She turned to Veronica. "Seriously, V. I feel terrible about what happened with Rachel, and I want to make it up to you."

"Don't feel bad. You were drunk, and whatever you thought she said, she didn't say."

"I wasn't that drunk."

"Can we just forget about it? I've moved on, and so has my mom. She finally stopped talking about her last week."

Tiffany let her head fall to Veronica's shoulder. "I'm glad you didn't move to California. I know we don't see each other that often, but still."

"That's my fault," Veronica said. "Let's do lunch next week. Have Bea schedule it when you go, okay?"

"Can I also have her schedule a date with this woman I met?"

Veronica let out a heavy sigh. "Is she for-sure gay?"

"Has been gay her whole life."

"Does she have any reptiles?"

"What?"

"You know, lizards, snakes, Gila monsters. Cold-blooded animals that shed their skin."

"A Gila monster is a lizard," Tiffany said.

"Oh my God. That is so not the point!"

"Oh. Okay, no, she doesn't have any reptiles. No rodents, either."

"I'm glad we cleared that up." Veronica stood. "Do you still want pizza?"

"Nah. I know you're busy." Tiffany held out her hand and let Veronica pull her off the sofa, then gave her a hug. "I love you, Double V. Too much to set you up with someone who wouldn't suit you."

Veronica held on tight for a moment. "Love you too, Tiff." She pulled back and said, "She better be so hot, I get burned when I touch her."

Tiffany grinned. "I need to go talk to Bea."

❖

Rachel hadn't been in the Prescott offices before. When she'd met previously with Madison and Ana, it was always at the estate. Even though she felt as if she knew them well, she was nervous because this wasn't a business visit. This was personal.

"Ms. Monaghan?"

Rachel turned from the huge painting she'd been admiring. "Yes."

"Please, follow me."

Rachel followed the young man down a long hall. Plastic was taped to the floor, and a man on a tall ladder was working on the lighting.

"Please excuse the mess. We're in the middle of a remodel." He took a closer look at Rachel. "I remember you from the wedding. You did the photography."

"I did."

He offered his hand. "I'm Kyle, Ana's assistant. Can I get you anything?"

Rachel's throat was dry from the nerves. "Water would be great."

Kyle entered the office first. "Rachel Monaghan, photographer extraordinaire." He smiled at her. "I saw the photos. They're amazing."

"He speaks the truth." Ana moved from behind her desk and gave Rachel a hug. "You sounded tired on the phone. I hope everything is okay." Rachel knew Ana was being polite. She looked far worse than she sounded.

Rachel didn't try to cover up the dark circles under her eyes. Why bother when she'd probably just ruin the makeup with tears? "I just got back from Europe. Couldn't sleep on the plane."

"I never sleep on planes," Ana said. "Madison falls asleep within minutes, and I'm stuck there all wide-eyed for hours, so I understand your pain." She motioned to a sitting area with two chairs and a small coffee table. "Please, sit."

Kyle set a tray on the table with two glasses of water. Rachel took a sip. She noticed her hand was shaking as she brought the glass to her lips. She hoped Ana hadn't seen it. "I won't keep you long, but I need some advice."

Ana waved her off. "Don't worry about it. I'd love a chance to sit and relax for a minute. This baby is taking all of my energy and using it for himself."

"It's a boy?"

Ana's eyes lit up. "Antonio Madison Prescott. It sounds presidential, doesn't it?"

"This country should be so lucky."

"We're naming him after my grandfather," Ana said. "And of course, his mother."

"I'm so happy for you," Rachel said. "And I can't wait to meet him."

"I'd love for you to be there when he's born, to take the photos. I mean, if you're available on short notice next January."

"I already have it blocked off. And I'd be honored. Truly honored." Rachel gripped the glass with both hands to keep them from shaking. She should've eaten something when she got off the plane. Instead, she'd put Justin in a taxi along with all of the gear and taken a different cab straight to the Prescott building.

"Tell me what's going on," Ana said. "Oh, do you want Madison in here too?"

Rachel shook her head. "If you don't mind, I'd like to talk to you alone."

"Of course." Ana leaned in and put her hand on Rachel's knee. "Talk to me."

"Okay." Rachel took a deep breath. "You were so candid with me about what you went through with Madison. How happy you were together and how torn up you were when Madison suddenly ended it."

"I was. We'd been by each other's side since we were seven and eight years old, and then she was just gone from my life like a puff of smoke. Sometimes I wonder how I got through it."

"You also said you never really moved on."

"I didn't," Ana admitted. "Not really. Moving on would mean I'd found a way to love and trust someone else and build a life with them." She tilted her head. "What is this about?"

Rachel had gone there to talk about Lauren, but she found it very hard to say the words. Her emotions were so close to the surface, she felt as if she'd break down at any moment, and she didn't want that to happen.

"Rachel, you can talk to me," Ana said. "Kyle knows not to interrupt me when it's a personal visit."

Rachel nodded. "I don't really talk about this, but I need to." She took another deep breath. "Four years ago, my fiancée, who I was madly in love with, left me standing at the altar on our wedding day."

Ana covered her mouth with her hands. "My God."

"Yeah," Rachel said. "It was, by far, the worst day of my life, and I haven't been able to love or trust anyone since, which I've been fine with. Until now."

"What's changed?"

"I met someone very special. It's all there. The attraction. The chemistry. The need to know her on a deep level, except I already feel like I know her on a deep level. The desire to love her the way I know I'm capable of if only I'd let myself. When she's hurt, I feel it just as much if not more. Same thing when she's happy. I'm connected to her."

"Ah," Ana said. "As you know, I've been there."

Rachel laughed. "Hardcore."

Ana laughed too. "That's a great word for it."

"My heartbreak seems trivial compared to yours."

"No." Ana shook her head. "Pain is pain. It's not a contest. It was a defining moment for you."

"I thought I was a strong person," Rachel said. "I saw myself as being able to handle anything that came my way, but I wasn't strong enough for that."

"But you obviously were," Ana said. "You're still here. You've made a success of yourself, just like I did. You've pushed through the pain every day, just like I had to do. You can do this, Rach. You can take back your life and stop letting the past control you."

Rachel blinked back her tears. "I've been trying to figure out how to do that."

"It's a process," Ana said. "But you came here for some advice, so here it is. Take it slow. Pretend you're an upper-class New Yorker during the Victorian Era and court her. Let her court you. You don't have to give her your heart all at once. Give her a little bit and see how it feels. If she treats it with tender care, give her a little bit more. Do you have a picture of her? I need to know who this woman is."

"I have a few." Rachel set her glass on the table and took her phone out of her back pocket. "Many, actually." She handed the phone to Ana. "I don't know if you'll remember her, but she assisted me on your wedding day."

Ana looked at the photo. "I do remember her." She scrolled through a few more photos. "She's beautiful." Then a few more. "Rach?"

"Yeah?"

"I think you're already long gone."

Rachel smiled. "I couldn't stop thinking about her while I was in Europe."

Ana handed the phone back to her. "So, here's another piece of advice. If this goes somewhere, and you decide to get married, don't wait for her at the wedding altar. Walk together. If she's that special, she's worth fighting your demons for."

Rachel felt a sense of relief. "That's good advice."

Ana stood. "Do you mind if I tell Madison about this? I have a feeling she'll be pretty excited to hear someone has caught your eye." She laughed. "Now I sound like my mother."

"Totally tell Madison." Rachel stood and put her phone away. "And I think you're right. She's already caught more than just my eye."

Ana gave her a hug. "Keep me posted. And call if you need to talk. We're both here for you."

Rachel left Ana's office feeling as if a huge weight had been lifted from her shoulders. She looked at Kyle and said, "Your boss is awesome."

"Rachel?" Madison walked up to them. "What are you doing here?"

Rachel gave her a hug. "I needed advice from your amazing wife."

Madison held on to Rachel's shoulders. "Did you get what you needed?"

"I did. She'll tell you all about it."

"Okay. Ana's mom is cooking Saturday night. You should join us. Stay the night, even. We'd love the company."

"I'd like that."

Madison kept hold of her. "Are you okay, Rach? You look—"

"Tired, I know. We'll talk on Saturday."

❖

Monaghan's looked busy. From across the street, Veronica could see Harry behind the bar. She glanced at the small piece of paper Bea had jotted the information on.

Monaghan's—7 p.m.
Drink—Kir Royale with Veuve Clicquot if available

And that was it. No profile. Not even a name. She was pretty sure the drink choice was an expensive champagne you had to buy by the bottle. It probably wouldn't come in a cocktail with crème de cassis. Yeah, Veronica looked it up. Would Charlotte even have it in stock? "This better be good, Tiffany." She stepped off the sidewalk and crossed the street.

"Well, aren't you a sight for sore eyes." Harry rounded the bar and gave Veronica a hug. "We've missed you, girl."

He almost lifted her off her feet, he hugged her so hard. "Easy, Harry. Someone might think you have a thing for me."

"Agh, the cat's out of the bag. How are you, sweetie? I heard you finally got that partnership. Good for you."

Veronica shrugged. "Yeah, it worked out in the end."

"Well, look who's here." Charlotte gave her a hug as well.

"Wow," Veronica said. "I should come around more often. I thought for sure you'd all be relieved to be done with me and all my drama."

"Not a chance," Charlotte said. "You're family now, which means your drama is our drama."

"I'm really hoping for zero drama tonight. My cousin, Tiffany, set this one up, and she promised me it would be someone I'd like."

Charlotte looked over Veronica's shoulder. "Looks like your regular table is available."

"What can I make for you?" Harry asked. "And don't say diet soda."

"Not diet soda." Veronica handed him the piece of paper.

"Kir royal…with…" He squinted at it. "Voo…ev…"

Charlotte looked at it. "Kir Royale, Harry. With Veuve Clicquot. Wow. Someone's feeling fancy."

"Do you have it? If not, it's fine. We can order something else."

Charlotte gave her a wink. "I'll see what I can do."

Carol and Joe weren't in their usual spots. Veronica felt sad she wouldn't be able to say hello. She sat at the table and took her phone out of her purse. There was a message from Mack, asking if this weekend would be a good time to get out of the city and go hiking. She'd forgotten about Mack. Her answer would depend on how this date went, but at least she had hiking boots now.

"Hi."

Veronica saw the belt buckle first, then the eyes. "You're back."

"I am," Rachel said.

"I…I didn't expect to see you." Veronica wasn't sure if she should stand and give Rachel a hug or stay where she was. "How are you?" She opted to stay seated so her body wouldn't give away how nervous she'd just become.

"I'm pretty good." Rachel folded her arms. "How about you?"

"I'm…" Veronica needed a second. She clasped her hands together and looked at them instead of Rachel. "I'm good." She couldn't do this again. She couldn't be expected to carry on a decent conversation with this person Tiffany knew when Rachel was right there, looking like her gorgeous self. Maybe a little bit tanner. She must've gotten some sun in Europe. God, she looked so amazing.

"Here for a date?"

"Yeah." It came out squeaky. "Yeah," Veronica said, a little louder this time. "I don't…"

Rachel sat across from her. "You don't what?"

Where was that drink? "I don't know that much about her. Tiffany set it up."

"Ah. You realize Tiffany is terrible at setting people up, right?"

Veronica finally lifted her gaze. "Is she?"

"The worst. Awful record. Really, really bad. She once set me up with someone named Kelly. It was a dude."

"Shit." Veronica looked to see where Charlotte was. Maybe she had to run to the liquor store. "Shit," she whispered. She couldn't handle another awful date. Not tonight.

"I'm kidding. I have no idea if Tiffany is good at setups."

Veronica gritted her teeth. "Fucking…damnit, Monaghan! You had me all worked up. I was ready to run out of here."

Rachel laughed. "Sorry, not sorry."

Veronica shook her in disgust. "I hate you. I really, really hate you right now."

Rachel put her arms on the table and leaned in. "Do you? Or are you really thinking that you'd like to push me up against a wall and kiss the hell out of me right now?"

"I'm on a date, Monaghan."

"Ooh, I love it when you call me that."

"She's going to walk through that door any second, and now I'm a mess because of you."

"No," Rachel said. "You're perfect in every way."

Veronica shook her hands at the ceiling. "Gah!"

Charlotte set a wine bucket by the table and lifted the champagne bottle out of the ice. "Veuve Clicquot. Should I open it now?"

"No, it's supposed to be Kir Royale."

"You look like you could use a straight shot first. How about we worry about the mixed drinks later?"

"God, yes," Veronica said. "Thanks to your cousin, I'm a nervous wreck now."

"Rachel has that effect on people."

Rachel threw her hands in the air. "Hey! Where's the familial loyalty?"

"Never heard of it." Charlotte popped the cork into a bar towel and poured two glasses. "I have a good feeling about this one, V. She has great taste in champagne." She put the bottle back in the bucket. "Wave me down if you need anything else."

"Will do." Veronica took a sip and closed her eyes while the bubbles soothed her dry throat. She needed to relax so she could fully engage in the conversation with this stranger. And she needed Rachel to leave. She opened her eyes. "You're still here."

"Your date is late."

"Yeah, um, those two things don't really have anything to do with each other."

"Or…" Rachel took a sip of champagne.

Veronica gasped. "What the hell, Monaghan! Put that down, right now."

"Maybe…" Rachel took another sip.

"I swear to God, if you take one more sip."

"She's already here." Rachel set the glass down.

Veronica whipped her head around. "Where? Did you see her come in?"

"She's right here." Rachel pointed at herself. "I hope you're not too disappointed."

"What?" Veronica leaned in and whispered, "Are you fucking with me? I don't have time for this shit."

Rachel's expression turned serious. "I know I don't deserve this after the things I've done. However, I'd really like you to give me another chance."

Veronica needed more alcohol. She took a long sip and set the glass back down. "Let me get this straight. You and Tiffany decided to go all covert ops on me?"

"Don't be mad at Tiffany. I talked her into it."

"Oh my God! I'll never be able to trust another word that comes out of her mouth."

"No. Don't say that."

"She came into my office acting all casual. 'Hey, there's this woman I met. She's really hot. Like, smokin' hot.'" Veronica growled under her breath. "I'm so mad at her right now."

"And you hate me," Rachel said. "So, I guess this was a really bad idea."

"I don't hate you, Rach. I just wish you would've asked me yourself."

"Would you have said yes?"

"Is that something you needed to know up front?"

"I'd rather not crash and burn."

Veronica nodded. "Yeah, I've done that a few times. It's no fun."

"V?"

Rachel reached across the table with her palm up. Veronica just stared at it. All she could think about was the times she'd crashed and burned with Rachel. This could end up being another one of those times. She gave Rachel one finger to hold on to. "Yes?"

"Would you want to have a drink with me?"

Carol and Joe rushed in. They stopped and looked at Veronica, then went to their usual spot. It was strange that they didn't say hello or even wave at her. She watched them get settled on their stools and whisper something to Harry. "Only if Carol and Joe whisper the whole time while they watch us like hawks, and you don't have any surprise snake tattoos."

"It's a camera lens."

Veronica turned back to Rachel. "What?"

"My tattoo is a camera lens."

"Oh." Veronica couldn't wait to see it, but she didn't say that out loud. "Not a snake. That's good."

"V?"

"Yes?" Veronica uncurled her fingers and rested them on Rachel's.

"I've been a fool. Because you're the most amazing woman I've ever met, and I almost let you go. And right now, I'm so scared that you're going to steal my heart, and I'll never get it back."

"I'm not Lauren."

"I know. And the thing is, I'm even more scared that you've already stolen my heart, but you won't want to keep it. I might backslide from time to time, so I'll need you to hang on to me."

This didn't seem quite real. Veronica felt as if she was in *The Twilight Zone*. She'd gone there to meet a stranger, and she was sitting across from Rachel, holding her hand. "I need a minute. I'm so confused right now."

Rachel got up and stood in front of Veronica. She put out her hand. "Let me explain it to you."

Veronica took her hand and stood. She wanted to grab on to Rachel and bury her face in her neck and hold her until she got her bearings. Until she understood what this meant. Until she knew she didn't have to let go anymore.

Rachel held Veronica's face with both hands. "I realized in Italy that I'm deeply, madly in love with you. I mean, I started realizing it in Tahoe and before that, in Connecticut and before that, my apartment and before that, in this bar. And I've got to tell you, I kind of love the fact that our first date is in the place I fell in love with you."

Veronica took a deep breath. "So, this is a date?"

"Hell yes, it's a date. And if you'll give me another chance, I'll prove it to you every day for the rest of my life."

Veronica felt like laughing and crying at the same time. And she did. There was no stopping the tears or the joyful laughter. She gripped Rachel's shoulders. "Rach."

"V."

Veronica didn't have words for this moment. She touched Rachel's cheek and whispered, "Kiss me."

Veronica didn't expect to hear applause when her lips touched Rachel's, but she knew who was clapping. And whistling. And hollering, "It's about time!"

Harry was the one yelling, and she couldn't have agreed with him more.

❖

Veronica paid the driver and got out of the cab behind Rachel. "You didn't have to bring me home."

Rachel took her hand and led her to the door. "I wanted to." The doorman let them in, and they walked to the elevator.

"Are you sure you don't want to come up?"

"If I do, I won't leave," Rachel said.

Veronica wrapped her arms around Rachel's neck. "I wouldn't want you to."

Rachel leaned in for a light kiss. "I'd like you to be my date tomorrow night. I'm having dinner with Madison and Ana. What do you say?"

"I thought you'd never ask." Veronica put her hands on Rachel's face. "Is everything okay?"

"Everything is more than okay."

"You sure?"

"So sure," Rachel said. "I'm just struggling because my mind is telling me to take it slow with you, so you can have time to learn how to trust me. I know you need that. Or at least you should, considering what a mess I've been. But my body has other things to say about it."

"I see. That is a problem. Would it help if I made the decision for you?"

"I guess that depends on what your mind and body are telling you."

"They're not battling. But I don't want you to be torn the first time we make love."

"I like the way that sounds, making love."

"I can wait." Veronica took a step back. "I've waited for you this long, haven't I?"

"I don't deserve you."

"You do, Rach. Your heart is bruised, but it's not broken. And I'll be right here when you're ready."

CHAPTER EIGHTEEN

Laughter filled the dining room. Sitting across from Rachel was Madison's ex-husband, Scott, and next to him was Gary. They'd been dating for three months and seemed very happy. To her left was Veronica, and Madison sat at the head of the table. Carmen sat to Veronica's right, and Ana sat at the other end of the table.

Scott tapped his glass with his fork and cleared his throat. "I have a toast to make." Everyone picked up a glass. "Six out of seven of the people at this table are gay. That is, unless Carmen has failed to mention that she has a girlfriend waiting for her in the west wing."

All eyes went to Carmen. She shrugged. "I may or may not, but I'll tell you this. If I do, she's a hot little Latina with a pretty smile and big *chi-chis*."

Everyone laughed except Ana, who had a look of shock on her face. Scott could barely breathe, he was laughing so hard. Madison stood and held up her glass. "Not to take away from Scott's thunder or Carmen's. Good for you, Carmen. And honey, close your mouth."

Rachel leaned over and kissed Veronica's cheek. "Having fun?"

"This is the most fun I've had in a long time," Veronica whispered.

"Okay, is everyone good? Because this glass is getting heavy."

Scott wiped his eyes. "Go, Maddy."

Madison smiled. "I always start every toast by thanking my wife for marrying me." Ana blew her a kiss. "And Scott, when he's here with us, for giving me an uncontested divorce." Scott blew her a kiss as well. "And Carmen, for letting me sneak into her apartment to play with Ana when we were little. And for walking her down the aisle on the best day of my life. No offense, Scott."

"None taken," Scott said.

"And to our new friends, Rachel and Veronica, we hope you will grace our table often. Cheers, everyone."

Madison refilled everyone's wine glass, and Ana walked over to Rachel and leaned down. "Will you help me with dessert?"

Rachel followed Ana into the kitchen and stood at the island while she took a pie out of the oven. "Ooh, what kind is it?"

"Strawberry rhubarb," Ana said. "One of my mom's favorites. We also have chocolate cake because since I've been pregnant, I require that to be present in the house at all times."

"My kind of woman," Rachel said.

"She's lovely. Veronica. Madison really likes her too."

Rachel smiled. "She is lovely."

"Aww," Ana said. "Your face just lit up like the Fourth of July."

Rachel blushed. "Shh. I'm trying to play it cool. Slow, like you said."

"Which brings up a question. Do you want separate rooms tonight? I can put your bags wherever you want. Then I won't have to ask later and make everyone feel awkward."

"That's a good question."

"You can think about it," Ana said. "Just signal me once you've decided. In the meantime, take this pie to the table, and I'll be right behind you with cake and ice cream."

When Rachel had texted saying she needed to bring an overnight bag, Veronica wasn't sure what that meant. It had been less than twenty-four hours since their "blind date," and she was still floating a foot off the ground. With her head in the clouds, she didn't want to make assumptions or have any expectations, especially after their conversation last night.

She knew they would be going back to the Prescott estate, but would they stay there or go to a hotel? Either way, she was packing two sets of pajamas: something sexy and something practical.

As she stood in a bedroom with a beautiful four-poster bed and a sofa that faced the fireplace with a small log burning in it, she still wasn't sure what to think. Both of their bags were sitting at the end of the bed, but Rachel wasn't in the room yet.

Madison had brought Veronica to the room and wished her a pleasant evening. The bags were already here, so maybe they'd put one of them in the wrong room. She was about to go see if a fire was burning in the room across the hall when Rachel walked in, closing the door behind her. She held up a plate covered in plastic wrap. "I stole a piece of chocolate cake."

"Just one?"

Rachel set it on a side table. "Unlike you, I share."

"Pancakes are sacred. Food of the gods. Breakfast of champions. And the only thing I ever put butter on."

Rachel furrowed her brow. "What about baked potatoes?"

"Sour cream."

"Corn on the cob?"

"I eat that maybe once a year."

Rachel wrapped her arms around Veronica's waist. "Toast? Bagels? Cornbread?" She leaned in and kissed Veronica's neck, right below her ear. Right on the spot that drove her crazy.

"Jam, cream cheese, and again, I hardly ever eat cornbr...Rach." Veronica had goose bumps all over her body. Rachel switched to the other side, and Veronica whispered through bated breath, "Oh God."

Rachel stopped suddenly. She pulled back and looked Veronica in the eye. "I just realized I didn't give you a choice."

"What?" Veronica could barely think. Rachel's lips on her neck had made her feel weak in the knees and slightly dizzy. Rachel let go of her and stepped back. "Oh God," Veronica said. "Not again." She put one hand on her hip and the other on her forehead. "You're going to kill me, Rachel."

"I'm sorry. It's just that Ana asked me if we wanted one room or two, and I made the decision without you."

"Okay. Why did you choose one room?"

"Because I couldn't stand the thought of being without you for even one second."

Veronica gave her a nod. "Okay. That's a good answer."

"What would you have chosen?"

"Rach, don't you know? How many times do I have to throw myself at you for you to realize I..." Veronica turned away from her.

She didn't want to cry. "You're right. We should go slow." She grabbed her bag. "I'm going to put on my pajamas."

Veronica had almost just admitted that she'd already fallen in love with Rachel. She leaned on the sink and looked at herself in the mirror. "Calm down," she whispered. But she didn't want to calm down. She wanted to go back out there and tell the truth, come what may.

She opened the door and found Rachel standing by the fire. "I don't care what your reason was for stopping us just now."

Rachel took a step toward her. "V."

Veronica put up her hand. "No. I need to say this. I'm in love with you, Rachel. I want you in every way I can have you, but not if you still don't trust me."

"I do trust you, V."

"I don't think you do, which is kind of too bad because damn, this room is romantic." Veronica went to the window. "There's even a full moon. And is that a horse out there?"

Rachel stood behind her. "Those are the stables. Madison and Ana both ride."

"Being in this mansion, it almost feels like we've gone back in time."

Rachel wrapped her arms around Veronica's waist. "I'd like to go back ten minutes."

Veronica rested her hands on Rachel's. "What would you do differently?"

"Can I show you?"

Veronica turned around. "Show me?"

"Yes." Rachel took her hand. "You were standing about right here." She grabbed the cake off the side table. "Don't move."

Veronica pursed her lips together to keep from laughing. Was Rachel really going to walk out and come back in? Yep, she was. Veronica tried to compose herself before Rachel came back in.

Rachel opened the door and closed it behind her. "I stole a piece of cake."

Veronica remembered her line. "Just one?"

Rachel set the cake on the side table. "I thought I would feed it to you later."

"No one's ever fed me chocolate cake before."

"Ah. Well, I hope we have a lot of firsts together."

"Such as?"

"Such as…" Rachel moved closer but still kept a few feet between them. "The first time we make love in this room."

Veronica smiled. "I like that one."

Rachel took her hand and brought it to her lips. "The first time I say the words 'I love you, Veronica Welch.'"

"Since when?"

"Hmm. I can't decide if it was when you choked on a piña colada or got drunk on Jägerbombs."

"Oh God." Veronica covered her eyes with her hand. "Will I ever live that down?"

Rachel took both of Veronica's hands and held them to her chest. "I hope we'll still laugh about it ten years from now."

"Is that what your Spidey sense tells you? That we'll still be together ten years from now?"

"V."

"Yes?"

"Once I get you, I'm never letting you go," Rachel said.

"Well, I have news for you, you've already got me." Rachel picked her up off the ground and spun her around. "What are you doing?"

"Another first." She set Veronica back down and held her face. "That was the first time you made me so happy, I had to pick you up and spin you around."

"And this is the first time I say I love you too."

"I'm going to kiss you again."

"And then what?"

"Then I'm going to—"

Veronica put her hand over Rachel's mouth. "Wait." Rachel's eyes widened. "I just need a minute. I brought something pretty to wear."

"Oh," Rachel said. "Well, don't let me keep you." She turned Veronica toward the bathroom. "God, I'm a lucky woman."

Veronica got to the door and turned back. "Or I could wear my Hello Kitty pj's."

Rachel clutched her chest. "My life will never be the same."

"What did you just say?"

"My life. I said my life will never be the same. You know, because of Hello Kitty."

"I have Wonder Woman too. And Snoopy."

"You're adorable, Veronica Welch. Hey, I just realized your initials are VW. I think I'll call you Bug."

"If you're going for firsts, you'll have to come up with something more original than that."

Veronica closed the door and stood against it for a moment. This was really happening. It felt like a dream, being in this old mansion with Rachel. She tried to imagine herself with anyone else—Avery. Lauren. Any of the women she'd met in the bar. No. This only felt magical because it was Rachel out there, waiting for her. "My future," she whispered.

She pushed off the door and stripped down to nothing. The little ensemble she'd brought was something she'd never worn before. While buying a new bra, she saw it on the mannequin and bought it on a whim. She held up the white teddy, but it felt like too many layers, so she decided to just go with the silk robe and matching thong.

She tucked her hair behind her ears and stood at the door. A part of her expected to walk out into the bedroom and find it empty. Would it be that big a surprise after what they'd been through? Rachel had all of the right words, but were they just…words? Was she really ready to open her heart and let Veronica live in it?

She took a deep breath and opened the door. She exhaled when she saw Rachel standing there in a T-shirt and those cute sloth pajama bottoms. "It's all I brought," Rachel said.

"I've never been so glad to see a sloth in my life." Veronica walked to her.

"I don't know what that means, but I strongly approve of this." Rachel motioned up and down Veronica's body. "You're gorgeous, V."

Veronica stopped and leaned her hip on the back of the sofa. "I wasn't sure you'd still be here. I'm glad you are."

"Think what I would've missed." Rachel stepped up to her. "I mean, my God." She ran her hand from Veronica's shoulder down to her hand. "This will be the first time I untie your robe and let it fall from your shoulders."

Veronica shivered at the thought. Rachel's gaze fell to her hardened nipples, which she was sure were visible through the light fabric. "I should confess that your voice really turns me on. I hope you're the talkative type in bed."

Rachel grinned. "I like your honesty."

Veronica tucked her finger into Rachel's pajama bottoms and pulled her closer. She ran her other finger over Rachel's bottom lip. "I will always tell you what I want. And right now, I want your tongue." She slid her hand behind Rachel's neck and pulled her into a not-so-subtle kiss. She let her tongue dance against Rachel's, then took it between her lips and sucked on it.

Rachel moaned and took control of the kiss while her hands slid down Veronica's sides and under the robe. She squeezed Veronica's bare ass and whispered, "Oh my God."

Veronica could hardly breathe, she was so turned on already. She found the hem of Rachel's T-shirt and lifted it over her head. She tossed it aside and put her palms on Rachel's stomach. Her mouth watered at the sight of pert breasts slightly smaller than her own. "You're perfect," she whispered.

Emotions bubbled to the surface as Veronica cupped Rachel's breasts and circled her nipples with her thumbs. It seemed as if they'd gotten past a point of no return, and that made her want to cry. Because this was real, and they weren't stopping.

"Are you okay?" Rachel asked.

"You're so beautiful, and I can't believe this is happening."

Rachel lifted Veronica's chin with her finger. "Turn around."

Veronica turned away. She felt Rachel move her hair to the side. She kissed her neck and reached around with one hand to untie the robe. Veronica leaned back against her and let the robe fall open.

Rachel pulled the robe off one shoulder and kissed and sucked, then did the same thing on the other side. There was a dressing mirror across the room from them. Rachel hadn't realized it yet, but Veronica was watching her, and God, it was turning her on.

Rachel pushed the robe down a little farther and held it in place on Veronica's arms. She was about to kiss her neck when their eyes met in the mirror. Rachel went still and stared for a long moment. The robe was open and barely covering Veronica's breasts. She felt exposed, but the intensity in Rachel's eyes told her she liked what she saw.

"Sorry it took me so long," Rachel said.

"Is this where you make it up to me?" Veronica gave her robe a little tug and let it fall away from her right breast. The flickering light from the fireplace danced across her skin. Rachel's grip on her arms tightened, and it felt perfect. Veronica wanted Rachel to be in control.

She wanted to be taken by her. She wanted to get lost in the moment and forget about the times they'd come close only to be left unsatisfied.

Rachel loosened her grip on the robe and let it fall to the floor. She untied her own pajamas and let them fall to the floor as well. The only thing covering Veronica was a skimpy white thong, and the only thing covering Rachel was Veronica.

They continued to stare at one another in the mirror. Rachel rested her hands on Veronica's bare waist, and said, "You're absolutely stunning."

Veronica's skin tingled under Rachel's touch. Her heart raced. Watching themselves in the mirror like this was possibly the sexiest thing she'd ever done. Rachel moved Veronica's hair to the side and kissed her neck.

Her eyes shuddered closed for a moment when Rachel's tongue caressed her ear. She opened them again as Rachel's arm slid around her waist and held her close. It was everything, this feeling. Rachel's strong arms holding her as if she'd never let her go. Her warm breasts pressed against Veronica's back. She needed more, but she didn't want to rush. She wanted to savor the feeling of Rachel's lips and tongue on her body. She wanted to remember the fire that burned between them.

Veronica reached back and slid her fingers into Rachel's hair. Her chest heaved as Rachel sucked hard enough to leave a mark on Veronica's shoulder. She turned and whispered, "Touch me, Rach."

Their eyes met in the mirror again. Rachel slid her hand up to Veronica's breast. She cupped it and kneaded it, then rolled her nipple between her fingers. Veronica felt a white-hot heat build between her legs.

Rachel did the same with the other breast and held them both in her hands. Veronica could feel Rachel's chest heaving against her. "I need to take those panties off," Rachel said. "I need to see all of you."

Veronica took Rachel's hands from her breasts. "Let me do it," she said. "You can watch." She felt emboldened and wanted to give Rachel a sexy memory of her own, so she tucked her thumbs under the elastic sides and pushed the thong down, but only an inch.

She pushed the thong down a little more while Rachel watched with an intense stare. She slid it down just enough so the top of her bare pussy was visible. Rachel lifted an eyebrow and licked her lips.

It was the reaction Veronica had hoped for. She slid the thong all the way down and let it drop to the floor. Rachel wrapped her arms around her waist. They stood like that for a moment, looking at each other in the mirror. Veronica felt silly even thinking it, but this was the first time she'd been turned on by her own body. Maybe it was the warm light from the fire or the way Rachel held on to her with such strength. Whatever it was, Veronica loved the image she saw and found herself wishing she could snap a photo.

Rachel whispered in Veronica's ear, "Watching in the mirror is off the charts."

Veronica nodded. "Uh-huh."

"I want to watch you like this while you come." Rachel moved her hand lower, over Veronica's abdomen. Her fingers teased just above her pussy. "I can't wait another second to touch you."

Rachel slid her middle finger into Veronica's folds. "You're so wet," she whispered.

"I've been wet for weeks. Oh God." Veronica writhed under Rachel's touch. "So many times, I've imagined having your hands on my body, touching me like this."

"You're so sexy. So fucking beautiful. Your pussy is so soft and wet. Keep your eyes open."

Veronica's hips bucked with every stroke of Rachel's finger. She tried to keep her eyes open, but she just wanted to throw her head back on Rachel's shoulder and let her whisper dirty things in her ear.

"Do you want me inside you, V?"

Veronica moaned. "Oh God, yes."

"Not yet."

Veronica put her hand on Rachel's and increased the pressure on her clit. They worked together to bring her to the edge of a climax while they watched themselves in the mirror. Veronica's nipples hardened as she got closer and closer to a climax.

"Are you almost there?" Rachel asked.

"So close." Veronica gasped as every muscle in her body tightened. "Oh God!" She reached back and grabbed Rachel's hair as she came in an intense wave that made her knees buckle.

Rachel held her tightly and didn't let her drop to the floor. After a few seconds, she whispered, "V, look how beautiful you are right after you come."

Veronica opened her eyes. Her face was flushed, and her skin glistened with sweat. She'd never seen herself in this state of satedness before. She looked relaxed. She looked as if she was in love.

Rachel loosened her grip and kissed Veronica's cheek. "God, that was hot."

"Whew…the mirror…" Veronica smiled. "That was another first."

❖

Rachel watched the rise and fall of Veronica's chest as she slept, just like she'd done in Lake Tahoe. This time was so much better. Mostly because Veronica was naked, and her breasts were only half-covered by the sheet. But also because of the sense of contentment Rachel felt. The fear and trepidation had been replaced by a feeling that she was right where she was supposed to be.

After they'd made love in front of the mirror, they'd crawled between the soft sheets, wrapped themselves around each other, and fallen asleep almost immediately. That wasn't like Rachel. The women she'd been with since Lauren were welcome in her bed while they had sex, but afterward, it felt awkward, and Rachel was usually relieved if they said they couldn't spend the night.

She wasn't sure what had awoken her. The fire had burned out, and it was still dark outside. She missed the fire. It warmed up the room and created an atmosphere that seemed perfect for their first night together. There were still a few embers burning under the ashes, so she got out of bed and tiptoed over to the fireplace and put some kindling down along with two small logs. She leaned over and put her hands near the embers to warm them.

"Nice view," Veronica said.

Rachel turned around. "I didn't mean to wake you. I just wanted to get the fire going again."

Veronica patted the spot next to her. "Yeah, I want that too. Get back here."

Rachel decided to slowly saunter back to the bed. "You're not talking about the logs, are you?"

"Legs, Rach. I'm talking about having your legs wrapped around me while I tongue kiss the hell out of you."

Rachel grinned. "And then what?"

Veronica got up on her knees and moved to the edge of the bed.

"And then I want to run that same tongue that just kissed the hell out of you down to your left nipple."

"Not the right one?" Rachel stood at the edge of the bed and let her eyes rake over Veronica's body.

"Focus."

Rachel cleared her throat and made eye contact. "Right. I'm with ya. Left nipple."

Veronica slung her arms over Rachel's shoulders. "And the right one. Don't leave out the right one."

Rachel shook her head. "Never. Both nipples. Then what?"

"Then comes the really good part." Veronica ran her finger down Rachel's stomach. "That same tongue that just devoured your nipples is going to spend a long time getting to know other parts of you."

Rachel wrapped her arms around Veronica and squeezed her ass. "Any parts in particular?"

Veronica leaned in and took Rachel's bottom lip in between her teeth and sucked on it. "All the parts."

Rachel felt a jolt of electricity shoot through her. She wrapped a hand around the back of Veronica's neck and kissed her deeply. Their tongues danced and fought for dominance while Veronica backed up, and Rachel got on the bed, also on her knees.

"Lie down," Veronica said.

Rachel lay in the spot where she had just been sleeping. Veronica straddled her and rested her hands on her stomach. Rachel reached up and caressed Veronica's breast. "You are a sight to behold, Veronica Welch."

"Will you still love me like this when I'm old and my boobs are down here?" Veronica pointed at her belly button.

"Will you still do what I know you're about to do when I'm old and gray and have whiskers growing out of my chin?"

Veronica giggled. "You'll still want me to go down on you when you have to wear bifocals?"

Despite what people believed, Rachel had been a big believer in happily-ever-afters. At the weddings she shot, it always put a smile on her face when the elderly men and women of the families would give the couples advice on how to make love last. She'd heard the typical stuff. Things like *say you're sorry every day, even if you aren't*. Or *never go to bed angry at one another*.

There was the advice she laughed at and the newly married couple usually cringed at—the advice about sex. One grandmother of the bride said *Don't ever stop having sex, even if it takes a lot longer*. Another said *Worship each other's wrinkles the way you used to worship their smooth skin. Find the beauty in every phase of your partner's life, and they'll always desire your touch.*

And then there were the people who belonged together. The ones Veronica would say perked up Rachel's Spidey sense. They said things like *Give her the best of you. Some people save their best selves for just about everyone else. Those people are doing it wrong.*

Rachel was ready to have that kind of love, and she was ready to have it with Veronica. She reached up and ran her hands over Veronica's hair. "That's the dream, isn't it? A forever love?"

Veronica laid her head on Rachel's chest. "I'm in if you're in."

Rachel wrapped her arms around Veronica and kissed her head. "I'm in, babe. I'm so in."

CHAPTER NINETEEN

"My parents are freaking out." Rachel pulled her overnight bag out of the luggage bin. When they'd landed in Rochester, she'd taken her phone out of airplane mode and had several texts waiting to be read.

"Why?" Veronica stood and straightened her heavily starched white shirt under her navy-blue cardigan. "Do I look too stuffy?"

Rachel leaned in for a kiss. "You look perfect, honey." Rachel loved it when Veronica left her dress shirt untucked and put a tight sweater over it. So sexy. "My mom is freaking out because we've only been dating a few months and I'm bringing you home. Also, she never thinks her house looks good enough for company, so a well-timed compliment would probably be a good idea. I promise I'll make it worth your while."

"Well, I'm sure as hell not going to turn down an offer like that. And if it prevents the freak-out, even better."

"Oh, that's just my mom's freak-out." Rachel gave her a playful swat on the butt. "My dad is freaking out because after the awful wedding that wasn't, he'd rather I never dated again."

"Can't blame him," Veronica said. "It must've been awful for both of your parents to see you get hurt like that."

They walked up the ramp and entered the airport. Rachel took Veronica's hand. It was a last-minute trip that she'd managed to fit in between two weddings she was shooting. She could've waited until mid-September to introduce Veronica to her parents, but she was so happy and in love, she couldn't wait another second to take this next step. "I'd really like to send Lauren a thank-you card."

Veronica's eyebrows shot up. "For what?"

"For dumping me so that four years later, I could meet the most amazing, sexy, smart, passionate woman on planet Earth."

Veronica let go of Rachel's hand and wrapped her arm around her waist. "Can I sign the card too?"

Rachel led Veronica to the side, out of the passenger traffic. "This is real, right? We're really going to do this?"

Veronica smiled. "It looks like we already are." She took Rachel's hand. "Let's go meet the parents."

❖

Tom and Hannah Monaghan were lovely, warm people. They'd both greeted Veronica with a hug and kind words. She stood in the living room of their quaint home, looking at family photos. It was obvious they were proud of their daughter and two sons, just like Veronica's parents were proud of her. The same grade-school pictures adorned their walls, along with photos of family vacations.

Hannah walked into the room. "Dinner won't be long now." She stood next to Veronica. "Wasn't Rachel a cute kid? Such a little tomboy who insisted on keeping up with her brothers." She leaned in. "The truth is, she could outsmart both of them and win any eating contest they would start. I don't mention that last part to most people."

They both laughed, and Veronica said, "You have a lovely home, Hannah. Very warm and inviting."

Tom and Rachel walked in. "Are you embarrassing me, Mom?"

"Your mother would never do that," Tom said firmly. "That's my job. It's only right that Veronica knows what she's getting herself into."

A sense of joy welled up inside Veronica as she watched Rachel and her dad pretend to spar. Tom pulled Rachel into his arms and kissed her head. "The truth is, Veronica, Hannah and I could tell you all kinds of embarrassing stories about our girl. But what we'd rather do is tell you all the good things about her and hope with all our hearts that you'll take good care of hers."

Veronica looked to the future and imagined her and Rachel bringing their kids here for Thanksgiving or Christmas. She imagined Tom getting down on the floor and letting them climb all over him. She imagined Hannah spoiling them with what Rachel described as "the best banana cream pie you'll ever taste."

She imagined both sets of parents being there for special moments in their kids' lives and how well they'd all get along together.

If felt so right, being in their home. She caught Rachel's eye and said, "Tom, I think I already know all of the good things about your daughter, but since my parents told every embarrassing story they could possibly think of the first time Rachel sat at their dinner table, I think it's only fair you do the same."

Rachel grinned. "I'm especially fond of the story forever known as that time in high school when you debated capital punishment with your shirt on inside out."

Hannah threw her hand over her mouth. "Oh no."

"I think it should be noted that I still won the debate," Veronica said.

"We can top that," Tom said. "Over Hannah's famous twice-baked potatoes and my not so famous but still very delicious grilled rib eyes. But first, let me show off my bartending skills."

"Dad helped Uncle John open Monaghan's back in the day," Rachel said.

"And that means I know how to keep a bar fully stocked for company," Tom said. "What's your pleasure, V?"

From the corner of her eye, Veronica could see Rachel stiffen. She'd spent the past three months trying to guess her drink of choice. It had become a running joke between them, but they usually just shared a bottle of wine when they went out. Rachel's wide-eyed expectant look made Veronica want to giggle. "I'm an old-fashioned kind of girl, Tom."

"One old fashioned, coming right up."

"Hey, I guessed that one!" Rachel exclaimed.

Tom froze. "Am I missing something?"

"Rachel's been trying to guess my drink since the day we met." She glanced at Rachel. "And no, honey, it's not an old fashioned." Turning back to Tom, Veronica said, "What I meant was that it's an old-fashioned type of drink. Passed down from my grandmother, actually."

"Ah, let me think." Tom rubbed his chin. "You don't seem like a scotch kind of girl. And definitely nothing straight up. From what my daughter says, straight is definitely not your thing." Tom laughed at his own joke.

"Oh God," Rachel groaned. "You're not going to get it, Dad. I've been at this for months, and I think I know her just a little better than you do."

"Let me think, sweetie." Tom motioned with his hand, suggesting Rachel should shush. Her turned back to Veronica. "A daiquiri is too sweet. Not that you aren't sweet, but you'd drink a grown-up drink. Something classy."

Rachel sighed.

"A gimlet," Tom said definitively.

Veronica smiled. "With Tanqueray, if you have it."

Rachel threw her hands in the air. "Is somebody frigging kidding me?"

Tom winked at her as he trotted off to the bar. "Try to keep up, baby girl."

Rachel stood next to her mom at the kitchen sink. She glanced at Veronica and her dad setting up the Scrabble board on the game table in the family room. "What do you think?"

Her mom leaned in and whispered, "I love her."

"Yeah, me too. Dad and V seem to have really hit it off."

"He had his concerns, but I think V has won him over."

"What concerns?"

"About you getting your heart broken again."

"It's worth it."

Her mom took her hands out of the soapy water and dried them. "What do you mean?"

"I mean, even if I get my heart broken again, being in V's world, loving her the way I do, that's not something I'd trade away to avoid a little pain."

"I feel like Garth Brooks wrote a song about this," her mom said.

"I'm sure lots of songs have been written about this. I'm not the first to realize that sometimes a person will come along and change everything you thought you knew."

Her mom opened her arms. "Let me know when I should start preparing for a wedding."

Rachel leaned in for the hug and whispered, "You'll be the first to know."

❖

"This was your room?" Veronica set her bag on the double bed. "Where are all of your trophies?"

Rachel closed the door behind them. "My room wasn't frozen in time like yours. They boxed up all of my high school crap and put it in the attic."

"Or maybe you lied about all of those basketball trophies you got." Veronica backed up until her legs hit the edge of the bed.

"You won them over," Rachel said.

"Changing the subject? I want proof that I'm really dating an MVP."

Rachel wrapped her arms around Veronica's waist. "You're dating a VIP."

"Oh, that much I know." Veronica leaned in for a kiss. "Wedding photographer to the rich and famous."

"I meant that I hope I'm *your* VIP."

Veronica cupped Rachel's cheeks with her hands. "Honey, why do I see doubt in your eyes?"

Rachel shook her head. "It's nothing. Just a conversation I had with my mom made me realize that even if we don't work out, I won't regret you, V. The last three months have been amazing."

Veronica pulled Rachel's shirt over her head. "If we're breaking up soon, I need to see you naked one more time."

"What? I didn't say we're breaking up. And besides, we're not having sex in my parents' house."

"Not ever? Or just not tonight? Because I think for future reference, I should know what the sex parameters are."

"Fine." Rachel put up a finger. "Wait. Can you take me seriously without my shirt on? Because what I'm about to say is super important."

Veronica gave her a big nod. "Oh, yeah. We'll call it titty talk."

"Oh my God." Rachel put her hands on her hips and giggled. "You always make me laugh at least once a day."

"It should become a thing between us. When you have something important to say, you'll take off your shirt, and I'll listen intently while ogling your breasts."

Rachel took a step closer and unbuttoned Veronica's cardigan. "I was going to list all of the places we wouldn't ever have sex, starting with our parents' homes, but I think I just changed my mind."

"Oh, good. Because I really think this thing between us might work out."

Rachel unbuttoned Veronica's shirt. "Oh, yeah?"

"Yeah. And what if we're here for Christmas or something, and I need it?"

"Need what?"

"You. All over me. Inside me."

Rachel urged Veronica onto the bed and kneeled over her. She kissed one side of her neck, then the other. "I think it's going to work out too."

"A gimlet?" Charlotte shook her head. "I never would've guessed."

Harry pulled the cocktail recipe book Rachel had shown him out from under the counter. "I need to brush up on my gimlet-making skills."

"It's easy, Harry. Gin and lime juice," Joe said. "Not my cup of tea."

"Oh, I bet I'd like it," Carol said. "Make me one, Harry." She turned to Rachel. "Sit and tell us all about it."

"Yeah," Charlotte said. "Stop holding out on us. Did they like her or what?"

Rachel loved their enthusiasm. Charlotte was family, but Harry, Carol, and Joe also felt like family to her. She put her bag on the barstool next to her and sat. "They loved her."

"Of course they did," Carol said. "V is a special woman. Someone just needed to wake up and smell the roses."

"I'm lucky I wasn't too late, aren't I?"

Carol gave Rachel her best mom look. "Damn right you are."

Harry set the drink on a napkin in front of Carol. "Be kind to an old man."

Carol took a sip and then another. She looked at Rachel. "Your lady has good taste."

"I'm calling Veronica *Gimlet* from now on," Joe said. "It suits her."

Charlotte set a diet soda in front of Rachel. "Where's Gimlet?"

Rachel glanced at her bag. It was unintentional, subconscious even, but a glance nonetheless. "I had to run an errand. Without her."

Charlotte raised an eyebrow. "What's in the bag?"

They all stared at her, waiting for an answer. She put up her hands. "It was an impulse buy."

"Those are the best kind," Carol said.

Rachel's hands started to shake. "I don't know when or if or how or any of that stuff. I just saw it in the window, and it called to me—"

"Honey, what called to you?" Carol looked concerned.

"Oh God. I don't even know how I'm supposed to know what her size is," Rachel babbled. "I just know it's the right one for whenever the time comes. I mean, at least, I think it is. Jesus. How am I supposed to know if it's right?"

Joe flashed a sizable grin. "Rachel Monaghan, if I didn't know better, I'd say you're in the middle of engagement ring insecurity."

Carol gasped. Harry had a twinkle in his eye. And Charlotte ran around the bar and put out her hand. "Cough it up. I'll tell you if it suits her."

"I just might keep it in my safe for a year," Rachel said.

Charlotte waggled her fingers. "Give it to me."

Rachel dug to the bottom of her bag and pulled out a black velvet box. Charlotte took it and ran around the bar again. She leaned on the bar so Carol and Joe could see it too. Harry looked over her shoulder.

Rachel waited for the oohs and ahs, but they all just stared at the ring. Finally, Charlotte said, "It's okay."

"Okay? What do you mean, okay?" Rachel got off her stool and stood behind Carol and Joe.

"It's pretty," Joe said in an unconvincing tone.

"It's the sentiment that counts," Carol said.

"The sentiment?" Rachel leaned in and looked at the ring. She thought an emerald-cut diamond set in platinum would look gorgeous on Veronica's slender finger. She felt Carol's shoulder shake next to her. "Oh my God, you all are fucking with me!"

They all burst out laughing. Carol wrapped her arms around Rachel. "It's stunning, Rachel. She'll love it."

Charlotte ran around the bar one more time and gave Rachel a hug. "I'm so happy for you." Then she slugged Rachel's shoulder. "But you're not keeping it in your safe for a whole year." She handed the box back to her and motioned with her head toward the door. "Heads up! Gimlet's here."

Joe picked up his phone and pretended to talk. Carol took a large sip of her gimlet, and Harry found a nonexistent dirty spot on the bar he needed to wipe away.

"Hey, guys." Veronica put her purse on the bar. "Who's glad it's Friday?" She smiled at Rachel and said, "Hey, babe."

Rachel's tummy did a tumble at the first sight of Veronica. That wasn't unusual. It happened every time she walked out of her apartment building and got in Rachel's car. It happened when they'd meet at what had become their favorite coffee shop. Rachel would see Veronica walking toward her, and she'd get all starry eyed and week in the knees. She was over the moon in love with Veronica Welch.

"We should go out tomorrow night." Rachel glanced at everyone. They were watching like hungry hawks. "Someplace nice. Maybe get some of that champagne we had on our first date?"

Carol clapped her hands. "Date night!"

Harry winked at Rachel. And Joe, who in all his years on this earth had yet to learn the art of subtlety, got choked up and said, "Aw, Gimlet." He tried to cover it up by putting a napkin over his mouth. "Sorry. Got a nut stuck in my throat."

Charlotte grinned and turned away from them. Veronica seemed to be unfazed, but Rachel felt a blush work its way up her chest. If she felt this way now, how would she feel tomorrow night when she'd have to say the words *Will you marry me?* But the second Veronica walked into the bar just now, Rachel knew that waiting another month or week or even a day felt too long.

Veronica hadn't replied to Rachel's idea. She was focused on Joe. It was only when he pulled himself together after his fake coughing attack that Veronica turned to her and said, "I'd love to." She wrapped her arm around Rachel's shoulder and leaned in. "Did Joe just call me Gimlet?"

Rachel cleared her throat. "I may have mentioned something."

"Ah." Veronica leaned in closer and whispered, "You'll pay for that later."

About the Author

Elle Spencer (http://ellespencerbooks.com) is the author of several best-selling lesbian romances, including *Casting Lacey*, a Goldie finalist. She is a hopeless romantic and firm believer in true love, although she knows the path to happily ever after is rarely an easy one—not for Elle and not for her characters.

When she's not writing, Elle loves working on home improvement projects, hiking up tall mountains (not really, but it sounds cool), floating in the pool with a good book, and spending quality time with her pillow in a never-ending quest to prove that napping is the new working.

Elle grew up in Denver, and she and her wife now live in Southern California.

Books Available From Bold Strokes Books

30 Dates in 30 Days by Elle Spencer. In this sophisticated contemporary romance, Veronica Welch is a busy lawyer who tries to find love the fast way—thirty dates in thirty days. (978-1-63555-498-4)

Finding Sky by Cass Sellars. Skylar Addison's search for a career intersects with her new boss's search for butterflies, but Skylar can't forgive Jess's intrusion into her life. Romance is the last thing they expect. (978-1-63555-521-9)

Hammers, Strings, and Beautiful Things by Morgan Lee Miller. While on tour with the biggest pop star in the world, rising musician Blair Bennett falls in love for the first time while coping with loss and depression. (978-1-63555-538-7)

Heart of a Killer by Yolanda Wallace. Contract killer Santana Masters's only interest is her next assignment—until a chance meeting with a beautiful stranger tempts her to change her ways. (978-1-63555-547-9)

Leading the Witness by Carsen Taite. When defense attorney Catherine Landauer reluctantly becomes the key witness in prosecutor Starr Rio's latest criminal trial, their hearts, careers, and lives may be at risk. (978-1-63555-512-7)

No Experience Required by Kimberly Cooper Griffin. Izzy Treadway has resigned herself to a life without romance because of her bipolar illness but wonders what she's gotten herself into when she agrees to write a book about love. (978-1-63555-561-5)

One Walk in Winter by Georgia Beers. Olivia Santini and Hayley Boyd Markham might be rivals at work, but they discover that lonely hearts often find company in the most unexpected of places. (978-1-63555-541-7)

The Inn at Netherfield Green by Aurora Rey. Advertising executive Lauren Montgomery and gin distiller Camden Crawley don't agree on anything except saving the Rose & Crown, the old English pub that's brought them together. (978-1-63555-445-8)

Top of Her Game by M. Ullrich. When it comes to life on the field and matters of the heart, losing isn't an option for pro athletes Kenzie Shaw and Sutton Flores. (978-1-63555-500-4)

Vanished by Eden Darry. First came the storm, and then the blinding white light that made everyone in town disappear. Another storm is coming, and Ellery and Loveday must find the chosen one or they won't survive. (978-1-63555-437-3)

All She Wants by Larkin Rose. Marci Jones and Tessa Dalton get more than they bargained for when their plans for a one-night stand turn into an opportunity for love. (978-1-63555-476-2)

Beautiful Accidents by Erin Zak. Stevie Adams doesn't believe in fate, not after losing her parents in a car crash. But she's about to discover that sometimes the best things in life happen purely by accident. (978-1-63555-497-7)

Before Now by Joy Argento. The instant Delaney Peyton and Jade Taylor meet, they sense a connection neither can explain. Can they overcome a betrayal that spans the centuries to reignite a love that can't be broken? (978-1-63555-525-7)

Breathe by Cari Hunter. Paramedic Jemima Pardon's chronic bad luck seems to be improving when she meets police officer Rosie Jones. But they face a battle to survive before they can find love. (978-1-63555-523-3)

Double-Crossed by Ali Vali. Hired thief and killer Reed Gable finds something in her scope that will change her life forever when she gets a contract to end casino accountant Brinley Myers's life. (978-1-63555-302-4)

False Horizons by CJ Birch. Jordan and Ash struggle with different views on the alien agenda and must find their way back to each other before they're swallowed up by a centuries-old war. Third in the New Horizons series. (978-1-63555-519-6)

Legacy by Charlotte Greene. In this paranormal mystery, five women hike to a remote cabin deep inside a national park—and unsettling events suggest that they should have stayed home. (978-1-63555-490-8)

Somewhere Along the Way by Kathleen Knowles. When Maxine Cooper moves to San Francisco during the summer of 1981, she learns that wherever you run, you cannot escape yourself. (978-1-63555-383-3)

Blood of the Pack by Jenny Frame. When Alpha of the Scottish pack Kenrick Wulver visits the Wolfgangs, she falls for Zaria Lupa, a wolf on the run. (978-1-63555-431-1)

Cause of Death by Sheri Lewis Wohl. Medical student Vi Akiak and K9 Search and Rescue officer Kate Renard must work together to find a killer before they end up the next targets. In the race for survival, they discover that love may be the biggest risk of all. (978-1-63555-441-0)

Chasing Sunset by Missouri Vaun. Hijinks and mishaps ensue as Iris and Finn set off on a road trip adventure, chasing the sunset, and falling in love along the way. (978-1-63555-454-0)

Double Down by MB Austin. When an unlikely friendship with Spanish pop star Erlea turns deeper, Celeste, in-house physician for the hotel hosting Erlea's show, has a choice to make—run or double down on love. (978-1-63555-423-6)

Party of Three by Sandy Lowe. Three friends are in for a wild night at billionaire heiress Eleanor McGregor's twenty-fifth birthday party. Love, lust, and doing the right thing, even when it hurts, turn the evening into one that will change their lives forever. (978-1-63555-246-1)

Sit. Stay. Love. by Karis Walsh. City girl Alana Brendt and country vet Tegan Evans both know they don't belong together. Only problem is, they're falling in love. (978-1-63555-439-7)

Where the Lies Hide by Renee Roman. As P.I. Camdyn Stark gets closer to solving the case, will her dark secrets and the lies she's buried jeopardize her future with the quietly beautiful Sarah Peters? (978-1-63555-371-0)

Beautiful Dreamer by Melissa Brayden. With love on the line, can Devyn Winters find it in her heart to stay in the small town of Dreamer's Bay, the one place she swore she'd never remain? (978-1-63555-305-5)

Create a Life to Love by Erin Zak. When sixteen-year-old Beth shows up at her birth mother's door, three lives will change forever. (978-1-63555-425-0)

Deadeye by Meredith Doench. Stranded while hunting the serial predator Deadeye, Special Agent Luce Hansen fights for survival while her lover, forensic pathologist Harper Bennett, hunts for clues to Hansen's disappearance along the killer's trail. (978-1-63555-253-9)

Endangered by Michelle Larkin. Shapeshifters Officer Aspen Wolfe and Dr. Tora Madigan fight their growing attraction as they work together to destroy a secret government agency that exterminates their kind. (978-1-63555-377-2)

Incognito by VK Powell. The only thing Evan Spears is focused on is capturing a fleeing murder suspect until wild card Frankie Strong is added to her team and causes chaos on and off the job. (978-1-63555-389-5)

Insult to Injury by Gun Brooke. After losing everything, Gail Owen withdraws to her old farmhouse and finds a destitute young woman, Romi Shepherd, living in a secret room. (978-1-63555-323-9)

Just One Moment by Dena Blake. If you were given the chance to have the love of your life back, could you ignore everything that went wrong and start over again? (978-1-63555-387-1)

Scene of the Crime by MJ Williamz. Cullen Mathew finds herself caught between the woman she thinks she loves but can no longer trust and a beautiful detective she can't stop thinking about who will stop at nothing to find the truth. (978-1-63555-405-2)

Fear of Falling by Georgia Beers. Singer Sophie James is ready to shake up her career, but her new manager, the gorgeous Dana Landon, has other ideas. (978-1-63555-443-4)

Daughter of No One by Sam Ledel. When their worlds are threatened, a princess and a village outcast must overcome their differences and embrace a budding attraction if they want to survive. (978-1-63555-427-4)

Lightning Source UK Ltd.
Milton Keynes UK
UKHW010630080920
369553UK00002B/199

9 781635 554984